The Book of Love

GUIDANCE
IN
AFFAIRS
OF THE
HEART

The Book of Love

GUIDANCE
IN
AFFAIRS
OF THE
HEART

a novel

Barbara Sibbald

ValleyCom
MEDIA ASSOCIATES

ValleyCom
MEDIA ASSOCIATES

www.barbarasibbald.com

ISBN 978-0-9949027-0-2 (pbk.)
ISBN 978-0-9949027-1-9 (ePUB)
ISBN 978-0-9949027-2-6 (MOBI)

Copyright © Barbara Sibbald 2011

Cover art, design, formatting: Magdalene Carson
Published in Canada

Cataloguing in Publication data available from Library and Archives Canada

 The author gratefully acknowledges the financial support of the City of Ottawa Arts Funding Program.

This book is dedicated to
my paternal grandmother, Lucille Banta,
whose life was a celebration of our capacity to love.

chapter one

Betting

THROUGHOUT MAY, Suzanne and Erica spend a few evenings every week at the racetrack, studying and debating the *Live Racing Schedule*, placing bets, and screaming at the horses. They linger with the sun later and later every evening. Both are reluctant to go home, each for her own reason.

Suzanne is dodging Michael, who is spending most of his time at his golf course dodging her.

"We've become the Bickersons," Suzanne says, but she can't tell Erica what lies at the heart of it. She's tried, but then she feels a fluttering tightness in her chest and her throat closes down. I can't do it, she thinks. At least not yet.

Erica lingers too, relieved to have a break from the singles scene but reluctant to spend yet another weekday night alone in her apartment.

Late in the month, Christina—the balancing third to their friendship triptych—is able to join them. "I feel like I'm escaping domestic detention," she tells Suzanne.

Between races, they sip over-priced gin and tonics—an optimistic harbinger of the warmer weather—and chat randomly about coq au vin and Murphy beds, belligerent colleagues, and the vagaries of love.

They aren't horsey women, but then harness racing isn't really about the horses; it's about betting on the basis of scant information, something all three women know about.

Erica thought it might be a laugh.

"It's been such a *tedious* winter." She rolls her eyes for effect. "The bars and blatant expectations, the give and take—and take. I haven't had a promising date for months. All I want is someone who can string two sentences together and goes to the clubs for the music, not in the hope of getting some. It's so facile. Don't they realize women need a reason to have sex not just a place?"

Christina laughs widely, revealing a mouthful of fillings courtesy of her childhood craze for toffee. Suzanne grins but wonders: is that what it's really like out there, being single?

"Well, at least you have some excitement: clubbing, getting tarted up, checking out the action," says Christina. "This is my first foray outside work and Don and the kids since I don't know when—February? Whenever it was that we saw that indie band at the Galaxy. I've missed you two."

"It hasn't been the same since you moved to the 'burbs, Tina," laments Erica. "Our trio is sadly diminished."

Suzanne nods.

The three women have met once or twice a week since second-year university when they found one another cackling in the back row at a film club screening of *Annie Hall*. Afterwards, over a Blue at the noisy campus pub, they agreed that their favourite part was when Alvie and Annie were each complaining about the frequency of sex: we hardly ever have sex, complained Alvie. Only three times a week. He wants sex all the time, said Annie. We do it three times a week.

"Vive la différence," laughed Erica.

They began hanging out together, mostly at galleries and clubs. And after graduating, they all stayed in Ottawa by choice and chance: jobs taken, love relationships begun, marriage for two of them, a family for Christina.

"Here's to spring," says Christina, raising her glass, "the start of the race season, and our friendship."

They raise their highballs, and as they clink glasses, they make deliberate eye contact—Erica told them years ago that if they didn't look each other in the eye, they'd have seven year's bad sex, so it's become part of their ritual.

"Ten minutes to post," says Suzanne, nodding towards the standings board. "Bets up, gals, for race six." She runs her finger down the list of horses. "I think I'll go with Postivelydangerous. Oh, but look at this one: Neversawhimcoming. Who makes up these names anyway? I want that job!"

"I'm taking American Hunk," says Christina. She laughs:

"Or That's Ideal."

"Hey, what name would you pick for Don?" Suzanne asks Christina.

"Hmmm, good question," says Christina, tracing the list with her finger.

Erica notes that Christina's cuticles are ragged. She's working too hard, she thinks. Erica keeps her nails clipped and buffed.

Christina pauses at Wild Ride. Not in this life, she thinks.

"How about EasyLivin' Smiley," she says.

"That's so sweet," says Suzanne. "Michael's definitely Workaholic. The pathetic reality of the junior partner. He's never home before seven, dragging his ass and a pile of dossiers."

These days this isn't strictly speaking true; he makes an effort to get home by six "so I can spend some time with you," he says. She wishes he'd made the effort a year ago when it might have mattered.

"For myself, I'd like Winning Decision," says Erica. "Just for a change of pace."

They all laugh and settle back into their chairs.

The bet-taker, a youngish woman wearing a faux-Western get-up replete with a slightly bent, red cardboard cowboy hat strolls up. They each make a two-dollar bet, all to place.

"We're not exactly big gamblers, are we?" asks Christina.

"It's a tough call," says Suzanne. "You bet on a sure thing, and the returns are low. You go out on a limb and you can lose it all."

"Or you can win big," says Christina, smiling.

But likely not, thinks Erica.

Her losses in love have mounted over the years—men won, lost, rejected—but at thirty-two, she's still willing to take a calculated risk.

"So what's up with you, Tina?" asks Suzanne. "What are you working on?"

"Painting? No time for that these days. Ever since the move to the hinterland. The commute's a killer: fifty minutes each way minimum. It sucks me dry. At the end of the day, I can barely manage to throw dinner together and get the kids settled. And then the weekends are jammed with errands and house stuff and family—I mean I want some fun time with Norris and Vita, too. I bore myself with all the nagging I do: pick up your toys, hang up your clothes, take a bath, yada, yada. It's mind-numbing. Anyway, painting's taken a tumble on the agenda."

"Have you set your studio up?" asks Erica.

Christina shakes her head. "All my gear's still in the basement, but I'm going to set up something," she adds quickly, as if to convince herself as much as the others. "I could always work in the kitchen with an easel. I did that for years at our Spruce Street apartment, remember? I don't need a studio per se."

"I hear you," says Suzanne. "What you need is time. Working five days a week really interferes with life." She's dying to mention the grant she has applied for to make her documentary, money that will buy her the time and equipment to make it happen; but she decides it might be bad luck—and besides, she doesn't want to endure their sympathy when it fails. If it fails, she corrects herself. I have to stay positive.

Christina nods: "Time. If only. But enough about that. It's the same-old, same-old. I have to decide to make the time, and then it will happen." She rattles the melted remains of her ice cubes. "Order me another?" she asks. "I'm off to the loo."

"Ditto," says Suzanne.

"Loo?" laughs Erica. "You're such girly girls."

She turns in her chair to see if the waitress is around. Of course not. The place has emptied out a bit; all the after-work gamblers have finally gone home. One of the businessmen sitting two tables away tries to catch her eye, and as Erica expertly glances away, her eyes land on a red book sitting on the chair at the table behind her. Its cover faces her: *Love* something or another. The table is clear, the book seemingly abandoned. She's found that reading a book is good for deterring wannabes, so she walks over, picks it up, and returns to her seat.

The Book of Love: Guidance in Affairs of the Heart by Jean Foster. Could be a man or a woman, she thinks. The cover is amateurishly designed: no visual, and the typeface is old-school. She flips it over. No author photo. She reads the blurb on the back cover:

THE BOOK OF LOVE
Guidance in Affairs of the Heart

by Dr. Jean Foster

The definitive guide to love's journey from pre-date pitfalls through courtship, and on to the nurturing bond. With remarkable insight, Foster combines commonsense and the latest research to steer readers through myriad emotional minefields:

♡ *E-dating dangers:* If you think this is the last refuge of the despondent, think again. It is *the* modern meeting place, and the rules of engagement have definitely changed.

♡ *Marital meltdown:* How to move from fusion (that melding-together phase of being "in love") to the more mature, long-term delimitation (separate yet together).

♡ *Sexual fulfillment:* Welcome yourself as a sexual "partner" and accept that sometimes you have to work at putting the play into playing around.

During twenty-six years as a relationship counsellor, psychologist Dr. Jean Foster has helped thousands of couples to develop nurturing, sustaining bonds. Her renowned "Intimacy Renewal" weekends attract couples from all over Western Canada and the United States.

THE BOOK OF LOVE: Guidance in Affairs of the Heart   Dr. Jean Foster

Erica flips to the catalogue-in-print page: the copyright date is listed as five years from now. How odd, she thinks. There's no publisher either, but then she sees it's printed by a digital press. Self-published, she thinks, or maybe a sample copy for shopping around to publishers.

Suzanne and Christina return.

"Hey, look what I found on that table," Erica says, flashing the book. "It's a digital advance copy not published yet."

Suzanne takes it. "I wonder, wonder, who-oo-oo, who wrote the book of love," she sings, turning the book over in her hands. She glances at the back cover. "Low-end psychobabble," she says and hands it over to Christina.

"I hate these self-help books," Suzanne continues. "The meat of it—I mean the actual nuggets of advice—would fit onto a single page. Double-spaced. My parents were really into that transactional analysis stuff, I'm okay, you're not, or whatever. They were always quoting from it when I was growing up: 'You're communicating like a child,' they'd say, and I felt like screaming at them, 'I am a child, you morons.'"

Erica and Christina laugh.

"Did you guys see who was sitting there?" asks Erica, pointing to the empty table behind her.

"A couple of women," says Christina. "Older, kinda dowdy, but in a nice way. Smart women, I'm thinking."

"Hey, look at this, there's a chapter on finding the perfect mate," says Erica. "I could use some help in that department. I'm going to keep it. I'm sure Foster has other copies—obviously an electronic copy at least—and besides, it's almost like it was meant to be." She raises her glass. "Here's to happenstance."

"There's nothing sadder than an empty cocktail glass," says Suzanne. "Where is that waitress?"

"I think you should turn it in to the lost and found," says Christina. "It's obviously not meant to be public yet."

"There she is," says Suzanne, waving her arm.

"I just want to read it. I'll return it in a week or two," says Erica.

The waitress arrives. Christina glances at the cover. "Foster's going to be looking for it. It's not like it was abandoned."

Easy for Christina to take the high road, Erica thinks. She has no idea what it's like out there. It used to be fun and flirty, but lately everyone seems on edge. It's the baby thing, she's decided: all those hundreds of ticking wombs. Except hers. She's never wanted kids. "We're overpopulated as it is," she argues, although there's more to it than that.

Lately, though, she's started wondering why she can't find a partner—Am I too particular? Too difficult?—and she envies Christina and Suzanne. Both found partners early and seemingly easily. Erica was a bridesmaid at both weddings. Christina and Don's was at Pink Lake in the Gatineau Hills. Her friend was stunning: blonde curls tumbling down over a halter-top dress that softened every curve. It was made from an exquisite fabric of white sateen covered with swooshes of giant green ferns. One of Christina's mom's designs. There was a lake-side, picnic potluck where everyone brought their favourite dish in lieu of a present. Erica had wondered about the match—a techno-nerd and an art-ist—but here they are, eleven years later and solid. Joyful even.

At least from the outside, thinks Erica.

Suzanne, on the other hand, seemed to find her soulmate in Michael. Three months after their first date, they were living together, and inside a year had a traditional wedding with one hundred and forty guests and a reception at The Chateau. That was nine years ago. Now, Erica suspects, their marriage is on the cusp of a meltdown or at least a good rattle. Not that Suzanne's said anything, Erica muses to herself, but she's sure spending a lot of time with me.

Suzanne finishes ordering the round.

"I'm sure the author has other copies, Tina," says Erica. "At least digital."

Christina shakes her head. "If I'd found it, I'd return it for sure. What do you think Suzanne?"

She shrugs: "A few weeks isn't going to hurt."

Erica changes the subject, anxious to avoid an ethics lecture from Christina. "You know," she says, "I've been thinking about how finding a good man is like betting on a horse. You study the incomplete facts, calculate the odds, and, fingers crossed for luck"—she crosses fingers next to each ear—"you place your bet. Then you sit in the stadium shouting encouragement as they trot around. And you hope you'll get lucky *this* time."

Christina smiles. "You can do more than cross your fingers," she says. "At least in theory."

"That's where the shouting encouragement bit comes in," says Erica. "But what do I know? After all, women might be able to fake orgasms, but men can fake a whole relationship."

They laugh.

chapter two

A Sporting Man

ERICA PICKS UP THE PHONE at work. It's Suzanne, saying she'd like to invite a friend to join them at the track that evening.

"Hugh's an old pal from Saskatoon who has just moved to Ottawa. You'll like him. He's the new sports editor at *The Star* so you might even have something to talk about. Plus, he's a laugh."

"That's always a bonus. And his status? Single?" asks Erica.

"I think so. Oh yeah, he mentioned something about it being easier to move 'cus he'd just broken up with his gal pal in Toronto."

"He'll be snatched up in a flash in this town. Bring him on!" says Erica.

As Erica waits on the bench outside her office for Suzanne to pick her up after work, she pulls *The Book of Love* out of her oversized, turquoise purse-cum-briefcase. She's been carting it around for a week now, thumbing through it during spare moments. She's put a Post-it at the section called "Finding the Perfect Mate.",

Finding the Perfect Mate

Before You Begin

If I had to give only one piece of advice, it would be, quite simply, don't expect to have all your needs met by one person. This sounds like a variation on the platitude, don't-put-all-your-eggs-in-one-basket, but this tendency is often the biggest stumbling block to finding a healthy love relationship—and keeping it. Women are particularly prone to a sort of monomania about romantic love, with a melody of Cinderella happily-ever-after stuck on an endless loop in their heads.

Cinderella is a fairy tale.

You will still need your friends, your family, your work colleagues. Each point of attachment—whether family, friends, or acquaintances—helps you to meet a different physical, social, intellectual, emotional, or spiritual need. These needs vary, but may include, for example, a book buddy, lover, confidante, film friend, professional colleague, work-out companion, etcetera. And finally—often principally—we are fulfilled through self-love that allows us to acknowledge our weaknesses, celebrate our successes, and be gentle with ourselves.

Ideally, our life partner should fulfill up to 30 per cent of our core needs, which vary according to the individual, but may include the need for security, sexuality, affection, and physical contact. The bottom line is that you have to take responsibility for meeting all of your needs[3] by identifying them and then determining how they can best be met by others and by yourself. Don't confuse needs with values such as trustworthiness, honesty, and political leaning. Shared values matter more than anything else—and are the most reliable predictors of the eventual success or failure of your relationship.

Of course, such considerations are pragmatic and unemotional—while dating is not. One study[4] found that people go into dating with an idée fixe about what constitutes the perfect partner, but all that goes out the window when they meet the "right" stranger. In other words, despite methodical plotting, we still follow our hearts and hormones—at least initially . . .

---

3   H. Bajramovic, Personal communication with author, Ottawa, 2006.

4   R. Kurzban and J. Weeden, "Do advertised preferences predict the behaviour of speed daters?" *Personal Relationships* 14, no. 4 (2007): 623–32.

A car horn blasts: Erica looks up to see Suzanne waving. She smiles and slips the book into her bag.

Erica finds Hugh's looks rather interesting. She notes his sculpted sideburns, strong shoulders, and dark Clark Kent–type glasses. He's broad-shouldered *and* semi-literate, she thinks. She prefers substantial, swarthy men; likes how they complement her slim figure and olive skin. She knows that's superficial, but it makes her feel good and it's at least a promising start.

Their eyes meet as Hugh gently shakes Erica's hand; it races through her head that he might kiss it. Then his eyes linger—just for a nano—on her breasts spilling ever so slightly over top of her orange T-shirt.

Erica welcomes this kind of attention and has laughed about it with Suzanne. "I'm the one displaying the girls," she'd said, propping her breasts up with her hands. She accentuates them in low-cut shirts or scoop-neck dresses that also reveal the small tattooed treble clef on her left clavicle.

Hugh asks what she does, and she tells him how she works days as a researcher for the Organic Growers Council. Describing it as pretty tedious, mired in endless footnoting and phone interviews, she explains that her real love is writing her freelance clubbing column, "In Tune," for *The Star*. She asks what music he listens to. His tastes are respectable, she thinks, though predictably mainstream—U2, Coldplay, REM—and quasi-old-school. They talk a bit about mutual colleagues and editors at *The Star*, agree the gossipy atmosphere there is poisonous, then he blithely adds his gossip to the fray with a long story about the managing editor. Seems she was meeting a business couple in her office, and the woman was admiring the display of family photos when the man picks up a portrait of the editor's husband and says, "Hey, there's Andrew, Sarah's boyfriend." And they knew all these details about him, like where he worked, what books he liked.

"And so that's how she found out that her husband was cheating on her," says Hugh. "What a betrayal!"

The story resonates with Suzanne, but she laughs it off. "Sounds like an urban legend to me."

"Actually, I heard something about it as well," says Erica. "Though not all the gruesome details. Good snooping, Hugh!!"

He keeps them going all evening with tales from work and a running commentary about the other spectators and sportsmen.

"Two o'clock: Man from plaid having the time of his life."

Erica slowly shifts in her chair so she can see. The man is wearing a yellow-plaid jacket. He has a receding hairline, round, red face with small eyes, but a nice manner. Friendly looking, she thinks. Maybe forty-five. He laughs then says something to the woman, a carefully made-up blonde wearing a stop-sign red jacket. Glam. In an over-the-top seventies way. Line-backer shoulder pads. The woman touches his arm.

Erica scans around, pretending to be looking for someone, then turns back to Hugh.

"He looks happy," she says. "Must be the red jacket."

"Nine o'clock: two jockeys in heated debate with an angry guy," says Hugh. "Owner maybe. Looks like an altercation in progress."

And so it goes.

At one point, she touches his hand and moves her head towards a frail old woman wearing a fuchsia coat over a lime-green, much-wrinkled dress. Oblong stains run down her front.

"Check out her brows," Erica whispers.

She has no eyebrows. Plucked into oblivion, they have become innocent victims of fashion. Two crooked lines are drawn over her eyes with a medium-brown pencil. Her blonde wig is matted at the part and slightly askew.

"Poor woman," Hugh says.

Erica feels hot with shame, cruel for pointing out the woman. She glances at Hugh. He seems sincere. It makes her consider that he has a gentle side under the veneer of sporting bravado, of masculinity.

Later, as Hugh leans forward to watch the race, Erica studies him. She looks carefully at his lush, curly hair, full lips, and broad chest. Sexy, she acknowledges. It's been a long time since she's felt so strongly attracted to a man. She can't remember when exactly. Usually, she's slow to warm. Wary of prevarication and pretence. Hugh puts his hand on Erica's forearm and asks if she wants to place a bet. He stands close to her at the counter. Erica can't help leaning against him ever so slightly. On the way back to the table, Hugh invites her out for dinner. "That would be lovely," she says, and they set a date for the following evening.

"You never know," Suzanne says on the drive back to the city. "He was sort of a loser in high school, a wannabe athlete, a rink rat, and hanger-on, but I always really liked him. He lived in my 'hood, and we'd walk home together when we didn't have sports or whatever. He's a fabulous listener. And he's hilarious."

"Yeah," says Erica, "and hot, too! Hey, let's see what the book says about dating."

"Do you always cart that thing around?"

"It's good for reading on the bus. Listen to this:"

Dating for All the Right Reasons

With apologies to William Carlos Williams, so much depends upon the first date. After "the ask," which is in itself a minefield, our egos and libidos run amok before the first date. No one can really prepare you for the specifics of the encounter — that is part of your personal growth — but I do have two pieces of advice: go slowly and think before you unzip. Imagine introducing your date to your most trusted friend. What would he or she say?

"You already know what I'd say," interrupts Suzanne. "All you really need to remember is the three-dates-before-sex rule."

"No worries there. I know the score," says Erica, laughing. "Besides, sex isn't the issue for me. My foible is the spell of control. Remember Frank? He thought I was his Barbie doll. All the time we spent shopping and poking around my closet, sheesh. He practically dressed me for six months!"

"Oh, yeah, the hapless-ho look," says Suzanne. "How could I forget?"

Erica laughs, shaking her head. "Another lucky escape! From what I remember, it was Tina who was prone to premature premarital sex. Not that she ever admitted it to us."

"Yeah, I've often thought it was strange," says Suzanne. "She probably thinks we don't know about all her little trysts in university. Obviously, that's what she wanted for one reason or another. I had a few spontaneous flings myself. Not that it matters. It's only premarital if you plan to get married."

As usual, Erica arrives twenty minutes late for the date. She spots Hugh sitting at the back of the dimly lit Indian restaurant reading the newspaper, a half-empty glass of beer in front of him. Erica is unapologetic about making a date wait for her. In her view, a half-hour is rude, twenty minutes perfect. Keep them waiting, keep them wanting, she tells the ladies. Tonight, though, she nearly exceeded the twenty-minute rule in her indecisiveness about what to wear. Pants, dress, skirt? Eventually, she settled on a lime-green slinky blouse with three-quarter length sleeves, open at the throat—but not too open—and black capris that fit great in the butt. Then she tucked a swirled purple and green silk scarf behind her collar and draped it down her sides to frame her breasts.

Hugh stands, smiling, bends to kiss her cheek, then embraces her for a moment, pressing his broad chest into her. She notes that he's actually just a little overweight, then chastises herself for being superficial. She finds herself hugging him back and pulls away surprised. Three dates, she reminds herself. They sit down.

"Placed any bets today?" she asks him.

"Only on you," says Hugh, winking.

"How droll," she says, rolling her eyes.

Hugh laughs nervously, says how glad he is that they met, how he's looking forward to getting to know her.

"I want to know all about you," he continues warmly and begins asking questions: Where were you born? Siblings? University? Hugh covers the five Ws and the H, his interest never wavering. He's a great interviewer, thinks Erica enviously.

She tries boomeranging the questions back to him—And where did you grow up? How did you get into sports reporting?—but he provides cryptic answers then turns the questions back on her, dodging her queries skilfully and professionally. She feels vaguely uneasy about this apparent game of duelling journalists. It's contrary to her experience that men love to talk about themselves. But his interest is flattering, and she begins to enjoy talking about herself. Doesn't everybody? she thinks.

His questions keep her monologue going through the pakora and beyond, into the channa, the palak paneer, and lamb vindaloo, and through two more rounds of Kingfisher. She yammers on, barely picking at her food, and is surprised at how quickly he eats. Like her father. Does he even taste it? she wonders as he dishes up another generous spoonful of basmati rice.

She tells a truncated version of her life story, picking and choosing the details that cast her in the best possible light. She reveals a bit, amuses a bit—he is, after all, a stranger. She tells how her parents emigrated from Italy and built up a construction business in London, Ontario. How they gave her and her brother Anglo-sounding names so they would blend in. She tells of going to Mass twice a week, of despising her life in the 'burbs, and how she became a fashion punk—the musical origins being well over by her adolescence—with multiple piercings and a short, spiky haircut. Hugh says he likes the little ruby in the side of her nose, and she points to the bar across her upper left ear and the multiple holes in both ears.

"Mom went nuts when I got my nose done," says Erica. "I was sixteen, but hey, I was mature about it. I went to a good place, clean and everything. But Mom! She starts lighting candles for my soul, thinking I'm doomed to become a drug addict, a welfare mom. She talked to the priest about it then shipped me off to her sister's in Toronto for the summer. It was the best thing that could've happened to me. Aunt Zietta owned a tiny bistro in the Annex. It had only six tables and was always packed. I *loved* it. I worked there every summer until I finished university."

They linger as long as possible, and finally, as the staff begin to lay out napkins and cutlery for the next day, they order a final Kingfisher to share.

"I left my car at home," he says. "Thought I might have a drink or two. Where are you parked?"

"No car," she says.

He raises his eyebrows.

"It's one of the advantages of living in the inner city. It's not as if being on top of the food chain entitles one to the best cuts of beef *and* a vehicle."

Hugh laughs and takes her hand from under her chin and holds it.

She takes her hand away ostensibly to sip their beer, pleased to be playing the game so well.

"Actually," she says, "I moved downtown partly to be close to the office, but wouldn't you know it, inside six months it was moved way down Bank Street. Dad offered me his old beamer—two door, bright red, and only six years old. I was tempted but said no. My parents can't accept that I like living in an apartment in a decrepit 1930s house, that I don't want a car or a TV, or that I like shopping at St. V. de P."

"What does your mom say?"

Erica laughs. "It's outside her scope. I remember coming home one Christmas, and when Mom saw my cracked winter boots and unravelling tweed overcoat—the kind geezers wear when they do yard work—she started crying: 'I don't understand,'" Erica imitates in a falsetto Italian accent. "'Why do you dress like a bum?'"

Hugh laughs. "You really are charming," he says.

She ignores his flattery, fending off another advance. "It's as if coats and boots were the most important thing in the world. I told her I was warm enough and not to worry. To her credit, she found a funky old fifties coat in the attic that I still love, and she dragged me to the Boxing Day sales, armed with Christmas loot from Dad's aunties—two older sisters who live together in Tuscany near Siena. Spinsters he calls them."

Hugh smiles. "Hey, sorry to interrupt, Erica, but the staff are lurking. It must be closing time. I heard there's a great little bar just around the corner. Well, actually, I asked someone at work. Want to go for a nightcap?"

As they stroll slowly down a quiet residential street, he takes her hand, and this time she lets him. She's feeling a little wobbly; realizes she should have eaten more or drunk less. In the shadows between two streetlights, he stops her and kisses her gently on the cheek.

"You're so beautiful," he says, caressing her cheek with his forefinger. He gathers her softly and sweetly into his arms like a bunch of roses.

She holds her body rigid then melts for a moment, relinquishes herself to the ample contours of his body. Strong. Comforting, yet exciting. Slightly breathless, she pulls away a bit too quickly and dodges his eyes, embarrassed by her response. It's too soon, too soon, her internal alarm bell is clanging.

They order single-malt Scotch on the rocks: he, Glenlivet, she, Bowmore. He takes her hand, stroking it gently. Kissing it once, twice. Again. He reminds her of someone. She struggles to think who and finally realizes it's Trevor. Way back in the day. She was twenty-one, and the sex was amazing: intense, intimate. Of course she had no terms of reference then, since he was her first lover. But even now, she thinks it was the best she's ever had. Then, after a year, he decided to go to school in Vancouver, and when she offered to move with him, he said she shouldn't bother. She was devastated at first, then angry: How dare he lead her on! The egotistical prick. She took the next day off work and lay in bed, watching tear-jerker films she'd seen a million times before, using up an entire box of tissues. Suzanne and Christina came over with Greek-on-wheels and trash-talked Trevor until well past midnight. She went back to work the next day. After a few weeks, she realized that there hadn't been much to it besides the sex and eventually reconciled herself to the fact that it simply wasn't the kind of relationship that would last.

Just as she's thinking this, Hugh asks if she's looking for a relationship. Tipsy now, approaching drunkenness, Erica decides to go for it. What the hell. Waiting around, playing it cool hasn't got me anywhere. She tells Hugh that what she's looking for is based on the fact that she doesn't have sex: she makes love. Hugh enthusiastically agrees as he caresses her thigh under the table. Erica calculates the odds and, although it's strictly against her three-date rule, asks him outright what his intentions are.

"I want to be your lover," he says, looking at her full on.

His straightforward response takes her by surprise, and she is thrilled by the strength of his desire.

They stumble to her apartment for a final nightcap, although both of them know this is only a pretence. She drops the keys then fumbles with the lock. Finally, she gets it open and stumbles over the threshold. Hugh steps in behind her, closes the door and kisses her gently, moves a strand of hair behind her ear, strokes her cheek, her breasts.

"Beautiful," he murmurs.

He kisses her upper lip, taking it between his lips, then kisses her full on, holding her close. Somehow they're on the bed. Her inner alarm is silent. Shirt unbuttoned. Bra snapped open. Unzipped. Lips on. Nipple. Ear. He licks Erica's neck, then his fingers, and readies her, making her squirm and cry out. When he drops his pants, Erica's thighs tighten at the sight of his penis—the size of a newborn baby's arm and fist. The fate of Catherine the Great and her horse paramour flashes through Erica's mind. But Hugh is sweetly gentle, holding his great weight off her, never once, even at climax, relaxing.

"I don't want to crush you," he whispers softly. He is a careful, attentive lover, giving more than he gets. Erica falls asleep sated but wakes with raw emotions, filled with self-recrimination. Have I blown it by breaking the three-date rule? she wonders. She decides she won't tell Christina and Suzanne how quickly it has happened. Suzanne, especially, after what she'd said yesterday. Erica is embarrassed by her lack of control.

After the first night, they are both hooked. Weekend nights she's usually out late, going to clubs for her column. He comes along a few times but says he doesn't like that "experimental stuff." He waits for the big shows at the Coliseum. She shrugs it off, tells Suzanne, "It's like the book says. You can't get everything from one person." But she had hoped for someone who shared her love of music. During the week, he works until nine or so most evenings, depending on which teams are playing what and when, and puts the sports section to bed before getting a bite to eat. She offers to cook, rhymes off the names of some of her specialties: spaghetti aglio e olio, radicchio risotto, Trenette con pesto allo Genovese. But he says, no, no thanks, it's too much trouble. And besides, he explains, he normally just has a salad or something.

"Have to watch the waistline," he says, pinching a tiny roll on his side.

"You've got nothing to worry about," says Erica. "You look great."

"I have to watch it, though. I gain easily. That's why I try to go for a run once or twice a day."

Jock, Erica thinks, pleased that he looks after himself. Still, she is offended that he doesn't want to eat with her. It's so anti-social.

He usually arrives at her place well after nine—depending on whether he's gone for a run first—and they have a beer or two for a bit of a buzz. Then he takes her to bed for a night of frenzy.

After a month, Erica is surprised that, while her sexual pleasure continues to grow, the bond does not.

"He won't open up to me. I hardly know anything about him," she tells Suzanne. "It's so frustrating."

"Maybe he's slow to warm," says Suzanne. "He treats you well, doesn't he?"

"Sure, yeah. He's really sweet, always giving me flowers and wine, complimenting me."

"Well, that's all good. I wouldn't worry about it," says

Suzanne. "I'm sure he'll come around. Maybe he's been burnt before and is a bit reticent . . ."

Maybe he needs some time to trust me, she thinks. I have to be patient.

Finally, Erica thinks maybe they're getting somewhere when Hugh enters her only remaining orifice and, with voluptuous words, fills her head and plants the hope that at last she has bet on a sure thing. He says how close he feels to her, that he admires how hard she works, how she fills him with joy. He says it all amidst sighs and moans, and sips of cold Creemore Springs beer, and licks of melting chocolate off her breasts. Gulping, snorting, panting. Erica thinks of it as lurving, Woody Allen's term in *Annie Hall* for longing, loving, and lusting all rolled together.

Hugh talks about lovemaking, about the need to give oneself fully.

"In giving yourself, you come to understand yourself," he says.

She thinks that he must be quoting someone—maybe a past lover—but she doesn't call him on it. What does it matter? It's true.

Then he tells her what a huge difference she's made to his life, how she couldn't imagine his loneliness before. Then he says it.

"I love you."

And Erica blushes. She is flattered but suspicious at the same time. It's too soon. I don't even know him!

She tells him she's very fond of him, that he's a close friend, a passionate lover. Hugh says nothing, but they both know he wants the L-word. And in pop-psychology lore, they both know Erica now has the upper hand: he has stated his love, but she hasn't.

He leaves before six the next morning, so he can get in a run. He's abrupt in his parting, barely kissing her cheek. She consults *The Book of Love* and finds a chapter that looks promising: "What they're talking about when they talk about love." She looks through the sub-headings until she finds the one she's looking for: "Premature Articulation."

Premature Articulation

When your partner says *I love you* too early in the relationship (for you, obviously, but also by any objective standard), it's often because he or she is feeling insecure in themselves or the relationship, or more likely both. He tells you he loves you (whether he does or not) because he wants to hear the same from you, then the relationship will shift into something more certain and comfortable. But if you don't oblige with the return *I love you*, it not only gives you the upper hand, it ramps up the tension for him, making him feel even more insecure, which can play out in some very unsavoury ways. But that's no excuse to lie. Wait. You'll know when the love is real. And knowing has everything to do with intimacy.

For many, implicit in the *I love you* is the *assumption* of intimacy, followed by an inevitable trajectory to cohabitating or marriage. But the fact is, intimacy does not automatically accompany the declaration of love or agreement to share space. Our universal need for closeness—for someone who understands us—takes time, shared experiences, and meaningful communication.

Maybe he's insecure, she thinks. Maybe that's why he needs me to tell him I love him. Communication. Both ways. That's what we need. She vows to get him to open up. Erica puts the book away and rushes off to work.

She starts asking Hugh more pointed questions about his childhood, his aspirations. And Hugh begins to respond with a bit more detail. He tells Erica about his two younger brothers and mother, about living in subsidized housing in Saskatoon. His mom worked nights at a local bakery. She'd arrive home at eight in the morning laden with a shopping bag of leftover bakery treats—half a pie, day-old muffins, bread—and exhausted after work. She'd put on her pink fluffy slippers and sit at the kitchen table, cup of tea at the ready, overseeing Hugh as he made lunches for his brothers and himself. Then she made sure they ate breakfast and all left in time to walk to school.

After this revelation, Hugh begins arriving even later in the evening; says he really needs the run to de-stress after work. Late into the night, they lie in Erica's bed, his arms engulfing her as she listens to these stories—vignettes really—from his childhood. Erica asks for more: his circumstances, the influences, his feelings. The how of the thing. He laughs and says she should have been a psychotherapist.

"You haven't mentioned your dad," says Erica.

Hugh laughs—falsely, it seems to her. Defensively.

"He was in and out of the picture," he says. "He stuck around until I was three or so, but he was mostly unemployed, so he went to Alberta to work on the rigs. He'd show up in Saskatoon every couple of years with presents—cowboy hats and footballs and macho stuff like that. He'd stick around long enough to get Mom pregnant again, then he'd disappear. I always assumed he sent her money, but a couple of years ago, she asked me for a loan and admitted that he rarely did."

"You must be so pissed at him," Erica says.

"It's complicated," says Hugh. "He is my dad after all."

She feels he's not being completely truthful with her or possibly with himself. He must harbour some resentment—perhaps against his mother, too.

He begins caressing her, and she notices an angry red scrape across the back of his right hand.

"What's that from?" she asks.

"The perils of office work," he says, laughing, and distracts her with a lingering kiss.

Hugh continues to ask Erica questions as well, but his scope gradually narrows. One night, she realizes that what he actually wants to know about are her past lovers. Erica has a rule not to talk about this. In her experience, these stories have invariably led to assumptions then to suspicion and jealousy—the scourge of the beautiful woman.

She upstages his questions with flattery. "You're an exception for me," she tells him. "Normally I wait at least three dates before sleeping with someone. But you, well . . ." She smiles.

He touches her cleavage gently and smiles in return. "Erica, all I want is to understand you. That way, I'll know how I can love you more fully. But I can't if I don't know where you're coming from, where you've been, and how your experiences have formed you."

"I feel the same about you," she says, but he doesn't say anything.

Reluctantly, over the ensuing nights, Erica gives out a few scant details, a truncated version of the stories of her half-dozen past lovers: who and when—that's it. This leads to more questions. She fights every step. "This isn't relevant to who I am now," she says. "There haven't been that many, and three were more than a decade ago."

But on another level, she is grateful that the focus is on her past lovers, not her family. It's easy to mock her mom's Catholic guilt trips and traditional views, but there's nothing funny about her dad's unpredictable temper and relentless badgering. How he would catch her as she left the house for high school in a short skirt and heels. He would pinch the soft part of her upper arm, leaving bruised reminders of his rule, and yell at her: "No daughter of mine," etcetera, etcetera.

He was relentless: she was clumsy ergo unfeminine; her perennially scabbed knees would scar, and no one would want to marry her; she was a burden to her mother. She wasn't allowed to play with the neighbourhood boys or, later, go to her girlfriends' sleepovers. He said he was protecting her, but, to Erica, it felt like he wanted to keep her cloistered. She escaped into her Discman, her wall of music, and into helping her mother in the kitchen and learning to cook—something they both approved of. After she'd gone through puberty, he could no longer look her in the eye, but that didn't stop him from telling her that she dressed like a slut. Nothing could be further from the truth. At school, she wore the regulation plaid skirt three-inches above her knee and the high-buttoned white blouses. And she didn't lose her virginity until she was twenty-one and only after dating Trevor for two months. Now, when she sees her parents, her father immediately demands, "Do you have a boyfriend?" And regardless of her answer, he says, "When are you getting married?"

She doesn't tell Hugh that she spent five years in psychotherapy, either. He doesn't need to know everything, she thinks.

Erica finds there's something akin to psychotherapy in this disclosure with Hugh. Sort of a live-action psychotherapy. Gradually, evening after evening, it becomes easier and easier to talk about her failed relationships, even though there aren't that many. She finds herself searching for a pattern, so she can avoid repeating her mistakes. She gets caught up in the telling; pat phrases left over from the original anecdote get embellished, the story grows, and she lives it all over again—at least this version of it.

Hugh binges on the details, asks more questions, dissects, and analyzes the endless fragments of these relationships and adventures. He is kind and gentle, holds Erica close when the memories are harsh. He comforts her through late-night revelations about a past lover who betrayed her. She is grateful for Hugh's concern. She says "I love you." But what she means is that she loves Hugh's seemingly unending, compassionate interest in her. Between his come-cries Hugh repeats that he loves Erica. She's not sure what he really means.

Erica still meets Suzanne at the track once a week. It's getting more interesting now as clear favourites emerge, and the audience swells for a significant stake race with a purse of two hundred thousand. Erica bets on Feisty Dan, Suzanne on Clearly Possessed. They take turns watching their horses through the binoculars that Erica has borrowed from Hugh. Feisty Dan starts out strong. Too strong in Erica's estimation. "Damn, why doesn't he slow down? Conserve his energy for that final stretch?" she says. And, of course, he comes in third. She tears her ticket and throws it in the air, consciously imitating some movie or another. A thought occurs:

If Hugh and I could relax the intensity, perhaps in the final stretch we could share intimacy not just bodily fluids. We slurp sex like it's melting ice cream on a sweltering summer day.

Between races, Suzanne finishes off her cocktail. "I'm becoming a lush," she laments.

Erica looks up from the race schedule, raising her eyebrows.

"I can't face Michael," Suzanne confides in a rush. "We bicker non-stop. And then we go to bed, and he wants to have sex and I can't, I just can't, not after all that arguing. I don't get how he can."

"Men always want sex. They're hardwired for it," says Erica. "It doesn't mean you have to put out." She's dying to ask what they're fighting about, but knows that Suzanne will tell her eventually. When she's ready.

"It's not only the sex part," says Suzanne. "We don't seem to have any connection anymore. On the weekend, he's in training for half-marathon, or he's off playing golf. We used to go out for long, boozy dinners and fattening brunches or to films, but now, he never seems to have any time to go out. Weeknights he still gets home at a decent hour—six or half-past—but then, after supper, he's back in front of the computer. And if I rent a DVD, nine times out of ten, he falls asleep on the couch."

"Maybe you should go on a holiday together, give yourselves some time to re-connect."

"Yeah, he suggested that. We're thinking of August."

Suzanne stops herself from blurting out the whole story. She's decided she needs to get settled in her own mind first and make a decision before receiving the partially informed advice of a sympathetic friend. Even a close friend.

At any rate, Erica has her own problems. She asks Suzanne what she thinks about the Revelation Sessions—her nickname for Hugh's insatiable questioning.

"He may be legit," says Suzanne. "He may want to know you better." She pauses. "I'd be careful, though, because the more he knows, the more you'll need to trust him. And vice versa."

Erica pulls *The Book of Love* out of her bag.

"I thought you were going to give that back," says Suzanne.

"Maybe later. You have to read the stuff on disclosure in relationships," she says. "I mean talk about a coincidence." She flips to the page and hands Suzanne the book. "My bladder's busting," she says, standing up. "Back in a flash."

Suzanne reads: "'The Perils of Too Much Information: Talking about the Past.'"

The Perils of Too Much Information: Talking About the Past

As Voltaire quipped: "The secret of being a bore . . . is to tell everything." And no one wants a boring lover. Keep your partner's interest — intellectual and sexual — by keeping aspects of your past to yourself. It will help to keep them intrigued, wondering and wanting. This doesn't mean you should keep deep dark secrets from them — the fact that your house burned down when you were eight or that your sister died of cancer — but there's a difference between being informed about essential aspects of each other's personal history — which helps others understand the factors that moulded your psyche and enables true intimacy — and disclosing the tedious minutiae of our lives; in particular, details about past lovers. Because this is the second thing about full disclosure. Not only does it make you boring, as Voltaire so astutely observed, but telling all can also be dangerous if your partner is prone to jealousy (wrought by insecurity and/or their propensity to indiscretions). Stories about past lovers, some of which invariably cast you in a negative light, can be regurgitated and used against you. You behaved in such and such a way in the past and you will again. If your partner is vulnerable, it can fuel his or her fear of abandonment or betrayal.

Remember these stories are about your past self, a self that has been replaced (one would hope) by a more enlightened version. These stories were the building blocks for a new structure. You.

Live in the Now.

"It sounds like the take-home message from a *Cosmo* article," Suzanne tells Erica.

"Well, it's news to me," Erica says, "and you have to admit, Foster's got a point."

Suzanne shrugs her shoulders: "It's way too simplistic. As if something like love can be explained in one little book. It's pretentious. Half the Hollywood films are about love with more coming ever year. And look at literature."

"That's because love is so complicated. Just look at my track record. I'm taking all the help I can get."

Hugh can never relax after their romps. One night, after plumping up the pillows, he goes to the kitchenette for a beer. Erica parts the drapes and looks outside. Clouds billow across the half-moon.

He comes back and sits on the edge of the bed, his back to her, sipping his beer and peeling the label off the bottle with his ragged fingernails.

"I've been thinking about your affair with John," he says at last.

Erica sighs: I should have known this would be regurgitated. Adultery. It's so easy to judge.

John was Erica's professor—deviant psychology 304—and he had a ready repertoire of clichés: "You're just what I've always wanted." "My wife and I are splitting up. Really, we're separated already, and she's looking for a place to live." Then he changed the story, told her his wife was depressed. "I'm waiting until she's healthy so I can leave her." Erica accepted this. He was loving and generous, gave her expensive perfume, silk underwear, books and flowers, and left passionate messages under her pillow. Erica was flattered and loved being pampered. Then John's wife found a letter Erica had written to him—a letter she had cautioned him to destroy after reading. He left Erica abruptly and, it seemed, without regret. She was distraught, not at the breakup per se, but at how he seemed to dismiss her so casually. Then she got angry at herself for being such a sap. Later still, she thought that he had wanted to get caught, that it was part of the game John played with his wife; a game designed to infuse passion into their dying relationship.

"What about John?" Erica asks, trying for an off-hand tone.

"I don't judge what you did, but it worries me," says Hugh. You obviously condoned his behaviour. You knew he was cheating on his wife, yet you say you value monogamy, that it's essential to you. I don't understand."

Erica stares at the mirror across the room, her reflection a slim shadow against Hugh's bulk. His tiny head peers over her shoulder. He's gained weight, she thinks fleetingly, then: He thinks I'm going to cheat on him.

She sighs. "I've already explained. At first, John told me they were separated, then it seemed they weren't but would be soon. You know what it's like once you get involved. Besides, that was a long time ago—more than ten years. I've learned a lot since then. It would never happen now."

He ignores her last sentence. "But why didn't you think about his wife? And she was ill, which makes it worse. Didn't you know it was wrong?"

"This is ridiculous," says Erica, flushed with impatience. "Do you think I liked being part of his cheating? He said he was leaving her, and I believed him. I was naive. And I didn't know about her depression, not until we were well into the relationship."

But Hugh cannot accept this admission of vulnerability, and Erica sees how their relationship is slowly turning as he aligns himself with the ghosts of her past lovers.

"I don't judge you, but . . ." he says and proceeds to take Erica's facts and feelings and to rearrange them in diabolical patterns, ". . . what you did was a massive deception."

He thinks I'm the sum of these past transgressions, Erica thinks, as if there are no other factors playing in the equation: n equals a plus b without accounting for the (c x d). It's just like *The Book of Love* says, disclosure can turn against you. Still, she hopes this is just a phase he has to go through to reassure himself. She hopes this relationship will work.

Erica changes the topic and mentions that she's looking forward to catching up with her friend Steve over lunch the next day.

Hugh asks who he is, and she explains that he was in university with her, Christina, and Erica, and that now he's an archivist at the National Library.

"What will you talk about?" Hugh asks, followed by: "Is he attached?" (Like some appendage, thinks Erica.) And: "Did you ever go out with him?"

"Aren't I allowed to have male friends?" Erica asks in exasperation, seeking the comforting, politically correct answer she's sure he will deliver.

"Of course," Hugh says, quickly.

"But I can't go out with them?"

Hugh pauses, says it would be different if he could be sure that Erica would tell him if something did happen.

"But you never would," he says, "because you know I'd leave you."

Erica takes a sharp breath. "That's so egotistical," she blurts out.

"If we were living together, I'd forbid it," Hugh replies.

Erica is dumbstruck by the *f* word.

"You're kidding," she says, staring at him.

He stares back coldly, says nothing.

She feels overwhelmingly tired, tired of the arguing, the constant need to defend herself. It's three in the morning. Erica tells him she needs to sleep, and that they'll talk later. She pulls the blankets around herself, turning her back on him, careful not to touch him.

I let this happen, she thinks. Damn it. Damn him. I knew better. The book even said so.

She stares into the dark room, focuses on Hugh's half-empty beer bottle, wondering if there is a middle ground between pure passion unencumbered by the past—the stark fantasy of *Last Tango in Paris*—and this nightmare. I'll break it off tomorrow, she vows.

Erica wakes to the sound of the front door deadbolt clicking. His side of the bed is empty. The digital clock beams: 4:17.

"Hugh?" she calls out, but there's no answer.

She stumbles into the hallway; Hugh's shoes are missing. He's gone, Erica thinks. Well, good riddance. She climbs back into the rumpled bed but can't find sleep. She begins crying. Why is it so fucking difficult? She can't bear the thought of starting over again with a new man. Yet again. Yet again.

A half-hour later, Erica hears the deadbolt opening. She pulls on her robe as she hurries into the hallway. Hugh's carrying a plastic grocery bag, tortilla chips sticking out top. He looks surprised then shamefaced.

"Whatcha doing?" Erica asks as she ties her sash.

"Nothing. I couldn't sleep."

"So you went grocery shopping?"

Now Hugh tells his secret: he's bulimic. At a single sitting, he can consume a half-dozen Venetian-cream donuts, three Snickers bars, a 250-gram bag of ranch-style potato chips, half a litre of Tracey's triple-chocolate ice cream, and a medium Mr. Za super-combination pizza.

"I eat standing at the kitchen counter," he says quietly, "shoving the food in as quickly as possible, mixing donuts with pizza, slurping down the Pepsi with each mouthful, and scooping in ice cream with a serving spoon."

"Then I puke, or I make myself puke." He holds out his hand. "That's where the scrape comes from—my teeth dig into the skin of my hand as I shove it down my throat. And then I have to miss work the next day," he says. "I'm pathetic."

"No!" Erica says. "No, you're not." And she holds him closely, reaching her arms around as far as they will go. He begins to cry, small tears forced out of his big eyes. It's the first time I've seen him cry, she realizes, and is drawn into his sadness, his need.

"You're being too hard on yourself, Hugh," she says. "You've got a disease. It's not your fault."

She is simultaneously repulsed by Hugh's lack of control and curious to know what lies behind it.

All the next day, Erica can't get Hugh off her mind. It's over with him, she eventually realizes, but it would be cruel to leave now that he's opened up to her, too cruel after all those nights when he listened to her fears and secrets. It's my turn to listen to him, she thinks, and the corollary: now maybe he'll stop picking on me.

Before meeting Suzanne and Christina at a patio in the market that evening, Erica pops into the library. She's shocked by the number of self-help books on eating disorders, volumes attesting to its prevalence. She checks out a couple, arrives early at the bar, and seats herself in the sunny patio. She opens a book to find lines that a previous reader has marked in screaming pink highlighter: ". . . the fruitless search for perfection of body, mind and action. . . . The constant effort of careful controlling leads to binges of total abandon, total loss of control."

The friends order Cuba Libras, a drink Erica had discovered at Club de Sip the week before. It's a concoction of dark rum and coke, juice of half a lime, slices of lemon and lime for garnish. The perfect summer drink.

"What about you guys?" asks Christina. "How are things going with the new man, Erica?"

Erica shrugs. "He's sexy as anything and amusing in bed, so that part is still great, but the rest, well, I don't know. He's a bit of a head case. I'm beginning to think all he wants is to control me."

"That's what we all want," Christina laughs, but there is a new edginess that both her friends notice. "We start out loving each other for how we differ, then we try to re-make each other in our own image. It's like we're all relationship demigods."

"Maybe," Erica says, "but Hugh's a lot worse than most."

She doesn't want to tell them about his eating disorder, but she needs something to back up her claim, so she tells them what Hugh said when she told him about the lunch with Steve.

"He what!" Christina screeches then lowers her voice to a whisper: "He 'forbids' you to see Steve? You're kidding, right?" she says, laying her hand on Erica's forearm.

Erica reaches for her drink, dislodging Christina's arm. She feels Tina's eyes on her and wishes she'd kept her mouth shut.

"He probably didn't mean it," says Erica defensively.

"Why'd he say it then?" asks Christina.

Erica shrugs her shoulders. Avoiding Christina's eyes, she says, "He's jealous, that's all. He's afraid I'm going to fool around on him."

"And are you?" asks Suzanne.

"Suzanne! How can you say that? We've only been together two months. If it wasn't working, I'd break it off with him. I'd never fool around. I learned that lesson a long time ago with John."

They all sip their drinks; ice cubes rattle in the highball glasses.

"It's like *The Book of Love* says about disclosure," says Erica, "especially with an insecure person. I've told Hugh all those stories about my past, and now he's using them as an excuse not to trust me. He probably thinks I'm only telling him half the story, and that I've had more pricks than a dart board."

Christina laughs: "Hey, you said you'd turn the book in."

"I will, I will. I just want to finish reading it."

"It's been a couple of months already. How long does it take?"

"If you want to stay with him," Suzanne interjects, "you'll have to call him on this forbidding business. That's way over the top."

Christina is surprised to feel annoyed at Suzanne's interruption. Chill out, she tells herself. I can take it up with Erica later.

"I'm sure he knows it was a ridiculous thing to say," says Erica. "He's probably embarrassed." Fat chance, she thinks and finishes her drink.

"It's just too funny that Hugh would be jealous of Steve," says Christina. "I'd bet anything Steve's a virgin. Mr. Androgynous."

"I've always thought he was in gay denial," says Suzanne.

"What do you think I should say to Hugh?" Erica asks.

"You're asking me?" says Suzanne. "I haven't had a date in eleven years, and before that, I was the Queen of Disastrous Dating."

Christina happily weighs in. "I'd tell him it makes you feel untrustworthy. See what he says. See if he cares, and if he doesn't, or if he denies your feelings, you might want to think about ditching him."

Erica nods mutely. She wants to defend herself, to explain the mitigating circumstances: Hugh's eating disorder and her sense of responsibility. But she can't. She shares his shame.

Erica means to talk with Hugh that night, but he arrives late, carrying a bright red shopping bag from Ooh, La, La, the high-end lingerie store on Edward Street. He pulls out a black and pink merry widow with garters and sheer black stockings and asks her, almost shyly, if she'll try them on. She puts on the costume, and he slowly begins undressing her: "You're the sexiest woman I've ever seen," he whispers in her ear then takes her lobe between his lips. He removes every piece of clothing, stroking her body all the while. It is the most erotic night they've shared. And afterwards, at two a.m. or whenever, Erica falls asleep quickly.

Early the next morning, Hugh leaves to catch a plane to a Toronto baseball press conference, and so Erica lets the confrontation slide.

That evening, she reads parts of several books on eating disorders and begins to understand the obsessive behaviour and its probable causes that stem from emotional neglect in childhood, leading to poor self-image. She speculates about her chances of helping Hugh. Popular culture has promised that love can overcome any obstacle: distance, disapproving parents, jealous, vindictive friends. She wonders if it can overcome a nasty obsession.

In one of the self-help books, the author encourages people with bulimia to reveal their underlying issues by asking them to identify the scariest feeling they can imagine. Erica puts the question to Hugh over the phone that evening.

Hugh replies: "Loving someone who feels mediocre about me, who doesn't love me." Then he adds: "Or being made a fool."

Erica hesitates. She knows he's waiting for a confirmation of her love, but instead she says: "I think that for me, the scariest thing, or at least the most disconcerting thing, is to love someone who is always questioning me. You make me feel untrustworthy, Hugh."

"Are you talking about the Steve thing? I'm just going by what you said," Hugh says. "You can tell a lot about how a person will behave in a relationship by seeing how they behaved in the past."

"People do change, you know. They learn," says Erica. "And what's with the forbidding? How can you forbid me to do something?"

There is a silence.

"I don't trust you, Erica," he says at last.

"You don't trust yourself," she retorts and slams down the receiver.

The tears overflow as the conversation replays through her head. She nearly calls him back a half-dozen times but instead dials Christina's number. She loves Suzanne to bits but values Christina's ability to cut to the chase on matters of the heart. Usually, anyway. She's been a bit testy lately.

When Christina picks up, Erica tells her about Hugh's eating disorder.

"He's got too much baggage. He needs a psychotherapist not a girlfriend," Christina says. "Why do you stay with him, Erica? Is it for the satisfaction between your legs?"

Erica is startled. "That's so harsh, Tina!" she says. "I'm surprised at you."

It seems harsh to Christina, too, but she finds she's unable to qualify or apologize. "I'm just asking," she says.

"There's a lot more to it than just that," Erica says defensively but is glad that Christina doesn't ask what.

After hanging up, she realizes that Christina is partly right. The sex is incredible, and as the Book says, there's an assumed intimacy with sex, an intimacy that makes her want to help him even though she knows she can't. Hugh stuffs himself with food while I stuff myself with his affection and attention. We're both insatiable. She wonders where her addiction comes from: Years of going without good sex? Desperation for intimacy? For a partner?

She shakes her head. It doesn't really matter. It's time to get out from under his weight.

Erica breaks up with Hugh over the telephone. She knows it's cowardly and lacks finesse, but she can't bear to see his hurt face. And, more importantly, she doesn't want to risk the temptation of his caresses and kisses, his hand cupping her breasts. Mostly, though, she can't bear to be subjected to his demented assumptions posed like questions but stated as facts: "There's someone else, isn't there? . . . You can't break your past patterns, can you? . . . Do you realize you're throwing away a great relationship?"

In the end, Hugh says all these things on the phone anyway. But Erica hangs up before she starts to cry. She lies on the couch, hugging a pillow, wetting it with tears, not of sadness but anger.

She should have known it would end badly and curses herself for imagining it could be otherwise.

chapter three

Otis Reveals

"WHAT I MEANT TO SAY . . ."

Suzanne's whispered words dissipate in the wind as she pedals furiously along the canal bike path. "What I *should'a* said . . ."

What? she wonders. What? What? What?

She pedals as fast as she can, outdistancing the uncertainty, the marauder on her heels, then downshifts, climbs a rise up to Lt. Pooley Drive, and stops for traffic. Words rattle in her head like shrapnel in a tin can: hurt . . . plan . . . love . . . best friend. A break between cars, and she zips across the road, careens up a side street to Greg's apartment.

"Coward," she mutters as she takes off her helmet. "I should'a stayed home and duked it out with Michael."

Instead, she bolted. What the hell, she figured. It might be a laugh watching the fifty-year anniversary episode of *Coronation Street*. Both she and Greg have been fans forever, and Greg's expecting her: "You're key party personnel," he said. She liked the sound of that. Her pannier holds a bottle of fairly pricey French wine and the fresh pita for the hummus Greg has made for the potluck brunch. He's invited a gang of friends; not all are Corrie fans, but they agreed that it was a good excuse for a party.

Suzanne fumbles with the key and locks her bike against a No Parking sign. She sees Greg across the parking lot and smiles vaguely in his direction; he's busy smoking and talking to a fat man with a pint-sized dog on a long leash. She pockets her keys, runs her hands through her clipped dark hair, and wonders if there's a depanneur around that sells Rolaids — she's popping them like mints these days. Then Greg spots her, waves, stamps out his cigarette, and bounds across the parking lot.

"Darhling!" he exclaims kissing one cheek then the other in

the French way. "It's so wonderful to see you!"

He's an exotic bird amidst the brutalist-style apartment towers and screeching traffic. His green shorts and pink shirt are topped with a massive mock Amazonian headdress featuring fluorescent feathers, flowers, and ribbons: hot pink, neon orange, scorching yellow. She feels dull in her ancient black biking shorts that have faded to a dank green. Her beige sport's top flattens her already small breasts and bleaches her already pale skin.

They're not close friends, Greg and Suzanne, more party buddies and complicit Corrie fans. His employer, Design-to-Die-For, does the graphics for the documentaries she researches and sometimes produces at Children's Network; occasionally he hangs out with her and Erica.

"Punctual as always!" Greg says. "Couldn't wait to pony up to the buffet, eh?"

"Yeah, I've been starving myself for days," she says, grinning as they cross to the elevators. "I didn't know it was dress up," she adds, tweaking his lei.

"You know me, any excuse will do."

I need this diversion, she thinks, but in the beat of a nanosecond, she hopes Erica will arrive soon—someone who knows what's going on. Last night at Echoes—the new place in the market with the high ceilings, stone walls, and burgundy velvet curtains—she finally told Erica what was up. Her Michael Moan (as she's dubbed it).

"We were so naive when we married," Suzanne said. "We had this romantic idea about being soulmates, that we could be everything to the other person: best friend, lover, partner. Everything."

"There's something in *The Book of Love* about that," Erica said. "Fusion or fission or something. Some need for delimitation."

Suzanne shrugged and turned her palms up, open to the room: "The bottom line is that we wanted it all from one person. We wanted a multiple personality, a relationship chameleon, who could change to meet our moods. You know, macho lover all the way to sympathetic confidante."

Suzanne sipped her gin fizz.

"How long since you found out? Three months?" asked Erica. Suzanne nodded.

"Maybe it's time to decide," said Erica. "Maybe it's time to push for some answers; find out how he feels. He's committed to you that's clear—he knows a good thing when he sees it—but you need to know where he stands, how he feels, what he wants."

More importantly, Suzanne thinks, I need to figure out where I stand. Whether I want to keep trying.

Greg pushes the up button: "Where's Michael?"

Suzanne scrambles for the right lie. She can't tell him about the impasse that propelled her out of their house. Greg isn't that kind of friend.

"He's playing golf," she says.

It's only a half-lie. Michael will make his way over to the club, eventually, after his fourth coffee and his *Economist*. June days are too fleeting to be wasted moping around the house, he would say. The old Michael would say. Nowadays, he slinks out the door with a perfunctory goodbye, afraid of her scowl. She's glad he didn't come with her, glad that she won't have to feign normalcy: the contented couple. Like cows, she thinks. Like those cows on tins of Carnation Evaporated Milk.

"Too bad. Michael's a scream," says Greg, "but I understand, totally. All those tight shorts and bulging leg muscles on the links. Yum."

"More like beer bellies and varicose veins," Suzanne says.

They laugh.

The easy banter with Greg. I used to have that with Michael, she thinks. Now their conversation is mired in the daily logistics of who, when, where, and so on. They are polite and accommodating, struggling to achieve a precarious marital balance. Meanwhile, the thing they're avoiding lurks behind every exchange: Will you be home for dinner? A seemingly innocuous question, but the subtext: What are you doing after work? Who are you going to see? As a junior partner, he often works late. She'd come to expect it. And she often worked after hours, too, developing proposals for her own documentaries. Turns out it gave him the perfect alibi and opportunity.

Suzanne and Greg step into the elevator, and she props herself up in the corner, dangling her pannier in front of her. Greg presses five on the control panel and stands beside her as other people enter: two young men, their painfully crafted physiques bulging beneath snug T-shirts, accompanied by two wispy women in halter sundresses and strappy high heels. Then two middle-aged women stride in as if they own the place, their bellies and thighs bulging out of their shorts like sausage escaping its casing. Greg raises his eyebrows towards the women and winks at Suzanne. His gay-dar is finely tuned. She nods, complicit.

The couples press their floors' buttons: seven, for the heteros; fourteen, for the gays. The elevator door closes.

"Fifth floor, lingerie," Greg whispers, and Suzanne grins.

Michael used to make me howl with laughter, she thinks, remembering one Halloween when she came home from work to find him dressed as the fat-era Elvis: half-unzipped white jumpsuit with sequins glued all over, oversized sunglasses, bad wig from the Giant Tiger. He kept it on all night, dishing out pint-sized chocolate-bars to bewildered kiddies clad in their ubiquitous Batman and princess costumes. They gaped in astonishment at him as he mumbled, "Thank you, thank you very much."

When they first started dating, his sense of humour propelled her forward, enabled her to put aside her concerns about their opposing political stances: he decidedly small "c" conservative, she decidedly left of mainstream. Opposites attract, she thought and tried to show an interest in the war histories he was always reading, the corporate cases that comprised the bulk of his practice, just as he listened to her talk about her documentaries, many of which focussed on safety or environmental messages, and about her passion for visual art. More than anything, they had fun together. And besides, they melded physically, couldn't stop smooching and hugging in public; they laughingly called themselves the "sickening couple." She tries to remember when that ended. Slowly, surreptitiously. Their relationship became infused with comfort, the physical urgency lessened, and they lived together well. At least I thought we did, she muses. But maybe we were more like roommates. With occasional sexual forays for sustenance.

The elevator clunks to a stop at the fifth floor. Suzanne clutches her pannier, shifts her body away from the wall. There's a collective pause as everyone waits for the door to slide open. Another second. Another. It doesn't budge.

Are we stuck? Suzanne wonders. Her stomach flips. We can't be stuck. Are we over the weight limit? She squints at the Otis elevator sign. Twelve, it says. We're eight. But twelve what? Dwarfs? Do those hard bodies put us over the limit?

The elevator jumps and begins moving again.

"That was weird," Greg says. He presses six on the panel.

I've exaggerated, Suzanne thinks. Like Michael says I always do. It's only some mechanical failure or something at the fifth floor. We can always take the stairs back down.

The man in front of her smiles at his girlfriend and brushes a nonexistent speck from her cheek. She catches his hand in hers and holds on. A tightness passes across Suzanne's chest. She wonders if he's cheating on her. She wonders this about every couple she sees now.

Discovered infidelity. The basic story line is always the same. Even the details come from a limited repertoire: fumbled kisses, groping in cars, steamy motel rooms, found notes. Such a tired old story, it defines cliché. Yet each incarnation inflicts fresh hell. For Suzanne, it was a modern variation on the found note: an e-discovery. In early March, she was dumping deleted e-mails on their home computer and found five messages from *her*. Suzanne checked them out because she didn't recognize the name. They weren't steamy or anything, just details of the when and where. Signed, however, with Love. Love, Angie. Oh, Angie. Just like that cloying Rolling Stones song. She printed out the e-mails and left them on Michael's empty dinner plate. Food for discussion, she thought wryly. Then she waited for him to come home.

She had a shot of Glennfiddich, tried to avoid coming to conclusions—there was probably a logical explanation. It was a joke or something. But despite this effort, an image of Michael and Angie together fucking formed in Suzanne's mind: he was naked, cupping her (probably large) breast, his other hand between her toned legs. Then his penis in her, the thrust and parry that Suzanne knew so well. Finally, his crying out at orgasm—something Suzanne adored in their lovemaking—but instead of calling out "Suzanne," his lips opened to "Angie, ooh, Angie."

This scene filled Suzanne's head then spread to her chest, bringing tightness, pain. She sat down at the kitchen table, thinking: I'm having a heart attack then realized that her heart was breaking. For the first time, she understood how her mother must have felt all those years ago. Suzanne was fourteen when her father left. At the time, all Suzanne could think of was how he was leaving her as well, and she turned her grief and hurt to resentment of him though never quite to hatred. Her mother never let go of the grief.

Michael came home. He flipped through the e-mails then sat at the table opposite her. Suzanne thought he didn't seem in the least surprised. The first thing he said was that he never intended for her to find out. Not, she thought coolly, that he was sorry he'd done it and hurt her, only sorry he'd been caught. He'd deleted all the other messages, he explained, and dumped the e-trash, but had overlooked these from her office address.

"There are no such things as mistakes," she told him. "You wanted me to know."

"I don't love her," Michael said. "She came after me, and I was flattered, curious."

"Shall I choose another adjective?" Suzanne yelled at him. "How about unfaithful? Disloyal? Cruel?"

Lurking behind her anger was hurt. Her feminine ego—at best only a half-inflated, week-old balloon—had been punctured.

Michael hung his head, assumed the penitent position of the adulterer revealed, muttered his I'm sorries. Then he looked at her and caught her eye. "It's over, Suzanne," he said. "I promise."

He has repeated this nearly every day since. Suzanne thinks perhaps he's telling the truth, but the damage is done: trust hangs like a tattered sail. They are adrift.

The elevator stops at six, but again the doors don't budge. One of the haltered ladies presses seven, and again they ascend. My lucky number, thinks Suzanne, but her luck fails. The door remains closed. One of the gay women presses fourteen again. Nothing. The others begin pressing their numbers. Still the elevator won't move. Suzanne breathes deeply in the heavy air. Too many people, she thinks. She closes her eyes, tries to concentrate on breathing, but she can't seem to fill her lungs.

"Anyone have a cell phone?" Greg asks.

For once, as luck would have it, no one does.

Suzanne leans into the corner, closes her eyes.

The other week, over martinis, Erica foisted *The Book of Love* on her. "I've been trying to learn from what happened with Hugh," she said. "The section on trust is spot on." Then her cell phone rang, which Suzanne took as an opportunity to dodge another discussion about the futility of self-help. She slipped the book into her purse as Erica talked on the phone. Back home, she put it in her lingerie drawer (he'll never look there, she thought ruefully), until she could reasonably return it to Erica. But one evening, when Michael was particularly late getting home from the office and her head was racing—Is he with her now? Or someone else?—she poured herself a Glenfiddich and turned to the book. Under "Adultery" she found pages and pages about the destruction, the patterns, the pathos. She considered a section on the biological imperative; how men are almost compelled to cheat in order to sow their seed as widely as possible. She read about the thrill-seeking personality, which seemed a little more likely with Michael. The author, Foster, explained how secrets fuel the sexual fire. But then, Suzanne noted, Foster pulled out the usual psycho-explanation and foisted the blame onto parents because they deliberately hid sex from their offspring and refused to speak of it. Naturally, sex came to be associated with deception and secrecy, and—the leap for Suzanne—now men and women think they can only have good sex in secret relationships.

A load of yada, yada babble, Suzanne decided. Nothing's that simple. There's no one reason for these things. So much depends on the particulars, the emotion. Besides, we always had good sex. At least . . . then she spots another passage in *The Book of Love*:

> When one partner finds affection—and sex—outside the marriage, they revive their sex life at home, too.

Of course, she thought, I'm such a fool. All the signs were there in November: those sudden tender bursts of loving. I should have fucking known, but no, I snoozed until April.

After she left the e-mails on his plate, Michael tried to keep their sex life going, but she couldn't let go of the fact that his sexual attentions—his penis—had been elsewhere and likely would be again. She kept telling herself that she should leave him before he left her, that it would be easier that way. But she couldn't bring herself to do it, kept hoping that maybe . . . maybe . . . After a month or so, he gave up trying to make love with her, and she wondered if she'd lost an opportunity to repair things, if making love was a necessary part of the healing. But I couldn't, she thinks, I just couldn't.

And now, it seems too late. All that is left are brotherly pecks on her cheek and perfunctory pats on her back, like a nurse might offer to an upset, irrational patient, as if to say: "There, there, you'll be all right, dear." That's what he did as she left this morning. Patted her shoulder like a favourite pet—a faithful, well-behaved dog. There, there, the words unsaid, but audible nonetheless.

Suzanne's eyes pop open. The tall, over-pumped man in front is prying at the elevator door with his fingertips, but he can't get a grip. He tries again and again, everyone watching silently.

"Fucking thing," he mutters, and begins jumping up and down like a three-year-old throwing a tantrum. The car vibrates and rattles. Suzanne envisions a cable snapping somewhere, the car plunging. The idiot!

"Don't . . ." she says before knowing the word is coming. Mercifully, it is muffled as the elevator moves again.

"We're going to fourteen," says the shorter man, who is standing by the panel. Fourteen. Which, of course, is actually thirteen, thinks Suzanne, the universally unlucky number. The flowers in Greg's headdress look wilted, faded, though they are made of indestructible plastic and will no doubt endure well into the next millennium. Long after we're gone, thinks Suzanne, when none of this will matter in the least.

She drops her pannier on the floor between her feet.

The shorter man makes a grab for his girlfriend's hand, but she crosses her arms in front of her chest and stares at the control panel. What are *they* quarrelling about? Money? Commitment? Sex?

Every day, Suzanne wills herself not to cry, remembering her mother's incessant wailing, her puffy eyes and blotchy complexion when her dad left them. She curses the irony of her situation, which mimics her parents' marital woes, and vows not to succumb to self-pity, to be practical and proactive. Shortly after the e-discovery, Suzanne suggested that they go for counselling.

"We can work it out ourselves," Michael said tersely. "I don't want to air our dirty laundry in front of a stranger."

"You say you want to fix this, yet you won't even come to counselling with me?" she said accusingly.

"I can't," said Michael. "Please, don't ask me to do that, Suzanne. The counsellor will just blame me, and I'll feel even worse than I do now. We can work it out, Suzanne. I know we can."

"I'm going anyway," she told him. "I can't do this alone."

She put her name on the waiting list with a couples therapist that her family doctor recommended, but her first appointment isn't until August—it might as well be five years from now, she thinks.

After three months of marital purgatory, she felt worn down by the uncertainty. She began listing towards him, began wondering if they—if she—could leave the "why" behind, at least for now, and turn to something new. If I forgive him will we survive? What's the saying? If it doesn't kill you, it will make you stronger.

This past week, she caught herself humming along to a Québecois song on the radio and eventually deciphered the words: A woman is telling her husband that the sign of true love is the ability to fall in love a second time. It gave Suzanne pause to consider. Tentatively to hope.

The other couple is still holding hands. The woman leans over and whispers something in his ear. He smiles into her eyes. They're still on the top of the roller coaster of love, that unsustainable, high-energy ride. Invariably, life intervenes, and you settle for the little kiddy-car version: gentle, no real surprises but enjoyable nonetheless. But the roller coaster, that rush, it's addictive, hard to forsake.

Michael's still with her, with Angie, Suzanne thinks. The thought jars her. She feels hot suddenly and fans her face with her hand.

Greg takes off his headdress and fiddles with a red flower. He twists its stem and holds it, but it springs back to its former unnatural angle.

"The future is in plastics," he whispers to Suzanne, a lame allusion to *The Graduate*, a joke to alleviate the stress. She smiles weakly. *The Graduate*. The allure of the older woman. The cougar. Is that my future? Or will I be a fruit fly, frequenting gay establishments and acquiring the lexicon of men who hold no threat—or potential.

Last night, bolstered by Erica's advice and three cocktails, Suzanne asked Michael how he felt about her.

"I've told you. I love you," he said, and she noted the impatience in his voice.

"And the passion?" she asked.

"Well, no," he drawled then quickly added, "but that's only natural after nine years."

This changed an hour or so later to an admission that he had no romantic feeling towards her. He said it as though it was the same thing as passion, as if the two were interchangeable. But they aren't, said Suzanne.

"You can have passionate, good sex without romance, but at the heart of romance, for me at any rate, is complete devotion to your partner. You want to be close to them, to spend time with them, to care for them." She held herself back from adding the final phrase "to lie with them, not to them."

He sighed and patted her hand. "I'm really tired, babe. That damn Driscoll case is driving me crazy. Let's talk tomorrow, okay?"

The elevator arrives at fourteen and everyone holds their breath. Nothing. The door is definitely stuck.

"This happens all the time with this elevator," says the tall man. "It stops, won't open, and then it suddenly does."

Is he trying to reassure us? Suzanne wonders. The dolt. Not only are we stuck, the elevator isn't well maintained. Someone once told her that if an elevator plunges, you should jump up and down and hope you're up in the air when it hits bottom. It seemed logical at the time, but now she realizes it's ridiculous. The impact would still be felt. It will jump to meet you, breaking legs, bodies. There are no tricks for avoiding the inevitable.

"Should I press the emergency button?" asks the short man beside the control panel.

"Yes!" Suzanne says before anyone. The others murmur or nod in agreement.

The bell is shrill and annoying yet redeeming at the same time. The short man varies the rhythm so she doesn't know when to next expect it. During a pause, they hear someone call to them, asking if they're okay.

"We're stuck!" Suzanne yells.

Idiot! Why am I panicking? Stare at the control panel or the doors like everyone else. At least they haven't noticed I've lost it.

The voice says the service people have been called and will arrive soon.

Soon. How long will it take on a Sunday? An hour? More? Suzanne closes her eyes and braces herself more firmly into the corner, feeling the reverberation of the elevator's faulty mechanism.

"Let's keep going up," suggests Greg. "My friends got stuck once, and it opened at the top floor for them. They said it always does."

So he knows, too! She looks at the control panel. Twenty-three! Twenty-three floors to fall! The short man presses twenty-three. This can't be right, she thinks.

Nothing happens.

"Try fifteen," one of the gay women says.

The elevator moves. Suzanne half-smiles. It's good to move, she thinks. It's something I know. Move, leave behind fear, supplant it with hope. No, that's too Pollyanna-ish. More likely movement is merely a diversion, something to take my mind away from the actual peril of the situation. In this case, the physical peril; with Michael, the emotional.

The man in front of her lets go of his girlfriend's hand and puts his arm across her shoulders, gives her a hug.

This morning she asked Michael: "How can I live with someone who has no romantic feeling for me?"

He looked at her. "Is that so important?" he asked.

"Yes, for me it's essential."

"I don't know what to say, then," he said. "I can't invent something like that."

"We have to do something," she said. "I can't keep going on like this."

There was a long pause.

"Is it over then?" he asked.

"No," Suzanne said quickly. "No, I want to keep living with you."

"You're my best friend," he said softly.

She frowned and turned away, thought of his myriad acts of devotion and kindness: making dinner, running household errands, bringing her breakfast in bed, each grapefruit segment meticulously cut out.

Suzanne turned to him. "You're my best friend, too," she said, because she was afraid and needed to buy time.

She thought about what was missing, what had been lost — not only trust but also the underlying emotional and physical intimacy that mitigates, softens the daily trials and grind of a life spent in proximity; the thing that allows you to pick up his dirty socks for the thousandth time without pause or complaint; pick them up with a knowing nod of your head and an inward smile at his foibles, which are, in every way, as much an accepted part of him as the things you first fell in love with.

He isn't my best friend, she thought. Erica and Christina. They're the ones I turn to. I should have told him that. We have too many secrets already.

But somehow she couldn't.

They inch up floor by floor. One of the gay women has taken charge from the short man and is pressing button after button. The younger women are perspiring under their foundation; their dresses are wrinkled. The elevator arrives at the twentieth. Again the doors won't open. Where are the repair guys? wonders Suzanne. Why are they taking so friggin' long? She wants to lunge across the elevator and press the alarm again and again. If we make enough noise, tenants will complain, and maybe the service guys will arrive more quickly.

They reach twenty-three, the top floor, pinnacle of hope, but the doors are still stuck. No one says anything. Suzanne is afraid to open her mouth, afraid some word of alarm will leap out, and she will be definitively exposed. Everyone will know the extent of her suffering, and their knowing will make it worse, give it a name and place.

The other gay woman presses twenty-two, and they start their descent.

There was nothing left to say after that. Nothing would be enough.

Twenty-one.

But Suzanne needed to mitigate the intensity and the potential finality this morning.

Twenty.

"Let's see what happens after this summer," she told Michael. "After we have our vacation together and some time alone."

"Okay," he mumbled.

Mea culpa, mea culpa, she thinks. He will agree to anything to salve his guilt. Anything.

Nineteen.

But what difference will a vacation make? Suzanne asks herself. A change of venue to distract us? We'll still be alone even if we're together. We'll try to connect with more earnest conversation: he, trying to justify/explain his actions; me, trying to find a place to move on to as I search for an answer to why. But I already know. It's another hackneyed tale from *The Book of Love*—as simple as falling out of love and as endlessly complex.

Eighteen. Seventeen.

Greg is giving her an odd look, one of concern tempered by his own half-panic. Have I been speaking aloud? she wonders. He smiles tentatively. Suzanne nods then looks down at her dirty white running shoes streaked with bicycle grease.

This summer won't make any difference. Once intimacy is gone, it can't be reclaimed, only reinvented as something else; something crass and calculated aided by sexual toys and lubricants, self-help books and therapists. The other is gone. At best, time will allow us to come to some agreement, some truce so we can stay together indefinitely without passion or romance but within the confines of friendship under the guise of coupledom.

Maybe we can live comfortably together, but what about having kids? A family? No, no, it's not enough, she decides. Not for me.

Her heart is pounding. The elevator stops abruptly at sixteen, and magically, at the behest of pulleys and gears, the metal door clunks open. Suzanne grabs her pannier and elbows her way out. She slumps against the hallway wall as the others race down the hall towards the stairs, chattering about needing to go to the bathroom, about taping Out of Order signs on all the floors.

"Are you all right?" Greg asks her.

"No, not really," she says. "But I'm glad it's over."

Greg pulls a lei of bright plastic flowers from his cargo shorts' pocket and smiles as he slips it over her head. The colours make her skin look even paler, nearly translucent.

"Welcome to the Land of Oz," he says.

She nods and smiles wanly up at him. He holds out his hand and helps her up. They make their way down the hall towards the stairs, she touching the bright petals.

chapter four

Fusion

DON WIPES HIS MOUTH with a wrinkled cloth napkin. "School's out for summer." He sings the Alice Cooper song slightly off-key to the children.

Norris and Vita giggle.

"School's out, forever."

Christina smiles.

"The whole summer off!" she says, making an effort of enthusiasm for the children. "Woo-hoo!"

"You must be looking forward to taking it easy," Don says to Christina. "Gardening, reading, lollygagging with the kids." He grins at her.

Christina nods and turns to her dinner, cutting off a piece of the pork cutlet, noting that he hasn't mentioned painting. Not much point, she thinks ruefully, I don't even have a studio.

When they first looked at their house, they'd agreed that she would take the south-facing fourth bedroom—she needs lots of natural light for her self-portraits and finds it better for illuminating her mirrored reflections. But when the mover came, she's the one who piled the seemingly endless boxes of kids' toys and games in that bedroom, relegating her art supplies and canvases to the unfinished basement—"For now." Sitting among half-unpacked boxes, they talked vaguely about building a play area in the basement so she could reclaim the upstairs bedroom, but eight months after the move, her canvases are still shrouded in brown paper.

"I'm thinking of setting up my studio," she says to no one in particular.

"That's a great idea, Tina," Don replies. "You could hire someone to do the renos in the basement for the kids' playroom."

Because clearly you're not going to do it, she thinks, then corrects herself. After more than a decade, she is coming to accept the imperfections of marriage, the compromises over logistics, the day-to-day domestic hustle, the long lags without intimacy — particularly long these days. And she's realistic. He's a good father and husband, but he's been frantically busy since his promotion a year ago to assistant vice-president in charge of IT product development. And she's been busy, too, settling into this house, adjusting to teaching full time instead of three days a week, plus the long commute. Still, his statement is a bit of a showstopper; it makes Christina feel overwhelmed. The thought of clearing away all those boxes, getting a contractor, designing a playroom in the basement — it's too much to cope with right now.

"Hey, Vita," Don says, "pass those peas, sweet pea."

She giggles. "Peas for Papa," she lisps.

Christina smiles in spite of herself.

After supper, the children go outside to play in the sweltering late June evening although it's cool, almost cold in the new house. Don loads the dishwasher while Christina unloads the dryer and folds and sorts the clothes into piles. After their chores, they sit at the kitchen table. Don reads the specs on his new BlackBerry; every so often a word escapes from his lips:

"Switch . . ."

"Portal . . ."

Christina consults her list of household minutiae, ticking off the things that she's done:

> ✓ call re. kid's vaccinations (need?)
> ✓ phone Vita's piano teacher
> ✓ order lamp shade
> ✓ hem V's pants
> ✓ b-suits for kids
> ✓ car in — oil change, brakes?
> — V's bike p-up Tues.
> — Ph. re. ins. for braces?

". . . multiple-portal internet access," Don murmurs.

Christina turns the paper over and starts a new list:

Must do this summer
- *sort basement (contractor) & clear playroom for studio*
- *call Erica & Suzanne & do fun stuff*
- *get friggin' act together*

Christina knows that soon Don will say "I wonder what's on TV?" even though he knows already. These days, he watches reruns of *Frasier* then *Law & Order*. She will put the children to bed then sit beside him doing something. Most recently, she's been sorting and labelling her mother's old family photos supposedly so she can make a scrapbook. Three of the other teachers are making scrapbooks. Scrapbooking they call it—as if making it into a verb adds to its importance, its legitimacy as a pastime—and as the art teacher, she feels pressure to produce the most creative, the best. But her heart's not in it. She finds herself thumbing through the photos again and again: her parents as their younger selves, her dad's arm around her mom's waist, both grinning their heads off; launches of lines of the furniture he designed, her father posed with a manufacturer—Steff or Georg, she can't recall which—against a backdrop of sleek teak sideboards, tables, and chairs. Then there are the annual photos of the family with Christina dressed like a little doll in frills and flounces, her hair twisted into tight curls, bow lips, miniature matching handbag. And other photos of her: perched high on her dad's shoulders; helping her mom decorate Christmas shortbread, squeezing garishly coloured icing from store-bought plastic tubes. She gets older, and her dad disappears from the family photos. Now it's her mother holding her latest textile design, the more commercially viable striped and circle fabrics, but also mid-century modern—crosspatch squares in exquisite shades of sea turquoise and green, whimsical lemons replete with tiny leaves on a grey background—and some opulent, leafy motifs in rich burgundy and green that echo themes from the forties, her mother's childhood. I could paste some swatches of fabric into the scrapbook, she thinks. Then mount the photos on them.

Don turns a page in the manual before looking up at her.

"Tina, maybe we should try to get a weekend away this summer, just the two of us," he says. "We could go up the Valley or across the river into the Pontiac—it's lovely there. Rent a cottage or something."

"Who'll look after the kids?" she asks.

"Erica, maybe. The kids love her. Or Suzanne. What do you think?"

"Sure, I mean, yeah, it would be great to spend some time together." But she wonders what they will talk about outside their domestic selves.

"Sometimes I feel like I hardly know you any more," he says softly. "I'm not blaming you. It's just that our lives have become so cluttered."

"Sometimes I feel like I don't know me either," she says.

"What do you mean?"

"Oh, nothing. I'm just tired. It's been a long year. I'm gonna go check on the kids."

"Sure, honey." He turns back to his manual.

She pulls her heavy blonde hair into a ponytail and wraps an elastic around it. I should have been more enthusiastic about going away, she thinks. I've become such a naysayer. I could have explained that I need him to help me with the studio; he would have been sympathetic. Why didn't I? Why am I so reticent, so stubborn? She steps outside into a wall of heat and humidity onto the new deck. Don built it the previous fall using pressure-treated wood because it's maintenance-free, though she argued against it, citing articles about arsenic leaching from the wood into the ground below. He read the articles, too, but pointed out that it's only dangerous if the kids play under the deck. He nailed white plastic lattice around the footings.

Don said she worries too much, and though he said it kindly, she detected a paternalistic undertone. Or thought she did. She wasn't sure and so chalked up her unease to fatigue. Her usual justification for what ails her. Fatigue that seems to begin inside her bones. "I'm bone-tired," her mother used to say on Friday evenings as she massaged her stockinged feet, "and there's still so much to do." Christina understands now what she meant. She feels her to-do list is never ending, a tumour weighing her down, sickening and impeding her life.

She hears Vita's high-pitched, excited squeal permeate the still evening and knows Norris can't be far behind.

Collapsing into the Adirondack chair, she notes that the lime-green paint is peeling rather badly. Another thing to add to the list. She gazes out over the neighbouring backyards. The trees are young, her view unobstructed. She sees a flash of blue—a pool; a splash of yellow—marigolds that, on closer inspection, are lined up like soldiers protecting vulnerable young shrubs barely poking out of beds of dyed-red cedar mulch. Red dye number two? she wonders. Clotheslines aren't allowed in the subdivision, and all the houses are a uniform palette of browns and beiges.

She can't help longing for her old yard, the compact, enclosed lushness of it. There were mature maples swooping over the table-sized lawn, out-of-control sumacs from the neighbour's neglected yard pushing against the fence, and her own clusters of ferns, astilbe, and hosta—especially the cool, meditative hosta—melding one into the other in texture and nuanced colour: smooth green-yellow, heavily ridged blue-green, flat dark green, curly lime-green. She had a great view of it from her studio in the old sunroom, which was really a walled-in porch that Don had insulated for her. She used to spend hours there, but since Vita's birth, there's been no time for art. No space in her head—or her new house. But maybe that's just the latest excuse.

She sees Don through the patio doors fiddling with his Black-Berry.

She didn't want to move but in the end agreed with Don that it was best for the kids. Their old street downtown had a boarding house and a messy corner shop crowded with tattooed tough-ies and people in sweatpants buying excessive numbers of lottery tickets that they obviously couldn't afford, but they needed the hope. The local school was thick with kids whose parents were on welfare—or worse, said Don: "It's not safe for Vita and Norris." And she countered with a news item she'd read about a recent child molestation in the suburbs. He persisted: "Vita and Norris need a good school with field trips and opportunities." Touché. Opportunities, yes, she agreed. The local school in their old neighbourhood wasn't the best. There weren't enough ESL teachers for the newly arrived Canadians and not enough services for the special-needs kids integrated into the regular system. The smart kids, like Norris, were basically left to their own devices, which meant he was bored. It would be only a matter of time until he got into trouble. This move was an opportunity for a better education, and so, reluctantly, she agreed. To do otherwise would have branded her as a bad mother, one who puts her own preference for inner-city dwelling ahead of her children's welfare. But now she wonders if there could have been a compromise rather than this extreme—this new subdivision, an outpost on the cusp of civilization. "The Wonder Bread blandness of it all," she'd lamented to Suzanne.

A rivulet of sweat escapes her armpit, trickles down her side.

"It's my turn!"

Christina jerks to the edge of her seat. It's Vita yelling, "It's my turn, Norris! I'm telling Mommy!"

Christina propels herself out of her chair and out the gate, meets Vita on the sidewalk halfway down the block. Strands of hair cling to her red, flushed cheek. She brushes them back impatiently.

"Norris won't share his bike with me," Vita protests.

Christina takes her small, grimy hand. That feeling of injustice is so intense in children. They still assume that life is fair. She envies this optimism.

"I'll talk to him, Vita," she says to soothe.

Norris is hanging out with some older boys down at the corner, boys who look tougher than any in the old neighbourhood. Boys with raw, angry gazes despite their designer play clothes. Maybe, in part, because of them, she thinks. She spots Trevor, Pat's son: Pat Tripp, she remembers. They met as they sorted books one February evening for the school book sale. Pat, a lawyer herself, talked about her job at the national association of lawyers. She was in line for the CEO job but then unexpectedly got pregnant with her third child and felt she wouldn't be able to cope with everything. She stroked her swollen belly: "Rob's great, but three kids and a demanding job with lots of travel—it's too much." Christina heard the regret in her voice. "It will come up again," Pat added as if to reassure herself. And Christina nodded: "Or something better," she said, although she didn't believe it. She felt sympathy for Pat, felt she might learn something from her. They agreed that they must go for coffee sometime and exchanged phone numbers, but neither called. And now it has slipped off the to-do list, thinks Christina. She vows to put it back on as soon as she gets home: I have to make some friends around here.

She tells Norris that it's time to go home, and he turns to talk to one of his new friends, all bravado and male dominance, asserting his new neighbourhood persona. She walks away, and he follows slowly on his bicycle. When they are out of earshot of his new buddies, she gently chides him for not sharing with his sister; says Vita's bike will be back from the shop on Tuesday and how would he feel if he didn't have a bike. And he turns sweet and gentle again, for a time—until testosterone and circumstance turn him into the boys at the corner, she thinks. It won't be long now; he's already eight. She gives Vita's hand a squeeze, smiles down at her little girl: seven last week, and she's already asked if she can wear makeup.

Back inside the house, Christina hears gunshots and shouting: *Law & Order* is starting. They step into the family room, and without thinking, she barks out: "Don, can you put the children to bed?"

He looks at her, surprise in his raised eyebrows not at the request but at her tone. She, too, is surprised at the anger in her voice. Anger supplanting depression. She'd read that somewhere.

"Sure, Tina," he says. "Come on you two, shower, teeth, then a story . . . maybe two if you're quick."

He runs his finger down Christina's arm on his way out, but before she can respond, he is gone. I should have smiled in return, she thinks, staring at his back as he goes upstairs. I should have flirted, said "later" or something. She thinks of her dresser drawer full of fraying cotton or flannel nightgowns, tries to remember the last time they made love. And before that, the last time she'd had an orgasm. She can't remember either. *I've become a hausfrau,* she thinks, with dismay.

She switches off the television and grabs the cordless phone, goes back outside, and speed-dials Suzanne's number.

"Hey, girlfriend, how's the heat of the city?"

"My underwear is welded to my butt," says Suzanne, "and I'm surrounded by half-packed boxes. Other than that, fine."

"Michael's move went well today?"

"Yeah. It's such a relief to have that over, though he was great about stuff. We didn't argue about anything. It was all very civil. Though I had a good cry when he closed the door. I know this is the right thing to do, but I don't want to talk about it yet. So, how're things in the 'burbs?"

"Languid and dull. First day of summer holidays tomorrow, and I'm totally depressed about it."

"Aren't you looking forward to painting?"

"And looking after the kids and the house and the garden . . . God, I'm such a whiner. It's all sort of slid out of control. I don't even have the juice to get my studio together—but you've heard this all before. It's boring. Even I'm bored with it."

"Not at all. It's important," says Suzanne. "Let me know if you need a hand moving stuff or setting things up. Seriously, Tina, think about it. I'll be an expert after this week."

Christina hears her taking a drag of a cigarette.

"Hey, you're smoking again?"

"Yeah, it eases the pain. I'll quit later," she says vaguely. "Oh, listen, I found something you should read from that *The Book of Love*—Erica lent it to me."

"She still hasn't returned it!" Christina says, raising her eyebrows. "That was months ago. I'm going to call her about it."

"I wouldn't bother," says Suzanne. "You know Erica. She'll return it when she's good and ready. No one can convince her to do something she doesn't want to do."

"But I'm sure the author—Foster, right?—I'm sure she's looking for it. It's wrong to keep it, don't you agree?"

"Of course, but it's Erica's problem."

"I guess it is," says Christina, "but I still feel somehow responsible because we were there. And I just don't understand why she's keeping it."

"She'll get tired of it," says Suzanne. "It's definitely just pap for the populace, though every so often, there's something sort of worthwhile. There's this section called 'Love's Progression' about the stages of love.

Love's Progression

The first stage of love is fusion: you meld together, lose yourself. This is what people seek because in giving yourself to the other person and through the wholeness you form, you come to understand yourself. Plato talks about this in terms of eroticism: two sides of a sphere come together to form a complete sphere. You fall in love with something unrealized in yourself and, in the best case scenario, you can use what you learn in that relationship to grow into a better person.

However, this growth depends on the essential second step of love: delimitation, from the Latin, delimitare or boundary. This is where you draw lines between yourself and the other to define who you are. In other words, you keep your separateness. Without this, there is a danger that you will become so incorporated into the "us-ness" of couple-hood, that you will stop growing as an individual. Change is the essence of life. If you allow it, inevitably the inertia will spread to your relationship and it too will wither and die. This demise is often masked by a sort of mercantile exchange (you do *x* and I'll do *y*), but this exchange allows you to only *function* as a couple, not to *live*.

Delimitation is fraught with difficulties. Our popular culture fosters a belief, from fairy tales to films, that fusion is the ultimate goal of a relationship. Without this fusion, couples often feel that their love has died, and they await the end. Or in an attempt to delimitate, one partner may significantly limit access; in effect, he or she closes off, sometimes to protect him or herself, sometimes out of neglect, but rarely out of desire to do so. Communication is the key to moving from fusion to delimitation.

The trick is to delimitate and, at the same time, keep connected. To instill separateness but not to separate. In genuine love, separateness is respectfully maintained and nurtured.

Progress in relationships is fraught with danger but essential nonetheless.

"I found it interesting in the context of what happens in a long-term relationship," says Suzanne. "You begin with fusion where you sort of meld together—you know all that joined-at-the-hip stage—then there's delimitation where you re-establish your separate self. I mean it's simplistic, obviously, but there's a kernel of truth to it. That's one of the ways I blew it with Michael. I put too much energy into the couples thing and stopped doing my own stuff, stopped growing—isn't that the most flaky new age word ever? Still, we both know what life without growth means."

"Yeah, the 'burbs," says Christina. "We've all sort of fused together—hubby, kids—melded like a big glob of marshmallow. Especially in this heat."

Suzanne laughs. She knows Christina's not really kidding, but she hasn't got time to pursue it. "We'll have to talk about it over a cocktail or two with Erica. Listen, I've gotta run, Tina, but I was going to call you anyway. I got the best news today. I applied for funding to do a documentary about Maura Kerby . . ."

Christina's bra feels suddenly too tight: Maura! "I went to art school with her," she says.

"Yeah, I remember you guys were buddies when we first met. And remember, we went to see her first show at the Bank Gallery in Montreal way back when? But you had some sort of falling out, didn't you? Listen, I hope you aren't upset that I didn't tell you sooner. I would have, but I was afraid it wouldn't come to anything. Anyway, the long and short of it is that I'm getting funding for the documentary! All of it. I'll start filming early next year."

It should be me, thinks Christina. You should be filming me. She knows how I feel about Maura. It's disloyal. She considers asking why Suzanne chose Maura, but she knows the answer so instead she says: "Congratulations. I know you've been wanting to make a documentary forever. Does it feel like a dream?"

"Yeah, yeah, sorta. And it's perfect timing, post-Michael. Something to get him off my mind. There's tons of prep. I'll have to get a filming crew together and take a leave of absence at work for a couple of months. Maybe in January or February."

I had at least as much talent as Maura, thinks Christina. *Have*, I *have* just as much talent. "I'm really pleased for you," she says to Suzanne. And she genuinely is.

"I've gotta run, Tina, or I'll be late. I just got off the phone with Erica and Greg, and we're meeting for a celebratory cocktail. Can you come? We're going to that new place, The Metropole."

"Oh, I read about it," Christina lies. I'm so out of the loop, she thinks. "I'd like to come, but it's such a trip into town. And it's so hot. God, listen to me. I sound like a Stepford wife."

Suzanne laughs. "Well, if you insist on moping around the house, there's a great documentary on channel two right now: *The Wounded Stag*. It's about the duende and art. I'm taping it. Check it out and we'll talk later. I've *really* got to run. Talk to you tomorrow."

Christina hangs up and immediately feels the disconnect. No one—not even their professors—would have guessed that Maura would be the one who made it big, although she was the only student with business cards. That alone should have been a clue. In remembering, Christina feels the sting of hurt. They were close friends, or so Christina thought, hanging out at the university studios for endless hours till one or two in the morning, drinking plonk, talking about art: contemporary, Renaissance, the merits of new directions like performance and installation. Christina had been immersed in it since birth, surrounded by perennially growing stacks of oversized art books throughout her childhood home and prints of famous works jammed onto the walls. Originals from her parents' friends and even a small David Milne hung in the living room. But Maura's father was a cop, and her mom worked as an executive assistant for an editor of a trade magazine—a mining mag, she thinks it was—and they had more interest in the Rolling Stones than Rembrandt.

She and Maura were inseparable that whole second year at university. They even dressed alike: shopping together at bargain stores that Maura knew, they perfected an artist bo-ho look with vintage round skirts and chunky jewellery. Then it changed. During the summer, Maura got a job as a gofer in a Toronto gallery and only managed to phone Christina once during the four months. And when Maura returned to Ottawa, she didn't call. They'd run into each other at school, Maura inevitably in the company of a grad student or one or another of the teaching assistants. She'd give Christina a big hug and say, "We must get together," but she didn't return her calls. Twice this happened.

Erica said Maura was probably one of those women who rely on friendships to move their careers forward. Christina thought there was more to it than that; that she had been judged and found lacking: boring or dull witted or conservative.

Christina cornered her in the studio one night as Maura was clearing out her things. Christina had heard she'd found a real space at an artist's collective near downtown.

"I haven't seen you around for a while," Christina said.

"Yeah, I've joined the Bronson Collective. It's great. I have a really big space with lots of windows."

"I don't mean just now," said Christina, "but generally. Since last spring."

"I had a great summer at the gallery. It really changed things for me. I met so many artists, and I learned so much about the business side of things especially."

Christina had the impression that Maura had repeated these lines many times. Then Maura continued.

"It's nothing personal, Tina. I'd like to keep our friendship, but I have so little time now. All I do is paint and study. It's not you—I don't have time for any friends right now."

Christina recognized the it's-not-you-it's-me line; she'd used it herself many times for romantic breakups. What crap, she thought angrily. It's just an excuse to off-load me without really saying why.

"You must have time for a coffee or a glass of wine," she said.

Maura shrugged: "You know how it is. You must be busy, too."

"Of course," she agreed, "but friends are important. Listen, Maura, if you've outgrown me or whatever, just say so, and I'll leave you alone."

Maura put a bunch of paint brushes into a box. "It's not that. It's complicated . . ." She paused.

Another classic line, thought Christina, but said nothing. She stared intently at Maura who held her gaze for a second then glanced at her watch.

"My friend with the van is coming in fifteen minutes, and I'm nowhere near ready. Steve's helping me move," she added.

"My friend, Steve?" asked Christina.

"Yeah, he's sweet. Not exactly a stellar conversationalist but sweet."

Like me, thought Christina. She's using him like she used me. Him, for his van; me, for my background, my knowledge. She considered defending Steve, but decided it would be pointless.

"Well, I won't keep you from your important work," she said.

Maura ignored her sarcasm: "Yeah, I'll see you in drawing class on Wednesday, Tina."

Christina went back to her studio feeling angry, used. Late that night, she awoke and wondered if she lacked the same drive as Maura, wondered if this was the way to success, and if she was being naive. But in the morning, she looked at her latest works, her first self-portraits, and decided that there were other ways through talent and hard work.

She talked to Erica about her anger, and Erica agreed she'd been used.

"She's a bitch," said Erica and gave her a hug. "You don't need her," she added. "You've got us, your long-haul friends."

And Christina agreed.

At the end of the year, Christina took extra pleasure in winning the class prize for her triptych of self-portraits. Maura made a point of congratulating her then said she must visit her in New York City where she'd got another job at a gallery. But Maura didn't send her address. And now look at her: solo shows in Toronto and New York. A couple of pictures in the National Gallery even. A rising star, they say. And me, me . . .

Christina blinks into the blinding summer light. Her heart bangs against her ribs, her throat swells, and tears pool. She blinks again. Delimitation? Ha. More like assimilation, she thinks. Then catches herself: it's too easy, too simple to blame Don or the kids or the lack of studio space or time. It's all these things plus something else. A loss of confidence? Of belief? In myself? In the need? Was it belief that propelled me into the studio for hours at a time? Hours that might be magical or, equally likely, totally unproductive—time better spent hacking away at the to-do list or reading to the kids. Creativity is such a crap shoot when there's so much else to do. Is that it? Is that the reason?

Christina clambers out of her chair back into the house and impulsively turns on the television to channel two. The duende show seems to be winding down. Images of blurry partygoers lounge in a nightclub as dawn peeks through the door. Eyes are closed, but no one sleeps. All bodies are taut. A man is singing, moaning in Spanish. The sound builds slowly then explodes in aural ecstasy, in lightness of sound.

The hairs on Christina's neck bristle as the deep-voiced narrator begins:

Serious flamenco singing seeks the duende, a mysterious power that embodies what is oldest in culture: the act of creation. Many have written on the power of duende, but none so eloquently as the Spanish poet Federico Garcia Lorca. These lines from "Poem of the Deep Song" embody the spirit of duende for him . . .

The screen goes black, then magnificent panoramas of the Spanish mountains appear. The narrator intones Lorca's words,

The wounded stag
peers over the hill,

then continues his narrative:

Any artist who climbs the stairway, searching for something new—the aspect that injects life into art—must struggle with duende. An angel may guide, endow, or foretell; the muse may dictate and prompt the intellect, but both approach from without. The duende comes to life in the nethermost recesses of the blood.

The ultimate denial of your faculties, an abject vulnerability, a progression fraught with danger, like dying and being reborn— **this** *is the duende. It is an ancient rite of passage for artists, an epiphany, and also a flash of personal freedom.*

The flamenco guitar begins again and credits start rolling.

I know that. That feeling, thinks Christina. The weightlessness of it, the sense of soaring above yet of the art. Frightening yet familiar. Home in the midst of the milky way. She presses the off button on the remote. The screen pops and goes black. Blank.

She exhales and realizes that she'd been holding her breath. Oh god, oh god, she whispers. I had it once. I really had it. She visualizes a painting she did years and years ago just after she had finished school. A portrait of herself in her artist's get-up—which she hadn't really abandoned post-Maura. Behind her on the wall hung a portrait of her family: her mother, her father, and her pre-pubescent self. A portrait within a portrait, showing her roots. There was something about that picture. A sense of being rooted in community. In something larger.

She sits perfectly still on the couch. Gradually, she becomes aware of the pounding of her heart, the ticking of the starburst clock, the resonance of Don's voice reading to the children upstairs: "The birds had eaten all the breadcrumbs, and Hansel and Gretel couldn't find their way home through the forest. 'Oh, what shall we do . . .'"

Her heart opens to a wash of love for Don and for the boy and girl they created together. And in that moment, she sees the years gone by, how she has been overwhelmed by this love, muted by it, subsumed by the imperative of motherhood, devoured by domesticity, and the false premise of what constitutes necessity.

She recalls someone once saying that if you don't listen to your muses, they will transform into furies and pursue you relentlessly.

I have to trust in that creative spark, she thinks. Get a room of my own — like Virginia Woolf — and make time to work away from casual interruptions, no matter how fleeting the results. I will let my hair grow long again, toss away those cotton-spandex pants and blazers, wear loose cotton trousers and blouses, and not worry if they are covered in paint when I pick Vita up at piano. The kids will grow up knowing that art is part of life, that there are other ways of living, even in this suburbia of sameness. The last rays of light catch her face, but she keeps her eyes wide open.

chapter five

Disco Doll

ERICA WALKS PAST THE LINEUP of chattering youths in retro disco get-ups and strides around the block towards the main entrance. She has an invitation from the DJ. "I'll put your name on the list," Thomas had promised shortly after meeting her the night before. But that was in a liquor-induced haze at an after-club party, so Erica's not sure if he's remembered, or even if she's remembered correctly. It doesn't matter anyway because the club's owners know her; she's there almost every weekend covering some band or another for her "In Tune" column in *The Star*. Still, she hopes Thomas has put her name on the guest list. He was rather delish—from what she can remember.

She speaks to the long-time bouncer who, as usual, cheerfully checks out her cleavage before letting her in. It's the inaugural Seventies Night. On a Sunday, no less, in staid old Ottawa. It's been marked in Erica's day-timer for weeks.

People are milling about the ticket kiosk, although no one seems to be actually buying a ticket.

"I'm on the guest list," she tells the clerk, someone new. He sports an intricate tattoo of Jimi Hendrix's guitar on his bicep and a ring through his nose. The staff seem to change weekly. "Erica Savone."

He scans the names with the chewed end of a stubby yellow pencil.

"Sure," he says, stroking out her name. "Lemme stamp you," he says and makes a star-shaped mark on her upturned wrist: she always gets stamped there to keep it hidden from her earnest co-workers at the Organic Growers Association. They know she writes the column, but by unspoken agreement, no one ever mentions it. Dr. M. used to say the root of her problems was her bad girl/good girl duality. Rock critic, earnest eco-researcher. She doesn't see it this way at all and prides herself on being a Renaissance sort of woman, who is interested in and knowledgeable about many things.

"Erica!" She turns to see Disco Tee, alias Thomas Jansen.

"Thomas! Thanks so much for putting my name on the list."

"How could I forget?" he says.

She sidles up to him; he's so good looking, she thinks, taking in his short dark hair and chiselled cheek bones — so masculine. And slim, she notes with relief.

"You're looking very disco-literate tonight," she says, giving his long, pointed collar a tweak. His purple shirt is unbuttoned to just below his nipples; a tiny silver spoon nestles in his dark chest hair. Interesting, she thinks, in a sexy-polyester, seventies-disco-meets-*Pulp Fiction* sort of way. Men dressed in those days not like now when a wrinkled T-shirt and scraped-off jeans are the norm.

Thomas kisses one cheek then the other, holds her hand, and looks her in the eyes.

"Blue sparkly eye shadow! How do you do it, darhling?" he drawls. "Let me see you . . ." and he holds her hand above her head while she steps back to do a twirl then faces him again. Her stretch-sequin, red bandeau top shows her off to great advantage, and Thomas's eyes linger momentarily at her cleavage. Lately, she's recognized her girls as not only a useful asset but also a liability, capable of attracting the wrong sort of men. After Hugh, she is very clear on this. There are two sorts of men: those it would be possible to have a relationship with and those who have too much baggage to unpack.

After a pause too long, Thomas's eyes scan downward to her short black lycra skirt and take in her shapely, muscular legs — the result of constant biking and walking, given her refusal to buy a car. Only the shoes are wrong: black sandals, Hercules-like and expensive. She has impossibly flat feet and needs sensible shoes with proper arch support, especially for dancing.

"You're gorgeous," Thomas says. "Erica-licious."

"You aren't so bad yourself," she says, grinning.

But Thomas is glancing over her shoulder, nodding at some-one; she's being dismissed already and feels a pang of disappoint-ment, which she immediately checks. He's got to get ready for his show, she thinks.

He meets her eyes again: "Come and see me in the booth?"

"Sure," she nods, "I'll bring you a beer."

"Great!" He kisses her cheek while gently holding her upper arm then leaves just as her friends, Suzanne and Greg, appear at her side, twittering at one another like cardinals in an early spring, pre-mating frenzy. Suzanne is dressed to the hilt in a black Afro wig and fake eyelashes, hoop earrings, skin-tight, leopard print, micro-mini-skirt, and black tube top. Greg is more understated but decidedly in theme with his tight black, shiny pants, black Beatle boots, a starchy white shirt open nearly to his navel, and a mass of gold chains. They peck one another's cheeks then bob downstairs and find a perch overlooking the dance floor and bar. Greg gets in the first order: Grey Goose Vodka shooters.

"To kick-start the evening," he says. "Cheers."

They meet eyes as they clink glasses.

"I wonder if *The Book of Love* covers the Disco era," says Suzanne.

"Probably in the drugs and sex chapter," Erica says.

They all laugh.

The room begins to fill. It's a grand space, a former live-per-formance theatre built in the nineteen-thirties. The seats in front of the stage have been removed to make way for a large dance floor. Overhead, a giant disco ball twirls from the vaulted ceiling and grand, gilt-edged floor-to-ceiling mirrors flank the walls on either side of the dance floor; red velvet curtains cover the remain-ing walls. It's opulent and serene — more suited to opera than the ear-shattering music that normally plays there, Erica thinks.

She tells her friends she's been invited to the DJ booth and recounts meeting Thomas the night before at a friend of a friend's party when the clubs didn't pan out.

"Do they ever?" asks Suzanne over the din. "That's the worse thing about being single again: I've become a commodity, competing with cougars with their poured-on blue jeans and propped-up illusionary cleavage. How do they keep those figures anyway? How much gym time are they logging at their age?"

"Meooow," says Greg, and they laugh.

"Cougars aren't all bad," says Erica. "For one, they're usually more interesting to talk to than the men. Besides, you can't blame them for trying their luck."

Erica nudges Suzanne: "Speaking of which, do you see any likely prospects?"

"Five o'clock. Standing halfway down the stairs," Suzanne says in her ear.

He's a decent looking bloke, blonde, nice features, and simply but well dressed — though not in theme — in black shirt and faded jeans. But something about him isn't right.

"He has the stink of marriage about him," Erica says with a smirk. "I was reading in *The Book of Love* how women are attracted to married men because they are proven providers — you know they're capable of settling down, making a commitment. There's even this study showing that married men get hit on more often than single men."

"What a load," says Suzanne. "It's more a matter of demographics and the availability of single fellas of a certain age."

She talks about an article on Ottawa's demographics that mentioned how there are far more single women than men; of course, the piece didn't explain why or provide more details.

"Typical journalism-light," Erica remarks.

The canned music is pumped up another notch, making it virtually impossible to carry on a conversation.

Suzanne's right, thinks Erica. It is more difficult now with the invasion of the cougars and their blatant desire for sex without strings. It significantly diminishes the odds for all the women my age who have "want baby" — and de facto all the scary trimmings — written across their foreheads. Except me, she thinks, but how's a guy supposed to know that? You can't exactly state it at the start. Hello, my name is Erica, and I don't want children. I want a reliable guy. At least I know what I want now, she thinks.

After the disaster of Hugh, she's decided to cut to the chase and only date potential partners. The rest is a waste of time.

She sees her acquaintances hooking up, but to her, they're settling in both senses of the word: a community centre manager with a plumber, a senior editor with a hydro linesman. It seems to her that these relationships start from a place of inequity. These couples have little in common aside from the coupling and a desire for children. But maybe that's enough, Erica sometimes thinks. Maybe, realistically we can't expect more. Suzanne and Michael seemed to be perfect on so many levels—intellectually, socially—and look how wrong that was. She's read that arranged marriages between people with similar socio-economic status actually have just as much chance of survival as romantic pairings. Then again, she thinks, consider the cultural background of arranged marriages; it'd be impossible to get a divorce—direly shameful at the very least—so the comparison doesn't really work: cream puffs and potatoes.

Finally, Disco Tee cuts into the canned music with a burst of enthusiastic patter: "Welcome to Ottawa's Disco Emporium with all the tunes for shaking your bootie—the latest and the greatest—and for those of you who are a little shy to hit the dance floor, here's an injection of inspiration from the Queen of Disco, Gloria!"

> At first I was afraid, I was petrified,
> Kept thinking I could never live without you by my side . . .

Suzanne nods to Erica at the choice and grabs Greg's hand. The three head down to the dance floor. Flashes of light from the disco ball twirl around their bodies like falling confetti. They grin and whirl. Great dancing tunes, thinks Erica. It was so simple then: you go to a club and you dance your face off. But then she remembers scenes from *Saturday Night Fever*: the coke, the loss of innocence, the superficiality, and her nostalgia disappears. Every era has its limitations. Greg winks at her, grabs her hand and gives her a twirl.

That's the way, uh huh, uh huh, I like it,
that's the way . . .

When "Funkytown" begins, Erica leaves the floor—she's always considered the song to be over the top; the falsetto makes her cringe in embarrassment. She buys a couple of bottles of Corona with slivers of lime forced down their necks and climbs up to the booth. The stairs are brutally steep, hard to negotiate even in her practical sandals. She peeks in at the booth, and Thomas glances up, flips open the latch on the gate, and waves her in.

"Hey, hey, have a seat," he mouths, gesturing to a collapsible grey chair. Erica hands him his beer.

"Cheers," he says and leans in for a kiss.

"Cheers," she says, holding out her cheek.

She sits down and wonders how this will turn out. The night before, she and Suzanne had used some stuff from *The Book of Love* to scrawl an outline of a play on cocktail napkins. They had called it *First Date to Home Plate*:

Act One: Main characters establish themselves on the first date. Protagonist (aka the woman) feels there may be an insurmountable obstacle (e.g., his politics are too right wing, he hates dogs, is moving out of town the next week, etc.), but she is nonetheless hot for him. They kiss, linger a bit. She can't help but lean (but not push) her breasts against his chest.

Act Two: Second date. Insurmountable obstacle is subject of intense debate. It seems they are doomed to part . . . but inexplicably she (protagonist) finds herself even more attracted to him. She decides one last kiss can't hurt, but this leads to passionate kisses soon followed by over-clothing fondling of the breast or buttocks or both. She leaves breathless and bereft.

Act Three: Protagonist (she) reluctantly (compulsively) agrees to meet one last time and —eureka—it seems he's had a change of heart (e.g., he has undergone a profound social awakening; he's discovered and resolved the childhood-based hatred/fear for dogs; he has gotten a better job offer and isn't moving after all, etc.). This results in passionate kissing, fondling, and, inevitably, shedding of clothes and consummation (with condoms). It's make-up sex *and* first-time sex. Oh my!

She balances on the precarious folding chair while Thomas tries to chat her up, but the music is so overwhelmingly loud, she can only hear every other word. Still, his body language speaks volumes: he touches her hand, her arm, smiles, looks directly into her eyes.

"My friends want to meet you," she says in his ear. "They're fans."

"Bring them up," he says, smiling. "I know the music is crazy loud, but that's the way, uh huh, they like it."

Despite the attention he pays her, she quickly tires of screaming at him and mentally crosses disco DJ off her list of potential occupations for men who could potentially be hers. She knows it's irrational, but she's disappointed: I just met him, she admonishes herself. Still, he's quite attractive and obviously loves music. It's such a shame, but she's determined to find a partner. Suzanne and Greg have teased her about wanting to get hitched. They say she already has the shoes. But when she talked to Christina last week, she was sweetly understanding: "I love being married. It's the little things like when he puts his arms around me in the middle of the night or draws a hot bath for me. We take care of each other."

Erica knows that her window of opportunity is at its widest right now; the choice is hers. In the back of her day-timer she has compiled a list of attributes she's looking for in a man.

good job (worthwhile, interesting)
willingness to travel
loves music
good natured
fair minded (does housework)
partner material

Hugh failed on all accounts. Thomas fails on the first. At the very least, she reminds herself, I hardly know him. He could be a total jerk.

But then the vagaries of circumstance and the human heart intervene as Erica accepts her part, and a new play unfolds.

A DATE IN FOUR ACTS

Act One: The pitch

The next day, Thomas leaves a phone message saying he'd like to get together. "Somewhere quiet this time," he says, then laughs. "Can I take you to dinner on Saturday?"

Date night, Erica thinks. She knows he's all wrong for her but sees him as a distraction, someone to have a laugh with. Better than the cougar bars, and you never know, he might have a friend. Besides, for once she's free the next Saturday; there's only one band worth reviewing this week, and it plays on Friday. It seems like this date was meant to be.

She dials his number and accepts the set up: the where, the when, the how. He suggests dinner at Papa Giovanni's, a choice that surprises her. She was expecting a hip bistro, and she's heard Papa's is traditional Italian — excellent but over-priced food in a plush, dimly lit setting. I'll let him pay, she decides.

Then he suggests that after dinner they go for a salsa dancing session at Club Sociale.

"I was watching you on the dance floor at the theatre," he says, "you really know how to move." She gets a little thrill from the idea that he was watching.

Dinner and dancing. How old fashioned, Erica thinks. How Italian. Dad would approve.

Act Two: The odds

She thinks of him off and on all week long: his disco patter and deep brown eyes with the small creases around the corners, his lean body, and sense of humour. Like a favourite CD, she keeps replaying their scant moments together at the disco night.

"I know he's not right, but I'm feeling really attracted to him," she ends up telling Suzanne by the week's end.

"Just remember Hugh," says Suzanne. "I know how those dark Latino-looking men turn you on!"

"I can't have two psychos in a row," says Erica. "I mean what are the odds?"

"In this town . . .?" They both laugh.

It rains all day Saturday and, come evening, shows no sign of letting up. Everything is dripping, soaked. Erica had planned to wear a short, swingy skirt, which would be good for dancing, but now there's the shoe problem: sandals are out because her feet will get wet, but closed toes look geeky in the summer. So she opts instead for tight-fitting, black slacks and a low-cut, dark blue T-shirt that accentuates her red hair and décolletage. She puts on a dangly red bakelite necklace she'd paid too much for at the annual vintage clothing sale. She wonders at the inordinate amount of time she spends on her makeup and coiffure. After all, according to the terms of the chase in *The Book of Love*, she has the upper hand. She's the one who walked away disinterested. Now he's pursuing her.

Normally she enjoys the game, but these days—since Hugh —her heart's not in it. It's all so same-old, same-old.

She calls a taxi, which is an extravagance, but she doesn't want to arrive soaking wet. She resolves to have only three drinks.

Act Three: The play

She is surprised by how handsome Thomas is. The disco getup didn't nearly do him justice. He wears a white shirt, simple and nicely pressed, and a black, well-fitted jacket, black Levis, polished leather shoes—instead of the ubiquitous runners. Erica loves a man who cares for his shoes, who takes pride in how he looks. His hair is combed back but isn't tight with hair goop; it's friendly looking, touchable, curling slightly at the nape of his neck. He kisses her gently on her cheek and holds her chair out for her. She smiles, pleased at this small attention. She realizes that good manners matter to her. Maybe because Dad's so old-school, she thinks.

The restaurant is as she expected: dimly lit and draped in heavy dark curtains. A pair of elegant ivory-coloured, tapered candles instead of the omnipresent, pedestrian tea lights, adorn each table. They look at the wine menu.

"Shall I order?" he asks, taking away her burden of trying to guess his price range.

"Please," she says, grateful, even though she knows a fair bit about Italian wine from her father.

He orders a fifty-dollar bottle of Farnest Sangiovese Daunia, 2001. A solid choice, she thinks.

"I think you have the wrong impression of me," he is saying just as she is thinking it. "Disco Tee, the party—that's all just an act, something I do for fun on the weekend."

And so she encourages him to talk about himself, remembering that *The Book of Love* suggests that the more men talk about themselves, especially on the first couple of dates, the more they like you. This seems facile and unfair to men because, after Hugh, she knows it's equally true for women.

"So, what do you get up to besides the DJ stuff?" she asks.

"Have you heard of Master's Voice?" he asks.

"Yes, of course. They've recorded a lot of local artists. And wasn't Tavia nominated for a Juno?"

"Yes, she's great. It's my studio. I converted a double garage in my backyard."

"Oh, you're *that* Thomas. I should have figured it out. Of course I've heard about you—all good!—but I thought John Boynton owned it . . ."

"He's my technician and he does the front stuff with the public. That's the part I really don't like, all that schmoozing and PR. I concentrate on the music."

"Well, I'm a primo target for schmoozers, which is why I've met John. It's a fabulous studio, Thomas. Very professional. How did you get started?"

As she listens, she curses herself for making assumptions, wishes she had worn a skirt and her best perfume. During a pause, she excuses herself to go to the washroom, adjusts her bra, prodding the girls into place, then does a quick repair job on her makeup and hair. Damn rain, she thinks. Oh well, it's brought out the curl in my hair. It looks kinda flirty.

She comes back to the table, and he partly stands up while she seats herself, which impresses her beyond anything he might say.

"You are so beautiful," he says and reaches across the table to squeeze her hand.

She squeezes back slightly, softly, and smiles at him. He smiles back and releases her hand. She feels a small surge of happiness.

Thomas asks her about her work, her passions. She talks about the granola queens at the Organic Council of Canada, about her work as a researcher, writing reports and policy papers for the executive director, who is trying to convince politicians and senior bureaucrats to regulate genetically modified foods, to adopt standards for organic growers, to lower barriers to organic growers in developing countries. She says she wishes she worked at an NGO helping AIDS orphans in Africa or something, but still, healthy food is important, and she gets to travel in Canada at any rate. What she really loves, though, is her column with *The Star*.

"If only it paid better," she laments. "Did you see my article on Thursday about the disco night?"

"Of course! It was fantastic, really insightful; all that about the allure of disco in the new millennium, the harkening back to an allegedly more innocent time. I think you were spot on. Your column's the only worthwhile thing in that rag. I always read it."

"Thanks," she says and, feeling herself blush, is glad for the dim light.

"It was one of the things that attracted me to you: you're hip *and* intelligent."

Now that's a bit over the top, she thinks, but feels pleased nonetheless.

The waiter glides up to take their orders. Thomas suggests starting with the Proscuitto e Melone, and she concurs. He orders the Polenta con Funghi, and she settles on Gnocchi alla Marinara.

"I love to cook," Thomas says. "Not only Italian, everything: Indian, Chinese, Canadian, whatever that is. Moose steaks and poutine? The perfect date for me would be to cook together then go hear some music."

Erica nods. "I've been cooking since I was little. My mother's one of those Italian mamas . . . you know—acres of hand-moulded gnocchi."

"Of course, Italian!" he says. "I should have known with a name like Savone. And here I was suggesting the vino and the appetizers. Duh!"

She smiles. "Yeah, and real old-school Italian with all the trimmings. Dad was in the construction business, and Mom looked after my brother and me, the house, and garden. There wasn't a patch of lawn in the backyard, just vegetables. The fall cook-offs lasted days. Before the first frost, we'd pick all the tomatoes and set them on newspaper on top of the ping pong table to ripen, then we'd make vats of tomato sauce."

But then, she explains, as her father's construction company prospered, such "peasant" activities—as he called them—came to an abrupt end. A swimming pool replaced the veggies, and the fall cook-offs ended.

"But during the summers in high school and university, I worked at my Aunt Zietta's restaurant in the Annex in Toronto. It was a small sort of fusion place before that was popular. Auntie travelled a lot, and she'd bring her food experiences home with her: schnitzels and tajine, boeuf en daube, curries. I waited tables, and during downtime, I'd help out in the kitchen, mostly with desserts. Auntie says I have a delicate hand with the pastries." She laughs.

"I'd agree," he says, taking her hand in his.

How corny, she thinks, but he seems so genuine, she thinks it's sweet.

The waiter arrives with their appetizers. Damn, she thinks, I've been talking too much.

Dinner is delicious; they linger, exchange bites. She says it's as good as her mom's. They skip dessert—they're both too full—but order cognac. As she twirls and downs the last of the amber liquid in her glass, Thomas glances at his wristwatch.

"We've missed the intro class. Do you still want to go?"

"I'm not really great at just watching and picking up new dance steps," she says. "Do you think you could teach me to salsa?"

He laughs, says it's only his second time, and that he's pretty pathetic.

"Still, I could lead you astray," he says, winking.

"Ha, ha," she says, arching her eyebrows and smiling.

They leave the restaurant, talking vaguely of going for a drink, but it has stopped raining at last. They decide to take a walk and discover that they both love to stroll around the city. Down they go to the canal then north alongside its winking waters towards the Disney-esque spires of the Chateau Laurier. Finally, they find themselves beside the locks to the path below Parliament Hill beside the expansive Ottawa River. It is deserted and wonderfully soft with rain transformed into a light mist, refracting the lights. He puts his coat—a very practical waterproof Gortex, she notes—on a wet bench, and they sit, admiring the view of the river. He takes her hand and kisses it.

She can't stop smiling at him, can't stop thinking how attractive he is.

"It's such a romantic cliché," she says to him, indicating the view but thinking of them sitting there.

He chuckles. "Cold?" he inquires, putting his arm around her.

She nestles into him. He kisses her, and she meets him, feels a thrill of recognition, expectation, and desire run along her body. Full, long, and deep, tongues touching. A kiss that supplants memories of others. She puts her hand on his thigh, his slips under her coat to caress the side of her body over her shirt. Finally, at the same moment, they part.

"You're really quite stunning," he says.

She feels herself blush. "Thank you," she murmurs—then feels phoney, coy. "Shall we walk some more?" he asks.

She stands, and he puts his arm around her shoulder. They walk and walk beside the river bank then up along Wellington Street, down Kent, towards her house. They stop for a glass of wine, then two, at a little tapas wine bar he knows and nibble on black olives. So much for limiting the booze, she thinks. He walks her home, and she expects him to make a move, to want to come in, and she is torn, because she likes him so much, but keeps thinking of Hugh. Before she decides whether to invite him up, he says he has a band coming in at ten the next morning and better be off. She feels relieved: no pressure.

They arrange to meet for coffee late the next afternoon, and he kisses her lightly. "Goodnight, Erica," he says.

She loves the sound of her name on his lips.

Act Four: The follow-through

Erica closes her apartment door. I was so, so wrong about him, she thinks, appalled at how superficially judgmental she had been. She wishes she could phone Suzanne, but it's late, after twelve, and Suzanne will either be out or in bed. Erica has a difficult time falling asleep, her mind awhirl as she replays the evening: holding hands, his compliments, the food, the kiss.

Thomas phones her the next morning before she's even had a chance to do the after-mash with Suzanne or Christina and tells her what a great time he had.

"I woke up thinking of you," he says.

She did, too, but she's not 'fessing up. She smiles into the receiver.

"So we're still on for this aft?" she asks.

He invites her to his house and studio for the coffee.

"I'd really like to show you around," he says. "If I have a chance, I'll make my world-famous oatmeal cookies."

"We could make them together," she says.

"Oh, I don't know," he laughs, "that's pretty intimate."

She laughs, too.

He lives on the edge of Chinatown, the last house before an industrial area that the tracks run through. It's a narrow two-storey brick building with a cramped front porch, like so many others in the area, but with a huge yard and large workshop out back.

She rings the bell and waits, adjusts the waistband on her skirt—maybe I should have worn jeans, she thinks. She's just about to knock, thinking the bell isn't working, when he appears wiping his hands on the white chef's apron he's wearing over a black ironed T-shirt and faded blue jeans.

"Sorry, I was just putting the cookies in the oven," he says.

"Well, you certainly know the way into a woman's heart," she says.

He smiles and kisses her softly on the cheek, slipping his arms around her body. They embrace briefly. She moves away first.

"Welcome to the warehouse," he says, grinning.

The living room is crammed with a fifties faux Eames chair, a large wagon-wheel coffee table, an overstuffed, slightly worn, dark-blue leather sofa, and a mannequin dressed in a forties cocktail dress with a string of Christmas lights wrapped around her body. A red wall is covered with dozens of black and white framed photographs. She follows him through into the kitchen and dining area with its chrome and green Arborite table and coordinated red Naugahyde-covered chairs. Even his stove and fridge are old: forties vintage.

"Recycled," he says, following her eyes. "I like to tinker with things. You don't want to see the basement."

"I adore retro," she says. "Especially the fifties." She also likes that he is handy, that he takes so much care with his house. She admires the décor, the creativeness of it all.

He makes them stove-top espresso, which is ready just as the cookies are done. He puts the cookies on a Limoges plate—"It was my granny's," he explains—and places everything on a tray, even sugar and cream in matching china, she notes.

"Let's sit in the living room. It's more comfy," he says.

They sit on the couch sipping coffee. She tells him how much she likes the room, his house. He promises to show her the studio out back, explaining how his father helped him with the down payment on the house in the eighties when he was at university.

"I had two roommates for years," he says. "The house only has two bedrooms, so the living room was the third. It was pandemonium but sort of fun, too."

"These are delicious," she says, holding up half a cookie.

"Help yourself," he says, holding out the plate.

There is a pause in the conversation as she takes another bite.

"I want to tell you something," he says, taking her hand. "I know we've just met, but I wouldn't be telling you this if I didn't feel myself starting to care about you. And well, I don't want to lead you on or disappoint you . . ."

And she knows exactly where this is going. That old saw explained in *The Book of Love*: he's already got a girlfriend, maybe even a wife. Estranged, perhaps, but entangled nonetheless. She appraises the living room more critically. Of course he's taken.

She takes her hand from his; a pre-emptive act of protection.

"Yes," she says coolly.

"Oh, I'm not married or anything like that," he says as if reading her mind.

She laughs: "Well, that's a relief."

"This may seem kind of premature and bold, but I believe in being honest and I don't want to lead you on with false expectations. It's just that, well, I can't offer you a complete relationship," he says, and he takes her hand again, caressing it slowly with his thumb, avoiding her eyes. "At least not right now."

"What do you mean?"

"I don't know how to put this delicately, so I'll just say it." He looks her in the eyes. "I can't have sex for a while. I had surgery for testicular cancer and some chemo, so . . . well . . . it's been kind of rough and it will be for a little while longer."

Sympathy surges through her: "Oh gawd, I'm so sorry, Thomas. Are you going to be okay?"

"Actually, I'm pretty lucky. The prognosis is very good. It's just that right now, I don't feel well a lot of the time. I've lost a lot of weight, and here's the kicker, my sperm may be affected by the chemo."

"Radioactive sperm?" Erica asks. She can't help wondering if it glows.

He laughs. "Well, they don't really know, so better safe than sorry. My oncologist says I can have sex when I'm ready, but I have to wear a condom for at least three months after treatment, which I would anyway in a new relationship, but you know, it just seems too weird to me right now. Too soon. I need to wait, and . . ."

"What?" she asks.

"Oh, nothing."

She smiles softly. "Come here," she says and wraps her arms around him. He rests against her for a minute then pulls away to look at her: "I don't want you to think that I'm not attracted to you, that I don't want you. Because I do. You're beautiful and so interesting.

"We have two choices that I see," he continues. "We keep things platonic for at least three months and drive each other crazy, which would be totally unfair to you, although I'm game. Or we call it quits for now, let me recover, and see if things work out later."

Erica feels disproportionately disappointed. This is only our second date, she rationalizes. She turns her head so he can't see a tear that has somehow escaped. She discreetly brushes it away and smoothes her hair.

"I'll go for door number one," she says. "I have a three-date rule anyway. They could be long dates."

"Really long in multiple parts," Thomas says, smiling at her.

"Look," she says, "why don't we just play it and see how it goes? I mean, people used to court. My parents did for two years. We could use the time to really get to know each other without the pressure, you know what I mean? It'll be nice for me in a way because, well, you know how it is with men . . ."

"Wanting sex?" he says.

"Yeah, I mean I'm . . ."

"Sexy," he laughs, "and that's part of the problem for me. You're drop-dead sexy."

She blushes. "We can pretend we're 'born again.'"

"Shall we do Bible readings?" he laughs.

"Every Tuesday," she retorts.

They're both laughing now.

"May I see your studio?" she asks.

chapter six

Java Jerk

SUZANNE IS HABITUALLY EARLY, afraid that life might pass her by if she is five minutes late—or even precisely on time. Inevitably, she is left cooling her heels—and cranky. She tries to delay her departure from the house, she amends her grocery list, puts away the dry dishes, sorts through the newspapers. Anything to avoid wasting her time waiting for someone or something. But such ruses rarely work. Today is no different, although she's particularly anxious not to appear anxious. She's meeting Liam. It's not a date, she tells herself, only a coffee. It's been nearly a decade since she's had an actual date. Michael was the last. And even then she was lousy at the pace of dating, too impatient to know Does he? Do I? Will we? Too anxious, always wanting to cut to the chase ASAP. She hopes she'll be better at it now, more able to take her time, to get to know the man and how she responds to him. She hopes that she has learned something from her marriage. Only two months since their separation, and she's already changed her lexicon; she no longer calls it a failed marriage. It's one that ended.

She tells Erica she's making progress, is moving on. "Make sure you deal with it," says Erica, "or it'll come back and bite you on the butt twice as hard."

Suzanne laughs. All I need is a new guy, she thinks.

She doesn't know Liam well. They met at Greg's birthday celebration, ate homemade chocolate cake together in a dimly lit corner of his apartment building's party room; a sad space with stained, avocado-green carpets and thread-bare modular furniture—the kind that was popular in libraries in the seventies. She was surprised by his interest in her, his questions—Where were you born? How long have you lived in Ottawa? Where do you work? What are you reading?—and was quite willing to prattle on about herself. Besides, he was cute. Actually, more than cute, he was downright attractive with a buff body under a fitted paisley shirt (she had noted the firm biceps), long legs in black jeans, wavy light brown hair, petulant lips, and wide hazel eyes that seemed to invite her into his world. She guessed that, like her, he was around thirty-four. They shared a couple of cigarettes on the balcony, laughed about the tawdry party room.

The day after the party, Greg phoned Suzanne and said Liam had asked about her.

"He wanted to know if you were single."

"And?" she asked impatiently.

Greg loves to string her along.

"I told him you were, but he didn't ask for your number or anything."

"If I don't get laid soon I'm going to burst," Suzanne says, then promptly regrets her words. Why am I always so crass? It's not only the sex. I can get that at any cougar bar. Liam's different. He's interested in me, in who I am.

"It's been months for me, too," says Greg. "Hey, I'm inviting some friends to the Ad Hawks awards ceremony. I'm up for two prizes. Liam's coming. Why don't you come, too? We're meeting for dinner first at Beijing Gardens, that Asian place on Willow. The ceremony's just down the street."

She agrees that this might work nicely.

It has been an anxious summer. Suzanne is smoking a pack of du Mauriers a day and is well into her second bottle of Glenfiddich. I should be allowed to claim them as a medical expense on my taxes, she joked to Erica. Every night, she reads for hours before falling asleep. This beats lying awake and obsessively second-guessing her decisions like she did during the week after the elevator incident at Greg's. By the following Friday, she'd decided that she had no choice: she had to leave Michael, not only because of his affair and her inability to trust him, but also because it made the underlying problem so blatant. The romance, the passion, the attraction—they were long gone for both of them. They used to have all of it in spades.

"He used to be after me like a chicken on a June bug," she told Erica over drinks on the patio at Ferns, a downtown wine bar.

"But after what happened, even if we had stayed together, I never could've had kids with him," Suzanne said. "What if he had another affair? What if he left? I don't want to be a single mom like my mother. It's way too hard."

"Omigosh, I never thought of that," said Erica, "this is exactly like your mom, isn't it?"

Suzanne shrugs. "Yes and no. I mean Dad had an affair, but he left and had no intention of coming back. Michael wants to stay. I'm the one who's saying no. When it comes down to it, I was married nine years, but he was married eight."

"Good one," says Erica, "Here's to a good ending and new beginnings."

They clink wine glasses. It doesn't feel like a new beginning to Suzanne, only a very sad ending. And now? And now what? She finds a new fear taking root.

A bus roars past on the busy street.

Suzanne had met Michael at an opening at Five Alarm Gallery in a former fire hall. A friend of Christina's knew the artist, and so she tagged along, knowing little about art—especially conceptual art—but thinking it might be interesting. The exhibit consisted of a bucket with a brick under it and a long artist's statement, which she refused to read. "I should be able to get it without ploughing through a dissertation even if it is conceptual art," she told Tina and went to the bar for a second glass of red wine. She returned to find Christina talking to an attractive man with stylish side-burns and Elvis Costello eyeglasses that framed his intense brown eyes. He shook her hand warmly, giving it a little squeeze. She squeezed in return and touched his arm to ask what he thought of the exhibit, how he knew the artist. He, too, derided the need for a statement, and they made their escape together to a nearby basement pub. They held hands across the table, played footsie underneath. Midway through their second beer, she told him her sheets were fresh.

Such a promising beginning, she thought at the time. But obviously it wasn't because gradually things eroded.

Over the past few months, she has obsessively dissected the progressive disassembly of their bond. Michael began jogging every morning and joined a hiking club, putting an end to leisurely weekend mornings in bed. She lolled around reading books, hating all exercise except biking and strolls to the neighbourhood bar. Then he got promoted to junior partner and started working later into the evenings, coming home exhausted. Their intimacy diminished from three times a week to once—"Weakly" she e-mailed Erica—then to every second week, once a month. A year ago or so, before he started his affair with Angie, she bought a sexy purple underwear set that cost her the equivalent of two weeks' worth of groceries; the clerk assured her it was just the thing for "kindling." She was worried that she was boring, that she was taking him for granted and felt it was up to her to put some spice back into their marriage. Erica said the set was uber-sexy. "But you know the true test is how it looks on the floor because that's where it spends most of the time!" Suzanne put the underwear on, and perfumed, slipped into bed with great expectations. He said it was pretty—not that *she* was pretty—rolled over, and went to sleep. She remembers crying, feeling even then that he'd lost his love for her, although in the morning, he denied that and held her tightly.

A few weeks ago, Erica had foisted *The Book of Love* on her: "But don't tell Tina," she said. "Man, she's so cranky these days. Did I tell you what she said to me about Hugh?"

"Yeah, that was extreme, even for Christina. I wonder what's up with her these days?"

"Work, time crunch, the usual. She seems sort of depressed, doncha think?" asks Erica.

"Temporarily, 'cus of the situation. I think she'll feel a lot better once she gets her life organized. She's had a lot of changes with the move and going full time at work."

"Yeah, you're right," says Erica. "Anyway, here's the book. There's lots of great stuff in it. "

Suzanne took it — "I'll try anything at this point" — and later skimmed through the section entitled "Adultery: An Overview" and, under "Relationships: Sex," read:

Relationships

Sex

Sex is a barometer of your relationship's health. During the fusing stage, those first couple of years, the sex is typically fabulous as you discover each other through physical intimacy. But the urgency, the intensity tends to diminish over time. You get used to each other. The sheen grows dull. Polishing requires work.

There are two keys to a healthy sexual partnership: communication and chemistry. Chemistry is mysterious, a combination of dragstrip hormones and love force that is either there or not, but its presence can be encouraged by good communication, which is an acquirable skill (see page 119).

Many couples don't make it. A survey of some 6,000 men and women who had been married three years or less found that 16 percent hadn't had sex in the previous month. The couples' stated reasons ranged from stress-inducing jobs to drug use, financial woes to problems with the children. Usually, myriad factors are at play, and the most reliable way to sort it all out is through communication. Talk about your problems, hopes, fears, loves, hates. Talk about sex specifically, your needs, your desires, your fantasies.

Suzanne felt reassured by the stats: at least I'm not alone. And, she reassured herself, I did try more than a year ago to talk with Michael about our sex life; he was the one who refused to engage.

"We're fine," he said, slipping some file folders into his briefcase. "It's just that I'm so busy at work right now . . ."

He left the words dangling, and distracted by disappointment and hurt, she failed to grasp the threads and weave them into a real conversation. She tried a half-dozen other times, even suggested couples counselling, which was the final straw. He told her to let it be. "Talking about *it* (meaning sex) isn't going to make *it* (also meaning sex) better," he said.

So, she bought her first vibrator and resigned herself to self-pleasuring. Then, last fall he was unexpectedly interested, wanted to try new positions, bought massage oil.

But, of course, that was because of Angie.

After the elevator epiphany, she returned to *The Book of Love* but found nothing about ending relationships. Of course not, Suzanne thought: Pollyanna pap! They tell us that everything will be great if you do x, y, and z, and if you don't, well, you just didn't try hard enough, and you have no one to blame except yourself, and you don't *deserve* any advice on how to end it. Implicit is the idea that we have complete control over our destinies, our minds, and our bodies. It's such bullshit, she thought. We control what we can, but there are always other factors beyond us: deceitful friends, ill parents or children, economic recession, cheating spouses. Could I have prevented that? No! Michael's obviously coping with his own demons, whatever they may be—his drive for success, for one, to prove himself. Who knows?

She chose Sunday morning, when they'd both be well rested (although she'd been sleeping on the sofa bed since Tuesday). Suzanne had loosely outlined her exit script, mapped it out, like she would a documentary, with essential dialogue points and body movement:

(In the kitchen of an upscale downtown condo. Michael is working on a file at the kitchen table; Suzanne enters right and sits down opposite him.)

SUZANNE
Not working out for us.

(SUZANNE grasps MICHAEL'S hand.)

SUZANNE
Our romance has gone its course.

(Both cry for the loss.)

SUZANNE
Love you as a friend.

MICHAEL
Me, too.

SUZANNE
Don't want to lose that. I'm angry now, but I'll get over it.
Stay in touch.

MICHAEL
Please do.

(*Embrace.*)

The end.

But her script rapidly disassembled in the verbal pull and pummel, the tinkering and tattling of the relationship-ending scene; loss and longing, habitual history, and wounded ego informed and twisted every phrase.

SUZANNE (*wanting to start on a positive note and ease into things*)

I've always valued your friendship.

MICHAEL
You are my best friend.

SUZANNE (*Omigosh, he's repeating that. What do I say?*)

I really want us to stay friends, Michael, but, umm. Damn.
This is so hard.

MICHAEL
Do you want a drink?

SUZANNE
It's ten in the morning.

MICHAEL
Who cares? Glenfiddich?

SUZANNE
Please.

(MICHAEL *pours them each a couple of ounces and hands a glass to* SUZANNE: *she downs it.*)

SUZANNE
Okay, here's the thing, Michael: your passion, your romantic feeling for me, are gone.

(*Damn, she thinks, I meant to say* our *romantic feeling is gone; it's not good to blame someone; gets their back up. Damn.*)

MICHAEL
But Suzanne, we've been through this. That's what happens after years and years of marriage. The passion diminishes, but it's replaced by something deeper, more sustaining.

SUZANNE (*Shit, I didn't want to get into this. I didn't want to debate.*)
Diminished, sure, but it shouldn't just vanish. Before Angie, we almost never had sex. Once a month, tops.

MICHAEL
I was waiting to see how long it would take for her name to come up. You're never going to forgive me, are you? Never.

SUZANNE (*getting her back up*)
This isn't just about forgiving, Michael. It's a question of lost trust. Don't you get it? I can't go on if I can't trust you. You know that. You know my parents' story. And added to that is this lack of sex, passion, even romance. We're like roommates. I want more than that.

(*She thinks to herself: I want us back.*)

MICHAEL
I want us back.

SUZANNE
That's not going to happen. We both know that.

(MICHAEL *nods.*)

MICHAEL whispers
I am so, so sorry, Suzanne.

SUZANNE (*ignoring this, rushing on, fearful of tears*)
But I want us to stay friends. Please, Michael. I'm angry now, but I'll get over it and we were so important to each other for so long. We know each other so well. It would be a shame to lose that.

MICHAEL
So this is it? No more trying?

SUZANNE
No more.

(SUZANNE *feels a wash of relief-tinged grief.* MICHAEL *puts his arms around her;* SUZANNE *hugs him, fighting back the tears—I will not cry in front of him again. Both hug too hard, as if to squeeze the sadness out of each other, as if brute strength could make up for everything they have lost.*)

Then he went out to play golf. With the click of the door, Suzanne began crying, sitting at the kitchen table, tears dripping onto her bamboo placemat. She used up the better part of a box of Kleenex before phoning Erica.

Over the next month, they sorted and packed and looked for apartments. Suzanne couldn't afford the mortgage on their condo, and he didn't want to live with the constant reminders of their former life together. During that month, Suzanne went out as often as possible, most often to Erica's place, where the two of them co-navigated the unfamiliar topography of marital meltdown. They dissected the details of the demise a hundred times. Erica always listened, steadfastly offering sympathy, drying Suzanne's tears, offering hugs, and reassurance. She knew that her friend needed to tell her story, and that in the telling and retelling, she might arrive at a place of comfort.

Christina had murmured the correct words of consolation, but her heart wasn't in it. She kept thinking about Maura, about Suzanne's documentary, her jealousy, her feeling that Suzanne was being disloyal, though she knew this was unfair. It didn't occur to Suzanne that Christina would be jealous, and she wondered why her friend was holding back when she was usually so supportive. For her part, Suzanne contemplated Christina's marriage: It's so damn perfect, she thought. Her happy family and one-two, boy-girl children—how could she ever understand? I can't even bear to hear about the kids. Who knows when I'll be able to contemplate having a baby. That's all on hold—perhaps permanently.

"He'll wake up one day and realize what a fool he was for refusing therapy, for not trying harder," Erica said.

"Do you think so?" asked Suzanne quickly. But then she is instantly appalled at the hopeful note in her voice. "I wouldn't have him back. No way."

Erica nodded. "You deserve so much better. We'll have to find you a new nail to hammer the old one out."

Suzanne laughed.

There are fifteen people at the dinner, all Greg's friends and colleagues. Suzanne had ransacked her closet debating the formality, the sensuality of her choice of clothes, settling eventually on funky-comfy: a scoop-necked T-shirt featuring red Japanese calligraphy ("Good luck"), a stretchy asymmetrical black skirt and red heels, which she hopes aren't too high. She can't quite remember how tall Liam is.

She manages a seat at the long table directly across from Liam and steers the conversation towards him. She gleans factoids about his job: master's degree in biology, works at the university lab, second in charge of a research project into endorphin stimulation of mice. They stimulate them in various ways, he explains, then extract brain tissue to measure the effect. Of course, removing tissue is a euphemism for killing the creatures, but Suzanne has no problem with that; certainly not if it's in the pursuit of science.

The woman sitting next to Liam has a new miniature digital video camera that she thrusts into everyone's face, asking them inane questions: "What's your idea of the perfect holiday?" "What's your favourite book?" As she turns to Liam, her elbow careens across the table, knocking a full glass of ice water into his lap. He leaps up. Suzanne hands him her napkin. His khaki chinos are soaked down the right leg and in the crotch. Suzanne can't help laughing, and he grins at her as he dabs at the water.

"At least it won't stain," he says.

Other people hand him their napkins, and the waitress comes over with a cloth. The woman keeps on filming, like it's a reality TV show, making no attempt to help out; she doesn't even apologize. Cow, Suzanne thinks. Liam adjusts his pants, pulling down the waistband and Suzanne catches a glimpse of the Joe Boxer logo, and her heart beats faster; she likes the loose fit, the innuendo of boxers, detests tighty-whiteys. With his pants wet, she can see the curve of his penis, a most satisfactory length. She looks up lest she be caught staring.

"It should be dry by the time we leave," she offers.

"You'll have to stand in front of me," he says, and she pictures herself pressing her ass into his groin. It's a good thing women don't get erections, she thinks.

They walk to the ceremony with the gang. She notes happily that he is a good half-foot taller than she is. In the crush to get in the front door, they get separated, and she sits in an empty section at the back. Just as the ceremony is beginning, he slips in next to her.

"Good spot," he whispers. "We can make an escape if we have to."

It's a tedious ceremony, full of lame-ass, acronym-laden jokes that neither one of them has a hope of understanding. Her bowels are turning—she curses the microwaved bean burrito she wolfed down for lunch, and she shifts her buttocks to release a fart, praying that it will be silent and not too deadly. No joy. The pressure builds. A man in a white suit and matching shoes yammers on and on about the difficulties of the advertising business in this day and age, yada, yada. She feels like her stomach has swollen to twice its size, that she will explode. Liam presses his knee against hers, one of those touches that could be accidental, but then it's held a nanosecond too long, and she knows. Instinctively, she presses back, leaning ever so slightly towards him, but then the fart escapes—silently, mercifully, but quite aromatic. She pulls her leg away, tightens her buttocks. Christ! She glances surreptitiously at Liam; his nose twitches, but he's too polite or horrified to say anything. Well, that's the end of that, she thinks. But then he presses his thigh against her . . .

Greg wins two first prizes for his advertising campaign for Ginko, a green recycled-fashion store, and finally, after interminable other awards, the ceremony ends.

"My brain's gone numb," whispers Suzanne as they stand.

Liam turns to her, smiling, but a tall man with a haggard face taps him on his shoulder, an old friend it seems. Liam introduces them, but the man ignores her and talks intently to Liam about a mutual friend who has lost his job. She soon grows impatient and tells Liam she's going to congratulate Greg. She races to the bathroom instead, and when she returns, she can't find Liam. She waits around until the crowd thins, but he's nowhere in sight.

Greg catches her arm: "Liam said to tell you he had to go, something about that guy he was talking to . . . but he wants to know if you'll give him a call." He winks and gives her a scrap of paper torn from the awards program. Liam has carefully printed his home number and the words: "Let's meet for coffee." She warms with pleasure and, on the way home, vows not to come on too strong and scare the guy away. As usual.

Suzanne's most recent disaster involved Greg's cousin, Matt. They met at a nightclub where she and Greg were watching a reggae band. She and Matt stood close to one another, swaying as they watched. During breaks, they talked while she kept adjusting her top to draw attention to her body and even lightly touched his arm so he would know she was attracted, but he didn't respond. They were talking about his eleven-year-old daughter and the imminent arrival of pubescence. Suddenly, she crossed the line with a misplaced sexual segue: "Speaking of hormones, we should get together some time." He gave her an odd look and headed to the men's room. She knew she'd gone too far. He dodged her the rest of the evening, but she couldn't stop herself from phoning him the next day. He never returned her call. His loss, she thought.

These advances have never ended well. Some men are appalled by her boldness and take it as a cue to be rude or sexually crude. Others are initially receptive—and why not if it saves them the effort?—but soon they grow unsure and nervous. Threatened.

This time, she resolves, things will be different. I've learned: I'll take it easy, respond to the pace, be cool, go against my natural urges. Last week, over a Saturday morning café au lait, Erica read her a passage from *The Book of Love* on the perils of dating:

> Men like to be in charge sexually or at least harbour the credible illusion that they are in charge. Pursuit is part of the game; fundamentally, it is related to their hunter's instinct. In such a context, it is incongruous—unseemly some might say—for a woman to adopt this role. Of course, there are men who appear to like it—in fact, many are initially flattered— but in the end, when a woman usurps their role, men are propelled out of their norm of experience into uncharted territory, and some may fear it, resent it, or even reject the woman. Happily, for the sexually confident woman, not all men react this way.

"Sexually confident," Suzanne snorted. "A euphemism for horny if I ever heard one. It implies that we're in charge, we have control, when the opposite is actually true."

"Some women have a lot of control over their sexuality," said Erica, remembering herself pre-Hugh, and now with Thomas.

"Or they're just not that interested," said Suzanne.

Ouch, thinks Erica.

Meeting for coffee. It's less intimidating than, say, dinner, where one has to sit through cocktails, appetizers, entrée, possibly dessert, before bolting (if necessary). Coffee is simple, quick. Dodging is easy; you drink faster and feign an appointment. Still, she changes outfits four times before deciding on a hip-hugging blue skirt that accentuates her slimness and a black ballet top with a slightly dipping—but not plunging—neckline. Not that there's much to plunge towards, she thinks, and considers the pump-up bra that adds a cup size, but dismisses it as misleading. False advertising. She spikes her short black hair with styling gel then worries it's too masculine.

Despite the dressing dramatics, she's five minutes early. As she's about to open the coffee shop door, she spies him walking up the street and smiles broadly; it is a positive omen that he, too, is anxious to be on time. She pauses to let him speak first; part of her new let 'em think they're in charge, male supremacy tactic.

"Suzanne! Perfect timing."

The possibility of mutual orgasms flashes through her brain.

She smiles. "It's good to see you, Liam," she says, holding out her hand, but he puts his hands on her shoulders and kisses her on the cheek. She blushes. Damn, she thinks, I haven't done that for years.

He grins. "You look great," he says.

She blushes again and lets him open the door for her.

The place is surprisingly empty for an early Friday evening; the Grabba Java staff have even found time to stack the newspapers, clean the counters, and empty the garbage. He orders a latte; she has a mango ice-shake, knowing that caffeine after five in the afternoon will mean another sleepless night. She's had terrible insomnia for months.

If I were getting laid, she thinks, I'd sleep like a winter woodchuck.

He chooses a table by the window, and they sit in the steel and plastic chairs, toying with their drinks, chatting about how they've spent the day: he, writing up some of the research results and lunching with his new boss; she, doing still more research for the Maura Kerby documentary so she can narrow down the list of interviews (and obsessing about this "pre-date"). Finally, she focuses the conversation on him, and they leap from one topic to the next: his job (he's been there two years), his parents (dad, deceased, mom remarried and living down East), and siblings (none). She thought he lived in The Glebe, a hippie turned yuppie 'hood near downtown, but it turns out he lives on the other side of Bronson near the freeway in a former working-class neighbourhood now frequented by minimum-age youth working at minimum-wage jobs. It doesn't matter, she thinks, but then realizes it does. She envisions his thin walls and patchy, gross carpet and knows that if they do get together, she'll never stay over at his place.

He shifts his body on the chair and looks her directly in the eyes.

"So, Suzanne, what are you looking for in a relationship?"

She is thrown off guard. This is the sort of question she normally proffers. She stumbles over her response. "Something that works." (What the fuck does that mean? she wonders.) "Intimacy." (Sex.) "Companionship." (With someone I can actually talk to the next morning.)

She is so surprised at his approach that it takes her a few minutes to get back to him. "It's my turn now. What do you want, Liam?"

"Come out with me tomorrow night, and I'll tell you," he says.

She laughs: "Aw, you mean I have to wait?"

He pauses: "No. That's not fair. You told me."

He pauses again.

"I don't know what I want," he says. "I've never had a long-term relationship."

Disappointment surges through her body.

"A year?" she asks.

"No."

"A month?"

"Some longer. I have a lot of skeletons . . ."

". . . rattling in your closet?"

Their laughter cuts the tension.

"Just fun then," she says. It's better than nothing, and he's the perfect body type for me. A new nail . . .

"I was so attracted to you at Greg's dinner," he says.

"I'm attracted to you, too," she rushes, feeling the impact of his interest.

It's like it says in *The Book of Love*, she thinks. That Freud quote: "Men desire women. Women desire men's desire."

They agree to meet for dinner the next night, then he says he has to leave to catch a bus to an appointment downtown. She offers to drive him and, after he accepts, nearly has two accidents on the way, though she's justifiably proud of her driving skills. She stops the car in a No Parking zone on a side street, and they sit for a moment making arrangements for Saturday. They decide to try out a new Thai place and maybe go to a film afterwards. "I'll see what's on," she says. He leans in to kiss her goodbye on the cheek, but she doesn't turn her head, and so his lips land on hers.

He pulls away. "Too fast?" he asks.

Desire dictates. She leans in and kisses him full on the mouth, teasing him with her tongue. He puts his arm around her shoulders, holding her close.

She ends the kiss just as she started it.

"Wow," he says. "Wow."

Her face turns deep red. She hadn't meant to do that. Damn.

"I'm so embarrassed," she says.

"Don't be," he says and leans over to kiss her. Slowly, he takes her lips — the top, then the bottom — into his mouth, then dips his tongue in, flicking, lightly teasing. She lets him do as he pleases, fights against her urge to take charge. She teases his tongue with hers, feels the thrill of contact, of possibility, reverberate down her spine, down to her vulva, up her vagina. All she can think of is having this man touch her, caress her dry skin, tap the spring that bubbles beneath her surface.

Sometimes, some rare times in this life, there are barely believable moments of sheer perfection when the stars are aligned or the goddesses are smiling or something, and a tiny moment crystallizes into an eternity.

He cups her small chin in his hand and gazes into her light brown eyes. This is more than arousal. She understands the word swoon. Her hand flirts over his thigh. His fingers trace the outline of her cheekbone. They change their plans and agree to meet at her apartment the next evening.

Saturday morning, she phones Greg to glean more information about Liam and gloat about the perfect kiss, although a nagging voice says she should keep such perfection to herself. Besides, she has to give Greg something in exchange for the set up and advice.

"He said something about having a lot of skeletons in his closet," Suzanne tells Greg. "Do you know anything about that?"

"I probably shouldn't tell you," says Greg. "I only know it second-hand from Jerry, and he's prone to hyperbole."

"Come on, please. I have to know before this goes any further."

"Okay, twist my rubber arm, but don't hold it as the gospel, okay? In high school, Liam's dad died . . ."

"Yeah, he told me."

"Well, Liam had some sort of nervous breakdown or something and started doing a lot of drugs and a few B & Es to support the habit. Ended up in a juvenile home, and then he lived in Hintonburg for a few years, doing coke and who knows what. That's where he knew that guy at the awards thing from: he was some old pal from the bad old days—met him in rehab or something. Anyway, Liam cleaned himself up somehow. I think he went to rehab first and then he went back to school, and here he is today with a good job, and you panting after him."

"And girlfriends?"

"I can't say I've ever seen him with a woman, which is kind of odd because he's gorgeous, but he's not gay, darhling, I can assure you of that."

She laughs. "Did you try something on?"

"Are you kidding? I knew immediately. Sad, though, in his case. Doesn't he drive you wild?"

"Unbelievably," she replies.

I'm moving too fast. She knows it. She feels it. And Greg's insider info means Liam is high maintenance, complicated. Maybe we could just chat and neck a bit or something, she thinks. But the implications of the post-coffee kiss are far greater. She has always felt a man's desire welded her to him and his needs. Having elicited this need, she must gratify it—and herself. At night her vagina aches for a man to hold. Masturbation takes care of the immediate, the physical need, but she finds it indescribably lonely. She wants the touch, the connection of warm skin-on-skin.

She feels the imprint of his fingers on her cheek as she tries to concentrate on buying groceries: a few things for us to nibble on between nibbling on each other, she thinks, acknowledging how corny that sounds but not caring. Grapes (always erotic with their subtle pop and juicy inside), soft brie and camembert, roasted red pepper dip and mini pita. She also buys two bottles of Italian red, thinking she may have a drink or two before he arrives, wondering if he drinks alcohol. When she returns from shopping, her answering machine is flashing.

The robotic voice informs in a monotone: Message one, 11:59 a.m.

"Hey, Suzanne, it's Liam. Ah . . . Are you there? Can you answer the phone? (Pause.) Anyway, I can't come over . . ."

"Noooo!" Suzanne cries, dropping her packages on the counter.

The message continues: ". . . afternoon. I've been doing some thinking and I just can't have the kind of relationship that we were talking about. (Pause.) I'm really sorry. It's so stupid and tacky to leave this on the answering machine, but I didn't want to chance that you wouldn't get this message. I'm sorry. I should have told you when we had coffee. It was really inconsiderate, and I was selfish. I just wanted . . . I just wanted to let you know, and if you're pissed off I understand, and if you want to talk about it, I understand, too. I'm totally open to being friends, but I don't think that we should go ahead and have a . . . the relationship we talked about. (Pause.) God, it's stupid to say it to a machine. I hope you understand. I hope you aren't too angry. Bye."

"You prick!" Suzanne says. Her heart pounds, a grape rolls across the linoleum, and she stomps on it. "How dare he reject me! He's the one with all the problems." Instinctively, she grabs the phone and speed dials Greg's number.

"Girlfriend SOS," she says and tells him about the message.

"He's a coward," Greg says. "The phone . . . my gawd, how déclassé!"

"I just don't get it, after that kiss. Should I call him back?"

"What's the point? If he can't handle the heat, you don't want him in your kitchen because, honey, it's steamin' in there."

"Yeah," she says half-heartedly. "Jesus, Greg, we had something. I know we did. Am I that unattractive or what?"

"Hey, if I was straight, you'd be first on my list, darling. You're lovely. No, it's the damn men you choose. They're the ones with defects. It's Liam's rattling skeletons."

She laughs. "And I guess it's good that he told me now instead of after we had sex."

"A stiff dick has no conscience. Most men would have done the post-coital sprint," says Greg.

"Yeah, it was the right thing for him to do, just the wrong medium."

" Besides, you have that kiss," says Greg. "I got a thrill myself when you told me about it. A moment of perfection, of pure sexual anticipation."

It's true, she thinks. A perfect moment. Just not enough.

"And now what?" she asks.

"Think of Liam as a beautifully presented, tasty appetizer. Delicious but insubstantial. Now it's time to head for the entrée section of the buffet."

"And this time I'm going to choose carefully, eat slowly," Suzanne says.

"Sample a bit of everything on offer and find the entrée that tantalizes your palate."

Suzanne laughs. "I've been treating it like an all-you-can-eat buffet!" Greg laughs, too, then starts in on a story about a lunch he'd had with an old friend, who might potentially be a new lover.

chapter seven

Art as Therapy

CHRISTINA NOTICES HIM AT ONCE. Not only because he's gorgeous—tanned skin contrasted by a crisp white shirt, straight black hair gleaming down his back, high forehead—no, the thing that most strikes her as he walks into the conference room at the "Art as Therapy" session is the way he holds his body—tall, fully erect—and the way his brown eyes sweep the room yet make full contact with everything they encounter, absorbing it—then her. She glances away.

He folds his long body gracefully into the chair beside her.

"Arthur," he says, holding out his hand.

"Christina," she says, giving his hand a perfunctory shake. The texture of his skin is familiarly rough; from the solvents used to remove paint, she realizes. Her mother used to say you could tell a lady by her hands. Same goes for an artist, a real artist, thinks Christina.

"Where do you teach?" he asks.

"Ottawa. Grades 4 to 6."

"I do some supply work here at the Kingston board," Arthur says. He looks at her face. "Let me guess,"—he pauses—"acrylics."

He gestures to her left hand—"Not so much as you'd like lately"—and her plain gold wedding band—"too busy with kids and stuff."

She laughs nervously. "Guilty on all counts," she confesses. "Two kids and a husband. And you?"

"Never married. I'm a devotee of the LAT cult."

"LAT?"

"Living Apart Together. Though I haven't had much of that lately either. Still one can Live In Hope. LIH."

They smile at each other.

It's a boring session, a superficial overview of things she'd learned years ago. I could teach this seminar, she thinks. She peeks sideways at the doodles in his notebook: a competent caricature of the seminar leader, a canoe flying through fir trees. She shifts, glances at his profile: weather-worn skin, deep eyes, big nose—masculine. He's so attractive, she thinks and feels a shimmer of guilt, but then figures, what the heck, no harm in looking.

During the coffee break, they agree that the session is tedious. "Let's skip out," he whispers. "Go for a real coffee."

She smiles. "You're on," she whispers, pleased at their complicity. It reminds her of the time she played hooky with Ann in junior high, giggling on the Queen streetcar as they made their way to the Eaton's Centre, elated at being rebels.

They edge their way out of the crowded hallway into the foyer of the hotel and out the front door. It is a fine day in late August, the sun, gently warm; the sky, piercing blue. She walks beside him across the busy street, down an alley to a hidden restaurant that only those in the know could find. It's too early for lunch, so they have their pick of tables on the cobblestone patio, a forest of green umbrellas protecting them from the sun's rays and intrusive eyes. A small bouquet of flowers—blue borage stars, wisps of Queen Anne's lace, and a single red bergamot—mingle beautifully in a blue glass bottle on the yellow chintz tablecloth. They remind Christina of the arrangements her mother always placed on her teak dining table. Sometimes the flowers were from her garden; sometimes, wild ones she picked on her daily walks in the nearby ravine. In the winter, she bought long-lasting, modest bouquets from the corner florist. After Christina's dad died of kidney failure, her mother placed a mahogany-framed black and white photo of him by the vase and moved both to the place at the table where her dad had always sat. At the time, Christina, who was seventeen, found it oddly comforting; it was as if her dad were still with them at their evening meals. Years later, she realized that the arrangement was a shrine. All it needed was the candle. Her mother still dusts the frame every morning, and though she has a full life—she still does some work as a textile designer from her home studio and volunteers two afternoons a week at the kidney foundation—she has never sought male company, and it has never come her way.

Christina orders a cappuccino, and Arthur does the same.

"I suppose it's too early for wine," he says as the waiter leaves. "Although I do feel like celebrating."

"Oh, yeah?" she asks, raising her left eyebrow.

"I sold a painting last night. The biggest one, too." He pauses. "And now I've met you." He laughs. His even teeth flash white.

She smiles at his cornball remark then is aware of a slight rise in her temperature, a subtle change in the colour of her cheeks.

"Are you blushing?" he asks.

She flushes fully, cursing her pale skin. "Not me," she says, with a laugh. She is flattered to have someone pay such close attention to her.

He laughs, too, and grasps her hand for a scant moment, completely enveloping hers. The masculinity of the gesture makes her feel physically vulnerable yet protected. These primal impressions crowd her mind, then his cell rings. He takes it out of his pocket and looks to see who is calling.

She wonders what it would be like to kiss him. The thought seizes her by surprise. She pushes it away.

"They can wait," he says, placing the phone on the table.

"Tell me about your work," she says.

He, too, paints with acrylics but adds bits of twigs and dried leaves and weeds to the composition. He glues them onto the canvas then paints over them in layers to add texture and an impression, a nuance of nature.

"We're so distant from nature now," he says. "It's there, but only in the background, to be used when we like and otherwise ignored," he explains. "I integrate it into the work. It's part of who we are."

He tells her about how he makes natural dyes from berries and plants that he gathers at his cabin in the bush north of Kingston.

He is part First Nations, Algonkian.

"Did you grow up on Reserve?" Christina asks.

"Half and half—up near Barry's Bay in the Ottawa Valley, then down here in Kingston with foster parents. It's a long story for some leisurely evening over a bottle of wine. Now, tell me about your work. What do you paint? Where do you sell?"

He sips his cappuccino and looks at her over the rim.

Sell? she thinks. Ha, I wish.

"I haven't been doing so much lately," she says tentatively, afraid he'll see that she's a fraud, a wannabe, or worse, a has-been. "Vita just turned seven and Norris is eight. Plus the job. Full time this past year." Despite her good intentions in June, the summer has slipped by with the kids, gardening, painting the living and dining room walls. She pulled out a sketch book a few times, but nothing much has come of it, and her studio is still one more item on her to-do list.

He nods, but says nothing, his eyes intent on her. She shifts uncomfortably in her seat and tears open a package of Sweet'N Low.

"The truth is, we moved a year ago, and I haven't managed to set up my studio yet." She pauses and intently stirs her cappuccino, thinking how lame this sounds. "But it's happening soon," she adds. "A contractor's coming next week to finish the basement so we can move the kid's playroom down there, and I'll use the fourth bedroom. It faces south."

This is not strictly speaking true: she has phoned a few contractors, but no one's shown up yet. They're all busy finishing up their outside projects before the weather turns nasty.

She smiles, ashamed by her need to justify, to explain, and by her art's future place in a spare room, as if it's not central to her life.

"And so, Ms. Christina, tell me about your paintings."

"They're portraits, self-portraits . . ."

"Such a beautiful subject," Arthur says.

She takes a nervous sip of her cappuccino.

"Sort of a Frida thing?" he asks.

She remembers Don saying exactly the same thing. Once.

Years ago. He was quite well versed, probably still is, but now there's nothing to talk about. Nothing new, anyway.

"There is that tradition," she says, "but I don't have her angst—at least not her physical angst, her pain . . ." her voice trails off. A flash of her constant self-questioning, her dissatisfaction momentarily blinds her before she rushes on. "My portraits are actually meant to be a commentary on the myriad roles women have in our society," she says, cursing herself for needing to explain instead of showing her work, "the costumes and masks of friend, mother, daughter, lover, employee, and so on."

"And are you near the end of that?" he asks.

She is startled by the question, having never previously considered the possibility. It occurs to her that she's recited her description by rote, and that it hasn't changed one iota in years.

"Maybe," she concedes. "Maybe that's why I haven't had the drive, you know, that urgency to set up my space, to take up a brush."

There is a pause between them. A couple sits down across the patio. Three women are looking around for the best spot to sit. Christina hears indistinct murmuring and piped in classical music that she can't quite identify.

"It's good to move on," he says. "I did modern landscapes for years, sort of a Thompson-meets-Morriseau-on-a-dark-night thing." He laughs; she smiles. "Forest scenes, Native imagery. It was comfortable and sold well, but I got bored. Then, about three years ago, I tried abstract interpretations, and it's so much closer to where I need to be."

"I have started something interesting in the garden," she says abruptly. "But I'm not sure where it's going."

It's the first time she's thought of her garden as a work of art. Maybe it is, she thinks. Or maybe I need to be an artist in Arthur's eyes. To be doing something.

"Andy Goldsworthy sort of stuff?" he asks. "You know, the environmental sculptor."

"No, not exactly. His work is beautiful and really inventive—I love the spirals—but he's more concerned with manipulating aspects of existing nature to create something new. And his work always decays, or he destroys it and returns it to nature. My garden grows and changes every day. Visual art, painting, is so static. So dead."

She finds herself excited by this explanation made up on the fly.

"And because my garden is alive after the initial creation, it's mostly outside my control aside from watering and some trimming. It's up to Mother Nature."

"Or the Creator," he says.

She nods, though she doesn't consider herself to be spiritual. "I make a graphic design and plant perennials in a pebble bed, then I see where it grows. I have three little beds so far."

Small, because she can't face the massive landscaping job of doing the whole yard.

"I'd like to see them," he says. "Could you send me some photos?" He opens his wallet and takes out a business card for her.

"Sure, sure I'll send you some," she says, taking the card. "I have a few, but I'm thinking I should take photos every week or so, always from the same angle, so I can get a sense of what works best at different times, provide a sort of progression—you know, like those sequential stills of flowers unfolding. But the primary works are the beds themselves. Eventually, they will die, but then in the spring, they will unfold again."

"So how will you exhibit it?"

"I haven't got that far yet. I mean, you can't exactly move the garden. I could make a video of stills as it grows." She snaps her fingers. "You know, I could do that. It might work."

"Funny how ideas come like that," he says. "You talk to someone who's not involved and there it is . . ."

"Sustenance for the muse," she says. "It's up to us to find the duende."

He smiles at her: "That's the difficult part," he says.

She feels a warmth spreading over her, gratitude for being included in this place where people can talk about the need to create; not just the surface, impetuous urge—the weekend-watercolourist view—but the deep-down demand of it; the feeling of unease when it is absent.

The waiter comes, and they decide to order lunch after all. The menu changes every day, the waiter explains, depending on the whim of the chef and seasonal availability. Arthur orders red pepper sauce with pesto, pine nuts, and a hint of goat cheese over hand-cut pasta, and a bottle of rosé wine: something light, he says. She has a fresh tomato, basil, and bocconcini salad sprinkled with virgin olive oil and brewed balsamic vinegar. A home-baked olive bread arrives, still warm, tucked into its white linen napkin. He plucks a nasturtium off her plate and hands it to her.

"For luck," he says, "in the art garden."

They clink glasses and continue chatting about art, the conversation developing a beat of its own.

"And that green, you know the one, that signifies spring . . ."

"The textures are more difficult, knowing how much is enough . . ."

"I listen to Charlie Byrd . . ."

"You need a beat, a pace for painting, it helps set . . ."

Christina can't help contrasting their banter to how it is with Don and their never-ending domestic conversation. The lexicon of art is gone. As is the lexicon of love, she realizes. Not the feeling—we do love each other—but it's a background wash, an underpainting. Suddenly, it's time to return to the conference, and he volunteers to pay the bill. "I'm flush with the sales from my show," he explains. They hurry back to the hotel and split up for their different sessions. "I'll see you at the break," he says.

She sits beside a middle-aged woman with flamboyant red hair (Clairol 104, she thinks) then takes in her slinky purple dress with a plunging neckline and a necklace of fiery pink and green beads. She looks like an artist, thinks Christina, and views her own outfit critically: black flared skirt and a white eyelet, sleeveless shirt, pearl stud earrings. Conservative. Safe. More like a librarian than anyone involved in a creative pursuit.

"I love your dress," she says to the woman, and they begin

chatting as strangers who are thrust together at events are wont to do. They talk about where they work and how many children and so on. The easy chatter surprises Christina; she'd forgotten how it works. Lately, she's been tongue-tied and in a hurry when any of the moms at daycare or Norris's school tried to make conversation. I must make an effort, she thinks. Maybe that woman from the book sale.

"I noticed Arthur has taken a shine to you," the woman says.

"Oh, I don't know about that." Christina laughs. "But he is very interesting."

"He's a bit of a ladies man," she says, smiling, then adds in an undertone: "He's basically slept with all the women artists around Kingston."

Christina raises her eyebrows, poised to ask for more details, but she is pre-empted by the symposium starting: "Getting grants: a guide to funding without fuss is no mean feat," says the be-suited man leaning on the podium.

Why would she tell me that? Christina wonders. Perhaps she's slept with him, too. A ladies man. A good, perhaps a great, lover, one who knows where, how, and how long to touch. A man who is familiar with the geography of the female body, the hills and valleys, peaks and grottos. Who loves the form. Oh, to have such a lover, even just once more!

When she was younger, she'd slept with many men. Dozens. Suzanne and Erica don't know this. Neither does Don. She never considered telling him. As far as she's concerned, it has nothing to do with her life with him. She agrees with Erica on this score and was totally empathetic with her about Hugh's revelation sessions. In her pre-Don life, Christina found it impossible to be faithful to one man. She'd be going out with someone she liked, who treated her well, listened to her, cooked her nice dinners, bought her small but thoughtful gifts, then she'd meet some pretentious artsy guy at her local bar, an art gallery, or in a class.

She thought she fooled around because she hadn't found the one yet, and why not have some fun? Later, she realized it had to do with losing her father when she was seventeen, with looking for male affection. Understanding didn't change things. She acknowledged that she was promiscuous, and though she never talked about it, she never felt guilty about it either, never felt it was wrong or harmful to her. Until the fall of her last year in university.

She met an architecture student one afternoon at the unfortunately named Mad Cow Pub. They drank beer and ate nachos, talked about his final project: a co-op apartment building. Late in the day, they went to his place, a crowded apartment in a dilapidated house, and had sex in his bed nook off the kitchen behind a beaded curtain. It was strictly bread and butter sex. Nothing worth tasting again, she thought soberly as they lay in bed. Then he gave her the lowdown, which came as no surprise to her; she had no expectation of seeing him again. But his story had a twist: He told her he had a boyfriend, a relationship.

"Omigawd," she said, jerking up in bed, "we didn't use a condom! What about AIDS? You should have told me. I can't believe you didn't tell me."

Christina was on the pill and usually used condoms, but not always, particularly when alcohol was involved.

"Hey, chill out," he said. "I'm safe, we're safe."

"You don't know that for sure," she said getting out of bed. He lay there, watching, as she pulled on her jeans and top, stuffed her socks in her knapsack, and slipped her bare feet into her runners. She fled the house without another word, without a glance. Totally preoccupied with What if? What if? she called Erica from a phone booth and told her what had happened. Erica said there was a clinic downtown where she could get tested quickly. She didn't give her hell, although she was tempted: "You've got to be more careful," was all she said.

"I know, I know," said Christina.

Erica sighed. "Shit happens," she said. "The thing now is to stay calm and wait for the test results."

Christina made a deal: if she wasn't positive, she'd be more careful, she would stop fooling around so much, she'd look after herself. Having sex without a condom is a death wish, she scolded herself. The fates complied: the test was negative as was the fol-low-up six months later.

She had a relatively chaste year—only a few dates and one brief sexual affair, and she insisted on condoms. Mostly, she stud-ied and began painting for herself instead of class assignments. She hung out with Suzanne and Erica, who were studiously being studious, and they all graduated that spring. Her friends found serious work—at least that's how Christina saw it—but she replaced her classes with painting and working half time at the Rendezvous Gallery, doing secretarial stuff and courting patrons.

She soon grew tired of her mingy life, of not being able to afford flowers, of her make-shift Salvation Army furniture, of the apartment with its slanting floors that she shared with a series of slovenly grad students, of not being able to go to the chic bars and restaurants that Erica and Suzanne had started to frequent. Christina joked with Erica about strategies for finding a sugar daddy: taking tennis and golf lessons, investing heavily in clingy clothes with plunging necklines.

A year after she graduated, she applied to teacher's college, a one-year program in Ottawa, thinking it would be a better way of supporting herself so she could paint. She never regretted it. Sure there are bratty kids and the disinterested ones, but there are also those who love to be creative. Whether they are accomplished or not, they take joy in the process. They inspire her.

At break, she sees Arthur across the crowded foyer talking intently to a tall young woman who tosses her dark hair in an annoyingly self-conscious way:

Swish, I am beautiful,

Swosh, I am young.

Swish, I am talented.

A flirt. But Arthur isn't responding. He keeps his distance, body erect, not leaning towards her.

"Christina?"

She turns. It's Joanne, a teaching colleague from Ottawa, who Christina has met at some board meetings.

Joanne begins chatting about grants: her previous failed applications, lamenting the time it took to write the damn things—time she'd rather spend doing her ceramic art. Christina nods, but has nothing to add; it's been years since she applied for funding, years since she had anything to apply for.

Christina feels her elbow being cupped and turns to find Arthur standing behind her. "Meet me after?" he asks softly. "I'll take you to my exhibit at the gallery then dinner. Five o'clock?"

She'd tentatively agreed to have dinner with the small group of Ottawa art teachers—unless I'm too tired, she'd said. She smiles at Arthur and says, "Sure, I'll meet you in the lobby." I need this kind of connection, she thinks. Then feels guilty: It's not only about art.

She sits at the back of the conference room and wills herself to think of Don and the good stuff. He's attentive, solid, and dependable, and there's much to be said for that. She closes her eyes and forms a picture of him: blonde, medium height, slight build. Arthur is barrel-chested, dark, strong . . . She feels a tickle between her legs and opens her eyes, considers going to the toilet. Then she remembers the sensation. It's been so long. She crosses her legs and tries to pay attention to what the lecturer is saying.

She leaves the lecture hall as the Q & As are about to begin, races up to her room to change into her new designer jeans—she hadn't bought jeans in years, kept hoping she'd lose some weight but then discovered the miracle of spandex. She pulls on a scoop-neck shirt. Black. Revealing her bosom—this is how she thinks of her breasts post nursing. They're larger than ever, but no longer perky. They droop, and in a bra under her clothes, they form a sort of shelf. I'm matronly, she thinks. She shakes her head to dispel this picture and pulls a single silver chain with an onyx pendant over her head. Simple, appropriate for anything. It's what I'd planned to wear this evening anyway, she justifies to herself. She'd taken pleasure in selecting her wardrobe for the weekend conference—her first trip away from home in five years. She and Don had not gone away for their summer weekend after all; after the initial mention, it never came up again.

As she slips in her dangly hoop earrings, she notices *The Book of Love* on the bed. Suzanne gave it to her last week, saying that, while it was mostly a laugh, there were a few good things in it.

"I still think Erica should've given it back," said Christina.

"Water under the bridge now. You might as well catch up. It's part of our lingo now."

And so she took it reluctantly but hadn't had time to even crack the cover. Ten minutes until she's due to see Arthur. She opens it to the Table of Contents, marks in light pencil—easy to erase—the chapters that might be interesting.

She flips to page 102:

We have come to interpret Platonic love as an asexual relationship, but this is not how the term was originally understood. According to Plato, the Platonic ideal of love is a chaste but passionate love, based on virtuous restraint, not disinterest. The Western interpretation of platonic love typically refers to opposite-sex, close friendships.

Boring, she thinks, and flips on to the chapter on adultery.

Adultery

Someone Always Loses

Of the 1,154 past or present human societies, nearly 1,000 have permitted a man to have more than one wife. Life-long fidelity is a Judeo-Christian invention, which likely came about for economic reasons: a way to guarantee paternity of offspring for men with property to bequeath and ensure financial stability for women embarking on the long child-rearing years. Eventually, marriage became the precursor to sex (at least in theory).

Nowadays, with modern contraception and larger, more anonymous communities, infidelity is easy. Among !Kung San village, 2 percent of kids result from cuckoldry; in some contemporary urban neighbourhoods, the figure is 5 percent to 20 percent.

Why is adultery so common? There's the sexual rush fuelled by the secrecy imperative. And the excitement of a new partner brings us back in a temporal slight of hand to previous emotional times, and so the tryst makes us feel young.

The contemporary pathos is also fed by the pervasive importance of sex—from cooking shows to comic books—and the belief that good, regular sex is our right. Added to this is the emotional comfort of sex: it is the one time when we are most assuredly living in the now, the most present.

This is the backdrop. There are a million personal variations on the reasons for having affairs, but usually it boils down to two things. First, we think something is genuinely amiss with the home relationship and justify the clandestine relationship as a way to fulfill needs that aren't met in the marriage; second, and more common (although few have the self-knowledge to see it), something is missing in ourselves, be it self-esteem, security, or the capacity for contentment, and we look for it in someone else.

Remember: One must be well to love well (see chapter 13).

Regardless of the impetus, adultery is fraught with peril. Clandestine betrayal—and that's what it is, make no mistake about it—is nasty. Once you have broken that promise, that vow of faithfulness, there is a terrible sense of loss, no matter how you dress it up. In addition to the betrayal of your shared intimacy, the lying takes a toll. Lying about the where and with whom. Taking furtive showers in the secret lover's bathroom, trying not to get your hair wet. And each lie adds a layer of deceit until you hardly know what to say to your partner anymore.

Then something happens. You may get caught and have to contend with fall-out from a battered ego and lost trust. You may face a gradual, painful, and long breakup. Or your partner may kick you out, physically and/or psychologically. Affairs are poignant tragedies if they lead to the dissolution of an arrangement that's good for raising children. If it's between adults, well, it's your call. But before you start, appreciate that there is a real risk that it will destroy your primary relationship. Decide whether it's worth it. Consider what you have to lose—socially, financially, and emotionally—because someone always loses in an extramarital affair (Work Sheet 3a: Should I have an affair?).

Christina has never considered cheating on Don. From the beginning, he was trusting and, in a way, sweetly naive—optimistic is perhaps a better word, she thinks. He expects the best of people, of life. They met while she was doing her teaching degree. One winter day, they shared a table in the crowded university centre cafeteria. He was upgrading by taking an MBA. A mature student like her but unlike her, he had a great job in an up-and-coming high-tech company; she'd seen it in headlines in the business section of *The Star*. He kindly fetched her a spoon for her raspberry yogourt then asked what she was studying. When he learned she was an artist, he told her he'd just been to New York City for the first time. He had visited the Modern Museum of Art, where he'd seen a Stieglitz exhibition of photographs.

"There were these beautiful black and white ones of his wife, Georgia O'Keeffe," he said. "I don't think I've ever seen anything more sensual. Even her hands . . ."

He looked Christina in the eyes then turned shy. "I don't meet many girls," he explained.

"Women," she countered intuitively.

"Yes, those," he stammered. "Would you, I mean, if you aren't busy, would you like to go out on Friday night to a movie? There's that new Woody Allen at the Downtown, *Everyone Says I Love You*, with Drew Barrymore and Edward Norton. It's supposed to be good, sort of a musical with dancing . . . and a love story, of course. It is Woody, after all. But you're probably busy . . ."

All the while he was talking, his hands folded and refolded his paper napkin.

She loved how he was so nervous with her yet wanted her in a way that made him take this chance, made him ask her out. She realized this was the first time in years that she'd been asked on a date without alcohol being a factor.

She was not used to pragmatic, useful men. She was curious about Don, about the type of man he would turn out to be. She accepted his invitation. Four months later, she accepted his proposal. They were comfortable in one another's company. They balanced one another.

We are fundamentally still well, she thinks. Except for the loss of intimacy, and I know he misses that, too. It's the mitigating factor that allows you to put up with life's imperfections, she thinks. His long hours at work and obsession with technology that keeps him up till all hours of the night, tinkering; and my moods and unspecified dissatisfaction, my impatience with the day-to-day drudgery of family life, despite adoring the children. She thinks maybe she'll have a look at the section "Better Sex than Sorry" she'd noticed in *The Book of Love*.

CHAPTER 8

MARRIAGE
Better Sex than Sorry

Sex, money, chores, and children: These are the four "hot topics" in most live-in relationships, sex being by far the hottest and—sadly—the most pervasively avoided. Stacks of self-help books and legions of therapists concur: good sex is a barometer of relationship health. Making love can help establish a bond of respectful kindness and is an opportunity to relax, put aside pressures, and reinforce emotional intimacy. Put in its negative: sexual inactivity is a reliable predictor of marital unhappiness and divorce.

So, why do we avoid communicating about it?

First, as the quintessential playboy Hugh Hefner opined: "Our puritan roots are deep. We're fascinated by sex and afraid of it." Plainly put, communicating about sex embarrasses most people.

Secondly, couples often fear that lagging sexual attraction is a sign that their relationship is failing. What they may not realize is that it's natural, even biologically inevitable, for attraction to flag. During the first two years of a relationship, both partners produce phenylethylamine, a natural amphetamine that could well be called the love potion.

Just four years into a relationship, the proportion of thirty-year-old women wanting regular sex falls to below 50 percent.[1] Among cohabitating American couples, one-third have sex twice a week or more, one-third a few times a month, and one-third a few times a year or not at all.[2] The reasons range from extra-mari-

---

1   D. Klusmann, "Sperm competition and female procurement of male resources," *Human Nature* 17, no. 3 (2006): 283–300.

2   R.T. Michael, J.H. Gagnon, E.O. Laumann, and G. Kolata, *Sex in America: A Definitive Survey* (Boston, Mass.: Little, Brown Co., 1994).

tal affairs, demanding jobs and other responsibilities, drugs, alcohol, and finances. The problem is so prevalent that lack of desire even has a medical moniker: hypoactive sexual desire disorder.

Libidos can differ wildly between the sexes, partly because of natural hormonal levels, but also because of the role sex plays in men's and women's lives. Generally speaking, men use sex to feel good, while women need to feel good before having sex. In other words, when life gets stressful, he wants it and she doesn't.

And so we have a paradox: sex is essential to sustaining a marriage, but sex and marriage are seemingly not simpatico. What can you do?

There are two keys to a healthy sexual relationship: **chemistry**, which is essentially beyond our control (Viagra and testosterone patches aside), and **communication and action**, which we can control.

Talk Your Way Through

Set aside your inherent reservations, make a date, and have mindful, respectful, and calm conversations about underlying issues, such as the division of household labour, job dissatisfaction or overwork, rearing of children, and money (Workbook 5. Initiating and sustaining tough conversations).

You'll also need to talk about sex specifically: what you like and don't like. A survey of people in long-term relationships found they were more sexually satisfied when they communicated their likes and dislikes to their partners than when they did not.[3]

Don't Talk Desire to Death

But beware, if you make sex a self-help project, with the attendant monitoring of frequency and reciprocity, essentially demystifying your erotic experience, it will become dull drudgery.

---

3   *S. Macneil and E.S. Byers*, "The relationships between sexual problems, communication and sexual satisfaction," *The Canadian Journal of Human Sexuality* 6, no. 4 (1997): 277–84.

Communication is not about words, it's about connection. Strive to re-mystify your eroticism; rediscover the power of flirting, wit, innuendo, and pacing. You know what draws your partner in. Non-sexual touching is a good example. A man needs two to three times as much touching as a woman.[4] Another way to kindle the spark is to enjoy fun activities together or just look into her/his eyes and smile.

Sometimes you have to consciously put the "play back into playing around."[5] In the classic how-to book, *The Joy of Sex*, Alex Comfort writes that "sex is a deeply rewarding form of play. Children are not encouraged to be embarrassed about their play: adults often have been and are still."[6] But as long as our play is not "hostile, cruel, unhappy or limiting," we absolutely should not be embarrassed. Make a play date with your partner and take turns providing the "sexual meal" to set the stage for lovemaking, using toys, games, and fantasy. Have an affair with your partner. Meet your partner in a bar and pretend to be strangers. Afterwards, act like cheating lovers and book a hotel room. There's nothing unusual in this: 58 percent of Canadians say they watch erotic material with their partners, and 43 percent have spiced things up with a toy.[7] Another survey reveals that 66 percent have done it in a car, 49 percent in a public park, 40 percent at a party, and 33 percent in the bathroom.[8] Your imagination is your gateway.

Don't let your relationship succumb to mutual sexual neglect: better sex than sorry.

---

4   P. Love and S. Stosny, *How to Improve Your Marriage without Talking About It* (New York: Broadway, 2008).

5   B.A. Chernick and N. Chernick, *In Touch: The Ladder to Sexual Satisfaction* (London, Ont.: Sound Feelings, 1994).

6   A. Comfort, *The Joy of Sex* (New York: Crown Publishers Inc., 1972).

7   G. La Giogia, "Intimate info.," *Canadian Health* (January–February 2008): 54.

8   Durex. 2005 Global sex survey. *The Ottawa Citizen*, November 9, 2005, sec. A1.

But, of course, it's not only the intimacy. She and Don have never had that riff, that symbiotic synchronicity that she quickly noticed with Arthur. She thinks of the back and forth, the intellectual aspect of it, how it excites her sexually. She hasn't felt this in years—pre-kids really. But I can't complain, she thinks. Don does his share of chores around the house and loves being with the kids. And he brings me my breakfast on a tray every Saturday morning. In the winter, the grapefruit sections are individually cut out; in summer he makes sure there is always fresh fruit, usually berries with a spoonful of vanilla yogourt. And we talk and touch and hold hands, although our conversation is domestic-centric. Always, she thinks.

The gallery is in a handsome limestone building a block off the waterfront. An ideal location for walk-ins and well-heeled tourists. Arthur also has a dealer at a Toronto gallery, and a Montreal place on Green Street is showing two of his pictures.

She acknowledges her envy and wonders what his work is like, envisioning something blue and bright.

The gallery is closed, but Arthur has the key to the back door. The show opened the weekend before, he explains, and he's already sold three paintings: two at the vernissage and another to a collector, a patron who buys a piece from every show.

"She's marking the so-called progression of my so-called career," he says. Then laughs.

"Wine?" he asks, holding up a half-full bottle.

"Please," she says, "just a bit."

He hands her a half-filled juice glass: "To new friendships," he says.

"Cheers," she says, and they clink glasses. The wine's sharpness pierces her tongue.

He takes her elbow—an old-fashioned gesture that she quite likes—and guides her from one painting to the next. The works are huge, the smallest six by six feet. She is overwhelmed by how grey they are. They make her long for colour, and she wonders at what drives him. There is always something of interest that he wants to tell her about: the particular placement of a feather; its meaning in First Nations mythology. She knows nothing about such things.

What she really thinks is that the feathers remind her of dead birds, the twigs of dead trees struck by lightning or chopped down to clear the way for other less important things.

Intellectually, she knows the works are important, but they don't excite her.

At the end of the show hangs a small self-portrait: Arthur, eyes cast down, his face a mournful blue. A portrait of a person burdened by immeasurable sadness, evoking Christ, the burden of man's folly, thinks Christina.

"This is wonderful," she says.

"Do you think so?" he asks. "I just threw it in, you know, to go with the artist's bio, instead of a photo. It's not even for sale."

He says this as if the entire point is to sell pieces, and anything that is not sold or at least *for* sale, has no value.

"When did you paint it?" Christina asks.

"Last year." He pauses then adds: "You're probably more comfortable with portraits, because that's what you do."

Christina is perturbed by this paternalistic assumption, as if she is limited in her understanding by the scope of her own work.

She's about to tell him what the painting means to her when the phone rings. "I'll just check and see who that is," he says. "The owner said she might call." He walks into the office: "Hello? . . . Yes . . . Of course."

She looks at the portrait again and feels sad. She looks around the room. The paintings are startling in their size and myriad textures and components, but they are cold, disconnected from anything emotional, several steps removed from a genuine response to the world. Is he afraid of exposing or even facing his emotions?

Am I? Christina wonders. Is that why I keep painting the same thing again and again? She considers the crowd of Christinas she has painted. But they do seem honest to her. I can be direct, genuine. But not lately, she thinks. Not with the demands of life, the groceries-mending-vaccine-everything-of-it that makes me feel like screaming. Just once, let me get to the end of my to-do list, just this once. Puh-leese!

Repetition without respite mitigated by love? Unmitigated?

So, how do I respond? Why, I cut out the thing that is most core to me—my scratchings, as Mom used to call them.

"I'd like to see your self-portraits." Arthur steps toward her. "You're such a beautiful woman."

She feels a wave of pure feminine pleasure, despite her . . .

And he puts his fingers to her cheek, stroking gently . . .

Without thought, she leans, ever so slightly, lightly, into him . . .

"Sweet," he whispers.

He puts a hand on her left shoulder blade, drawing her gently towards him. Before she can think, he is kissing her, his lips large and pliable against hers. Slightly moist. His practised smoothness simultaneously attracts and repels. He slips his hand lower onto her back, and a flash of Don comes to her: his hand on the small of her back, guiding her to their bed. And in the remembering comes knowing. She steps back. Arthur releases his hold but keeps his face close.

"I'm married," she says.

"I know, I know," he says, stepping back, raising his hands. "I'm attracted to you," he says, catching her eye, "but I respect that you're . . . happily?"

"Yes, happily," she says, meeting his gaze, profoundly relieved.

He sighs: "Happily then."

He's a gentleman after all. He offers to take her to dinner, but she says she has arranged to meet some colleagues. He walks her back to the hotel, and they say their goodbyes in the lobby. "Remember you have my card. Call me if you ever want to talk about your work. Or just talk." She goes on tiptoe to lightly kiss his cheek and is momentarily surprised by its softness. Then turns and walks away without looking back. She waits by the elevators until she's sure he has left the hotel. After a suitable period of time, she goes outside into the waterfront park. The grass is already damp with evening dew.

She is sweetly happy to be alone. Reflected lights glimmer on the water between the sailboats resting in the harbour. She thinks of her conversation with Arthur at lunch, how it pleased and inspired her, how she needed this connection with a fellow artist, although not Arthur; that would be wrong. He'd made his intentions clear. And not Don. No. You can't get it all from one person, she thinks. So, I'll find other people—other art teachers, old classmates, someone.

She strolls across the damp grass as her eyes adjust to the dim light. Distinctive shapes of trees and bushes emerge around her, and, as she retreats into that place where art comes from, begins to wonder how she can mimic those in the miniature. Perhaps a dwarf lavender for a bush alongside the cultivars of sempervivum and *album* "Murale" sedums she has planted in one bed. Rocks as a central point as mountains. Like in a Japanese garden? No, that's too derivative. Too rigid. Perhaps garden gnomes.

She smiles to herself. Perhaps not the garden. Painting's my medium. Yes. She notes her hand is in a curved position as if to hold a brush. Self-portraits but with context in my milieu. Me with my family, with Suzanne, and Erica. Gardening. Cooking in the kitchen. Portraits of the ordinary but extraordinary human condition.

And even as she imagines it, she knows it.

These plans may change a hundred times before anything comes to pass, but she is excited by their prospect, the trying.

Facing the Music

WITHOUT THE PRESUMPTION OF SEX, Erica relaxes into the Zen of dating Thomas: the now, the flirt, the fun of it. That assumption, after the third or fourth date, that if you don't put out you must be frigid, or have some psychological twitch, or undesirable trait, belief, or affliction—that pressure's off. Although they've certainly had their passionate moments. Late night kisses and groping sessions while her taxi waits outside. A couple of times, she's nearly stayed over with promises on both sides of chaste sleeping together, but in the end, they've reluctantly agreed that the "chaste" part would be highly unlikely; the allure would overcome. Attraction buzzes like static electricity between them. It's been nearly four months—four months in the normal course of dating would be untenable. But Erica and Thomas have the perfect delay strategy: a physical problem, a serious malady, but with a positive prognosis.

Meanwhile, they happily spend most weekends and one or two evenings a week together. They cook—even take a class in Thai cuisine; they take long walks through downtown and alongside the river, always stopping at the bench where they lingered on their first date and, depending on what's happening and how he's feeling—most of the time he's fine, but occasionally he's overwhelmed with fatigue—they go to see bands. After years of going to the clubs on her own, she's glad of the company, but more than that, she's excited to have someone to discuss the groups with afterwards, especially someone who is in the business, who knows so much, who can put the music in its cultural context. She finds herself jotting notes for her column during their discussions. For his part, Thomas invites her to sit in on auditions and recording sessions at his studio. She loves being part of this side of the business, the genesis of a recording. Together, they riff on mixes and the musicians.

She feels as though she knows Thomas better than she's known anyone for a long, long time. Maybe forever. But she doesn't tell anyone, not even him — especially not him. It feels too soon; we're at the preverbal stage, she decides.

Yet, in spite of all that is good, Erica sometimes feels lost, wonders if she is on the right path in this unchartered territory. She is used to being desired, pursued, and wooed by men who are seemingly bewitched by her red hair and generous breasts. "Men are so predictable," she'd told Suzanne. But now it seems that they are not. She looks for her whereabouts in *The Book of Love* chapter called "Chaste Dating."

A period of dating without sex is an excellent way to establish a foundation for an intimate relationship. Chaste dating guards against using sex as a shortcut to intimacy. In reality, the physical bond of premature consummation fosters an assumption of know-ledge, and is frequently a shortcut to a short-term relationship. We all know that the meeting of hips does not equal the meeting of minds, much less hearts or emotions. But the physical is power-ful, fulfilling sexual and, to some extent, emotional needs. The problem is the physical novelty doesn't last, limerence wanes, and without a sustainable emotional and intellectual connection — the bond of personality — the relationship will fade.

Erica shows the passage to Suzanne as they slurp up pho one noon-hour in a crowded Vietnamese café.

"It makes sense to me," says Erica. "It gives us a chance to know each other without sex distorting everything."

"Yeah, but what if you aren't on the same grid?" says Suzanne. "I mean if it doesn't work out sexually — well, that's gotta be a deal breaker. Isn't it better to know that right from the get-go? Well, maybe not the first date, but you know, soon, before you're all caught up emotionally? 'Cus you can dick around forever — excuse the pun — thinking you can make it work, but in the end, the fit is either there or it isn't."

"Yeah," Erica ventures tentatively, "but it's also dangerous if you have sex too soon because it's like the book says: there's this assumption of intimacy and emotional attachment without anything more substantial than orgasms to back it up. And besides, isn't there a better chance of great sex if you are already emotionally together?"

"Maybe," Suzanne admits. "I think it's a question of what's reasonable. What works for you."

"Well, in my case, it's purely academic," says Erica, "because Thomas isn't ready yet. Though he said three months, and now it's been four. I mean we do fool around, and for sure we're both aroused, so at least that's there. Whether our parts fit together — well, that remains to be seen."

"It's like a jigsaw," says Suzanne. "You can have two bits of sky, seems good, lots in common, but then they don't fit. Sometimes, though, it's a perfect fit and it's heavenly." She rolls her eyes for effect. "Hey, did you read in the paper about women getting designer vaginas so they can perfectly fit their partner's penis?"

Erica shakes her head: "That's perverse. All that expense and bother. And for what? A better orgasm? Probably just for the guy. Maybe. And maybe not. Meanwhile, kids are dying of stuff like malaria. It's all out of whack."

Thomas is leaving on a two-week tour around Ontario with Impulse, a band he's recording, so they arrange for a farewell dinner at Erica's house. She thinks this might be the night that they sleep together, but more than that, she thinks about how much she's going to miss him. She's taken aback by the strength of this feeling: it's too soon, she rationalizes. We haven't even slept together yet. She leaves work an hour early and carefully prepares a creamy pesto and fusilli entrée and a salad with baby spinach, pine nuts, and mandarin oranges. For dessert, she's bought cannoli — taste bud orgasms, Suzanne calls them.

As Thomas opens the bottle of Val Muzzol he's brought, he casually mentions that he has had his six-month follow-up with his oncologist that afternoon.

"Why didn't you tell me?" she asks. "How did it go?"

"Good, good, it's all good," he says. "No sign of any evildoers, and I've been feeling great." He smoothes his fingers over her upper arm. "We talked again about fertility."

Erica's heart leaps: children—the one subject throughout their endless chatter that she's consistently avoided. He's avoided, too, she realizes.

"Oh," she says calmly, turning to stir her pesto cream sauce.

"It's a bit iffy," he says. "The chemo stops the sperm production for a few years. I may get it back afterwards, but maybe not."

A wave of dismay engulfs her, followed by thoughts of Vita. Vita and her little girl smell, which she loves. Still, she affirms to herself: I don't want children.

"I know we've never talked about kids," Thomas says. "I've been dodging it. I talked to Dr. Wright about it before the surgery, and, well, he recommended that I store some sperm—nasty business that, but I did it just in case . . ."

She exhales, though she hadn't realized she was holding her breath.

"So," he continues, "if I did want kids it would have to be by artificial insemination." He pops the cork and pours them each a glass of wine.

"And do you?" she ventures. "Want a kid?"

"Fifty-fifty. It depends so much on my partner," he says. "It's early days, Erica. Let's leave this one for a while, okay? Unless you want to talk about it. I just wanted to let you know what's going on. I've been meaning to tell you for ages, but it never seemed to be the right time."

"Early days," she agrees. "Let's wait."

"Sure," he says, wrapping his arms around her from behind. She turns from the stove to embrace him. Why don't I just tell him I don't want children? she thinks. Am I afraid of losing him?

"So," he says, "what delectable concoction have you come up with this evening?"

They linger over dinner and post-dinner cognac, and he's finally pulling on his jacket at midnight followed by a half-hour of kisses and embraces. Finally, he says he still hasn't packed and he has to go. Erica surreptitiously wipes an escaped tear from her cheek—she had hoped he would stay the night—and forces herself to smile at him.

"Don't forget to call me," she says.

"Every day," he says, returning her smile. Then, with a final kiss, he is gone. She closes the door behind him, pulls the bolt. Two weeks. It looms long. But it will give me time to think.

She crawls into bed, her mind whirling, twirling with feelings; feelings that recall memories, that trigger other feelings and questions, questions about Thomas. And the big WHEN? When will we sleep together? Except for Hugh, who was a total nut-job where sex was concerned, she has always been rather indifferent to lovemaking. She was pursued—she'd been able to count on that—and after three dates, she'd usually sleep with the man, not so much because she really desired him, but because it was expected. Usually, she wouldn't have an orgasm and never the first time (except with Hugh and that whole affair was a sexual aberration). But with Thomas she is longing for the physical connection. She even wonders if she should buy a vibrator. Four months, going on five, and still he doesn't seem ready, never spontaneously brings up the topic. She wonders if there's more to it—impotence, fetishes, fears—or if he's not attracted to her. Then she remembers a recent groping. Standing in his front hall, he slowly unbuttoned her blouse, kissing her neck, her clavicle, her breasts as he went, but never touching her with his hands. It was hot, oh yes, and she wanted him so badly. Is he toying with me? she wonders. Why didn't we do it before he left? But then she realizes it would have been weird with him going on the road for two weeks. No matter what the outcome—great, mediocre, or impotence—we'll need some sort of follow up the next day. And so she puts that aside, but still sleep won't come. She ruminates obsessively over the question of children. He wouldn't have bothered banking sperm if he didn't want kids. Am I changing my mind? she wonders. Would I with him? She tries to push the subject out of her mind, tries the mindful breathing she learned in yoga. But instead she imagines Thomas as a father, totally involved, playful, nurturing. But you never know with the pressure of parenting and the sleep deprivation it brings, along with the possibility of a cranky kid. What if he goes all self-righteous and bossy like Dad?

I won't impose the misery of my childhood on my own kids, she thinks. It's such a crapshoot. You think your partner will be okay as a dad, then he turns out to be rigid, unforgiving, overprotective. And I'd have to fight—I'd never stand by like Mom. An enabler, Dr. M. called her, who was complicit in Dad's barrage of verbal berating, especially where Alan was concerned. Dad's expectations were impossibly high for his only son: perfect grades, excellence at sports (soccer in particular), hard work, devotion, ambition. He cajoled Alan until he bolted at sixteen—ran away really, although Mom and Dad would never admit that. Now Dad talks about how proud he is of Alan, although all he ever mentions is his lucrative construction business. But I know he's struggling with his second marriage already. Thankfully, there are no kids in the mix.

Their father gave them Anglo names—Alan and Erica—with the hope that it would help them integrate into North American society. But in the end, he did everything he could to make sure that didn't happen. His past—the religious conservatism, the emphasis on respect and obedience—was part of his present, and he was helpless to stop himself from visiting these expectations on his children in a new world. Erica is fearful of sharing his folly with her own children.

Erica immerses herself in her work: the last-minute details of organizing a three-day national retreat for the board of directors so they can finalize their position on certification of Canadian exports. The retreat goes well, logistically, but the proceedings are cut throat. The fundamentalist foodies—the old guard—shrilly arguing that all exported products must meet the Canadian standards, which they worked so hard to develop. And the upstart realists berating them, saying why bother with the expense when the food won't be consumed in Canada. It'll only put processors out of business and, in turn, producers, too. Besides, they say in their irritating, placid manner, imports have to meet our standards; if we demand that exports meet them, too, and if other countries adopt a similar stance, everyone will be bogged down in trying to meet these standards, and either nothing will move or businesses will go bust. Either way, the international movement will suffer.

Finally, during the last afternoon, there's a coup of sorts, with some of the old guard joining the realists, and a resolution is narrowly passed: exports do not have to meet the Canadian standards. The fundamentalists are outraged, and two resign on the spot, including David, a sixty-something grower from British Columbia and one of the council's founders. Erica's always been very fond of David; he was so sweet to her when she first started at the council and helped her to understand the issues in a way that none of the documents could. The resignations shake everyone up, and the meeting ends on a low note with board members wondering if the cost of this win has been too high. But Erica has to press on now to revise their platform document. The thought of this chore makes her weary.

Christina calls on Tuesday and invites her over to visit.

"Don's away at a meeting in Silicone Valley, and I'm desperate for some adult company."

"Is Suzanne coming?"

"Nah, she's busy. Some NFB film screening; she's still on the prowl."

"She'll find her guy soon, I'm sure. She's so systematic about it."

"I love hearing her stories. It brings back the bad good old days. Hey, do you have the book?"

"Yeah," Erica says tentatively.

Christina realizes her faux pas. "I know I've been ranting about it, and I still think you should return it, but Suzanne showed me this section that I thought might interest you. Can you bring it along?"

"Sure, no problem." Erica says quickly, glad that Christina's not going to nag her about returning it.

"So, around seven?" says Christina. "You can help me tuck the kids in. They miss you, their zany Aunt Erica."

Erica thinks maybe Christina is more or less okay about the book. She's felt guilty every time it was mentioned, conscious of Christina's disapproval. She thought about returning it, but figured Foster must have other copies, digital at least, and she loves the book; it seems to answer so many questions for her. I've been reluctant to phone Tina, Erica realizes. It's been weeks. And it's not just the book, she thinks. She's been so cranky, so belligerent lately. She remembers Tina's crass remark about her relationship with Hugh. Way over the top and not like her usual self. Still, Erica finds herself looking forward to the evening, to seeing the kids and reconnecting with Christina. And she thinks Christina may have a different take on Thomas and the dating thing. Erica appreciates that post-marriage, Suzanne's libido is primed, and that waiting so long to be intimate must seem almost perverse to her. Although she hasn't said that in so many words.

It takes Erica over an hour to get to Christina's by bus, but Vita and Norris are still up, waiting in their PJs, when she arrives. She jazzes around with them for a bit, admiring the Lego castle and drawings of horses, then reads the good-night stories, lying on Tina's king-sized bed — "family sized," she jokes. Then it's kisses all around, tucking in, and night lights switched on before she and Christina head downstairs.

"They're adorable," she whispers to Christina.

"Maybe you'll have to change your mind," Christina laughs.

"Maybe," she says. It's bound to come up again with Thomas. But first things first: sex.

Christina pops the cork on a bottle of what she calls her vin ordinaire, Mezzo Mondo, and they settle at the kitchen table each with a glass and some biscotti that Erica has made and brought along in a cookie tin. They talk about the kids, especially Norris's problems settling down at school and the teacher asking Christina to get him tested for attention deficit disorder.

"I swear, I listen to the teachers talking in the lounge, and they'd like all the boys to be on Ritalin."

Gradually, the conversation veers to Thomas, and Erica confides her fears.

"At first, I thought it was okay, you know, waiting. But now I'm starting to feel like maybe it's going on too long."

"Are you happy with him?"

"Yes, yes, I am," says Erica. "And in my mind I just think, well, when the sex comes that will be another piece to our relationship. In theory, it doesn't seem weird to wait. What seems weird now is the three-date-to-screwing route—or even less in the case of Hugh, which was an unprecedented disaster. I mean you hardly know the person. What's their middle name? Their mom's maiden name? Did they have a pet when they were a kid? All those details. There should be a pre-coital quiz!"

Christina laughs.

"Well, I'm hardly an expert," says Christina. "I barely remember dating. I mean we've been married forever. And we certainly didn't wait—we made love on our first real date. I don't know. It probably depends on where your head is and what kind of relationship you want. Of course, with Thomas, there's the medical thing. Would you be waiting if he was healthy?

"I don't know. Probably not. Moot point, though."

"Well, you do seem happy. This waiting seems right for you—it seems to suit you. But you're not used to it. Men are always trying to lure you into bed and suddenly, with Thomas, that's not happening. So that must be a bit of a shock, even a blow to your ego."

"Well, he does want me, I know that. This waiting, I don't know . . . maybe it's just that it feels so square, so unhip."

Christina laughs. "You'll never be less than supremely cool. Impossible."

"Is that the right time?" Erica says, tapping the face of her watch. "My bus is coming in fifteen minutes. I'd better move."

"Hey, did you bring the book?" asks Christina.

Erica hands it to her, and Christina leafs through it as Erica pulls on her retro black and white checked coat—only five bucks at the Sally Ann.

"Ah," Christina says, "here's the section I thought might be interesting for you; I couldn't remember what it was called, and the book doesn't have an index. Anyway, it helped explain a few things for me. Read it and give me a ring tomorrow. And don't forget about returning the book, eh?"

On the bus home, Erica reads the section Christina has marked. It's under the main heading, "Lexicon of Love."

> Although English has more words than any other language, it is woefully lacking in words to describe different *types* of love. Our sole word is loaded with myriad meanings: a parent's love, love among family members, charitable love, love for a friend, and, of course, romantic love. Perhaps this is a reflection of English speakers' reticence to talk about their emotions. In Greek, there are four words, but, remember, the types of love defined by them aren't mutually exclusive. Sometimes one quality dominates and sometimes another.
>
> **Storge** (affection, τοργη): fondness achieved through familiarity, like the love between family members or people who find themselves together by chance rather than by choice.
>
> **Philia** (friendship, φιλια): the strong bond between people who share a common interest or activity.
>
> **Agape** (charity, αγαπη): selfless, altruistic love; for example, the love towards one's neighbour.
>
> **Eros** (ερος): love in the sense of "being in love." This passionate physical and emotional love has become the archetype—and stereotype—of our contemporary construct of romantic love.

What about children? Erica wonders. Where do they fit in? That's more than storge, which is basically happenstance. The bus turns onto the freeway towards downtown, and she continues reading.

In keeping with our culture's obsession, this book focuses on eros. John Lee identified six basic love styles[1] and further research postulates that people often seek partners with the same love style, and that relationships based on similar love styles last longer.[2] Given the vagaries of the human heart and mind, it seems likely that a person may well be a combination in varying proportions of any or all six.

1. **Eros**, or the love of beauty, encompasses the romantic ideal of love. Adherents to this highly sensual love select their lovers on the basis of intuition or chemistry. Marriage is an extended honeymoon and sex, the ultimate aesthetic experience. They may be hopelessly romantic or unrealistic. Eros love is fraught with danger given the inevitable decay that occurs in a fantasy-based relationship.

2. **Ludus** lovers view love as a game with conquest as the goal. They play the field, seeking as much action as possible, rebound rapidly from breakups, and view marriage as a trap. They may have excellent sexual technique, but are highly likely to be unfaithful or promiscuous.

3. **Storge** lovers share interests and are friends first. Commitment is essential, and sex less important. While there is a high degree of intimacy between these lovers, the relationship can lack passion and be boring.

4. **Pragma** lovers are driven by their heads, rather than their hearts, and have practical and realistic expectations. They select their partners, using a shopping list of desirable

---

1   J.A. Lee, "Love styles," in The Psychology of Love by M.H. Barnes and R.J. Sternberg (New Haven, Conn.: Yale University Press, 1988), 38–67.

2   C. Hendrick and S.S. Hendrick, "A theory and method of love," *Journal of Personality and Social Psychology* 50, no. 2 (February 1986): 392–4

attributes, and carefully weigh the costs and rewards of a relationship. Pragmatic lovers view sex as a reward or a means of procreation, and are, typically, undemonstrative and unemotional.

5. **Manic** lovers typically suffer from low self-esteem, anxiety, and insecurity, and place excessive importance on their love relationship. They tend to be volatile, obsessive, possessive, and sometimes extremely jealous. They *need* their partners and view love as a means of rescue and reinforcement of their own value: I am loved therefore worthy. Sex reassures them of this love. Mania is a typical love style among teenagers. This type of love is intense and often passionate, but also obsessive and, ultimately, insatiable.

6. **Agape** love is unconditional, selfless, altruistic love. Agapic-style lovers are often spiritual or religious people, who view their partners as a blessing and want to take care of them. Agapic love is self-sacrificing and all encompassing. Sex is a gift between them. Eventually, however, Agapic lovers may feel they are being used.

Erica sees herself as some combination of storge and eros, the latter being put on hold for now with Thomas and the former developing rapidly. Hugh was manic and insatiable sexually. No question. She was a vessel, a non-participant, a spectator until the finish and he had the technical skills to bring her to orgasm. Many of the men she's known haven't even had that. I have an element of the pragma, too, she thinks, remembering her list of attributes that she's seeking in a man. Suzanne is the true master of the pragma nowadays with her lists and endless scouting missions. I mean what could be more practical than that? And Tina? Eros—initially at any rate. Then maybe storge now, and of course, agape, 'cus of the kids.

Will Thomas and I be lovers in the sense of eros? she wonders.

Like Hugh, but sane. I want that, she realizes. She turns to the back of her journal and adds to the list.

> *good job (worthwhile, interesting)*
>   *willingness to travel*
>   *loves music*
>   *good natured*
>   *fair minded (does housework)*
>   *PASSIONATE LOVER*
>   *partner material*

The second week slowly wears on. She arrives at the office Friday morning to find a message from the arts editor at *The Star*, asking if she can come in for a "chat."

Erica dials right away. "Anything I should be concerned about?" she asks.

"No, no," says Joan, her assigning editor, "not at all. I think you'll be pleased. But let's keep it for face-to-face."

Erica wishes she could talk it over with Thomas, knows it would help to quell her nervousness, but he's driving home and his cell is out of juice.

After work, Erica takes a cab to *The Star* offices and finds herself in a large office facing Joan and two other editors, including the managing editor. They cut to the chase as journalists do and ask her if she'd be interested in a job, four days a week.

"We've noticed a real progression in your work," says Joan. "It's more thoughtful, more analytical. We've had good feedback from readers, too. We'd like you to be our contemporary music critic. You'd write more pieces about the local music scene—you know, profiles of newcomers and established people, programs in schools, recording studios—and you'd write a weekly column that would be a review of new CDs, national tours, international trends, and so on. That would be for the chain across Canada."

Erica is stunned by the job offer; *The Star* is notorious for laying off reporters, for scrimping on coverage, and underpaying freelancers. The salary they mention, even pro-rated to four days a week, is more than she's making working full time at Council, but something in her hesitates.

"I didn't see this coming at all," says Erica. "It's a great offer but a big step for me."

"Of course, you'll want to think about it," says the managing editor. "Why don't you take the weekend and let us know by Monday?"

"Yes, sure, that would be great. Thank you," says Erica. "I'm very interested, don't get me wrong, but it would be a big change for me. I'd have to quit my job. I need to talk to my partner."

That's the first time I've called Thomas my partner, she realizes. Well, he is.

As she waits for her cab, Erica calls Thomas at his house, hoping he's made it home, and feels an electrifying surge of relief when he answers. She tells him what's happened and asks if she can come over and talk about it. As she hangs up, it occurs to her that a few months ago she would have called Suzanne or Christina first.

He greets her at the door, waving a bottle of Prosecco. She smiles at him, can't stop smiling—they've talked on the phone every day, but it's so good to see his face.

"Way to go, babe!" he says, giving her a long hug.

"Yeah, I'm amazed," says Erica as he pours them each a glass.

"Here's to you!" he says. They clink glasses, and he kisses her before they each take a sip.

"You know, it's funny. I always thought this was what I wanted," says Erica, "but now that it's on offer, I'm not so sure. It seems so superficial somehow, covering bands and pop music. I mean the council isn't exactly changing the world; there's so much in-fighting, and now the two board members have quit. But it feels more worthwhile. It matters to the health of people and the planet . . ."

"Music helps people, too," says Thomas, "not physically but in other ways. It lifts their spirits. It can unite a protest. Just think of the sixties. And sometimes it helps them express their feelings or make sense out of things that happen to them. It's less concrete—it's not food—but it's still important. It's art."

"You're right in theory," says Erica, "but then I think of the specifics: Mighty Mouth, rap, disco—so much of it is self-indulgent and superficial. What broader purpose does it serve?"

"It's a mix, and even that stuff, kids identify with it. It expresses how they feel, their frustrations. It's always a mix, just like your work at the council. Some of it is self-serving, helping the farmers make a profit. In principle, how can you argue against the good of organic food? It's like arguing against motherhood. But the reality is that a lot of people can't afford the extra expense of organic food. Or they don't care. And it's one small piece of a political change that has to take place. Music is part of those politics, too."

She leans against him: "This should be a no-brainer for me."

"You know," he says, "you could volunteer the one day a week that you're not working for *The Star.* That's an option."

"That's an interesting idea," says Erica. "There are loads of organizations I'd like to work for—CARE, the Red Cross . . ."

He nods. "They'd love you. You're such a talented writer. You have to be happy with your decision. You have the weekend." He squeezes her hand. "Hey, I picked up a few things at the market on the way home. Shall I make dinner while we talk?"

Erica feels like there has been a shift, a progression between them during this two week separation. It's like *The Book of Love* says, love isn't a constant progression. It moves forward a bit, then back, or stalled, then forward. Or it loses momentum like it did with Hugh. But she feels closer to Thomas than ever before and still can't stop smiling at him. They finish the sparkling wine, chatting as he chops and cooks their shrimp and baby bok choy stir fry.

"No sense in changing to red now," he says and pops open a second bottle of Prosecco.

She laughs and holds out her glass.

"I'm feeling so good these days," he continues as he fills it. "I mean being on the road was tiring, but it also made me realize how much I care for you."

He hands her the glass, and their fingers touch. Their eyes meet: "I love you, Erica."

"I love you, Thomas," she says, smiling into his eyes.

"Come here," he says. And they hold each other close.

"I know it's early days and all," he whispers, "but I was thinking we might want to sleep together tonight." He laughs. She feels his joy and presses gently into his body.

She wakes early Saturday morning, marvelling at how they've managed to sleep intertwined all night long, their arms wrapped around each other. Peaceful, she realizes, I feel peaceful. And so happy. She snuggles into him. He shifts ever so slightly then moves his hand over her breast in his sleep. She stays still so as not to disturb him, thinks about the night before, the laughter and passion. It wasn't a case of parts fitting, as Suzanne said. It was more like meeting at a new place. She smiles, puts her hand over his and moves it down over her belly.

chapter nine

E-love in a Po Po-mo World

SUZANNE LONGS FOR CHANCE ENCOUNTERS, for fingertips brushing the back of her hand and a glance that lingers, posing a question that requires no punctuation, knows no limits: I want you.

Outwardly, she is practical, pragma, as Erica has observed; she keeps a list of places to meet men, for instance, but draws the line at e-dating, sees it as the antithesis of this allure, this snapping of synapses—the super-charged starting point of intense mutual physical attraction. She's holding out for happenstance rather than a calculation of cyberspace: two people available and posted at the exact moment—$x + y = xy$.

"It's not only about having the same hobbies or favourite books," she tells Erica. "I want the potential of romance. The potentiality!" They laugh.

Suzanne's parents met at a community dance, a Saskatoon fundraiser for a family who had lost all their worldly belongings in a house fire, but not each other—that's how her mom put it. Suzanne remembers them telling and retelling the story of their meeting: the looks across the hall, the sweaty first dance. It's a story that is infused with romance. Suzanne would sit on her father's knee, playing with the links on his gold watch as her mother did the crossword while sitting in her chintz-covered easy chair, listening and interjecting small details: the particular cornflower blue of her dress, the boughs of forsythia decorating the hall. They told the tale in tandem; it was their mutual legend. Suzanne doesn't remember when they stopped telling it—certainly before she was fourteen, the year her dad had an affair.

Before the divorce and her mother's unwanted confidences and constant crying. Before alliances were drawn, and Suzanne found herself siding with her mother and refusing to see her dad. He phoned every Tuesday evening when her mother was at aerobics class, and he'd chat away, trying to pry a few words out of his petulant teenage daughter. Finally, after two years, Suzanne started meeting him on the sly for lunch every second week or so, never more; and he never pushed. He was busy with his new family, and then he got a massive promotion—VP finance at the wheat pool—and she joined the volleyball team. She hardly saw him at all in her last year of high school. Then she moved to Ottawa for university. He's never visited but sends a fifty dollar cheque at Christmas and her birthday. The card is always signed "Hope you are well. Love, Dad."

This meeting at the dance was her parents' legend, perhaps their sole legend.

Sitting at her kitchen table, Suzanne lights a du Maurier and takes a sip of her Glenfiddich. Pushing aside these memories, she fingers the list that she and Erica had compiled:

Where to meet a man

— *church*
— *family*
— *community events*
— *work*
— *take a course?*
— *volunteer?*

She strikes them out one by one; those avenues of connection are lost to her. She doesn't go to church and has no time to volunteer or take a course. There's no one interesting at work, and her parents live two thousand kilometres away in Saskatoon. Before Michael (BM as she thinks, conscious of the bathroom humour) she met men through her friends, but these days most of her friends are women, and none of them *admit* to knowing any single men. She suspects they see her as a little too needy, too risky to be foisted upon a friend or relative. There is an implicit responsibility in matchmaking akin to saving someone's life. She recognizes she has an edge these days. She wakes every morning cloaked in loneliness. Stretching her arm under the covers to the cool white sheets beside her, she feels the void inside. Since Michael, she's had only one quasi-date and that was a big mistake (although she can still taste Liam's perfect kiss). It seems impossible that this is happening to her. BM, she had her share of dates, men calling, hanging around. Though they were mostly friends, she concedes. It has been four months since she and Michael split up; over ten years since they met. A decade since my last actual date, she thinks. Married couples talk about going on dates with each other, but it's not the real thing. It's not that edgy pre-sex date, laden with hope and potential.

She steps out onto the balcony of her second-floor apartment. An uncharacteristically warm late fall breeze strokes her bare face and neck. A sweetly familiar tingling begins, and her vulva swells. Warm skin against mine, she thinks. That's what I want. Physical memories—prehistoric memories—of Michael take hold. Him, trying to undo my slacks; me, re-doing them, teasing, straining against him, challenging him to get what he needs. All the while both of us knowing it is what I need as well. A red cardinal flashes across the street against the dark brown brick and overgrown cedars.

. . . you unearth me, resplendent in a similar red bra and panties that drive you to distraction. You, you want them stripped off, love the way they look on. Needs overwhelm, you click the bra, it falls. Your hands find my breasts, full nippled . . .

Suzanne shakes her head, goes inside to her bedroom, to her bedside table, to her vibrator. Her partner these past months. She'd always thought it was singularly pathetic to use one, but now she sees it as uncomplicated and necessary. Perhaps, she thinks, it will slow me down, keep my pants zipped for a couple of dates, allow me to keep a clear mind without the oxytocin effect. She's read about it: a neurotransmitter critical for bonding and mating. Men get it in tiny doses after sex, but it floods women's post-coital brains making them go all warm and fuzzy. Too fast, too soon. And too irrational, Suzanne has decided. Yam gel. Fresh batteries. Close enough for a minute or two.

Afterwards, in the bathroom, she washes herself and her cylindrical pal then stands in front of the mirror searching for new fine lines around her mouth (laugh lines; that's okay) and eyes (life lines; not okay). She spent half a month's rent on restorative creams and gels—a "facial routine," the clerk assured her in hushed tones—to try to erase the inevitable tread of living. She tracks her periods meticulously, lamenting the departure of each egg—a finite number, she's read. She only hopes there are enough.

She takes another small sip of her Glenfiddich, lights another cigarette, and opens *The Book of Love* to one of the yellow Post-its that Erica had placed, this one at a section about following your passions to meet your kindred spirit.

> People often try too hard to meet that perfect someone. More often than not, it's a question of being who you are, only more so. Invest your time in yourself, in following the passions that you hold dearest: dance, music, theatre, literature. But get out there, go to events, get on invitation lists. You'll meet like-minded people who may share more than your passion for something; they may well share your politics, your philosophy. Socialize mindfully at these events. Have fun, but keep your radar tuned.

Hackneyed advice, she thinks, I've read it a zillion times in women's mags. And I've been there. This past month, she diligently filled her calendar with events: film openings and script workshops. She ran into old friends but didn't meet anyone promising.

Tonight, she's invited to a launch of a new children's book. Maybe, she thinks, maybe. She downs her Glenfiddich—her preferred social lubricant—and dresses carefully in a low-cut aubergine T-shirt that shows off her clavicle in lieu of cleavage, and form-fitting, stylish grey pants. She crimps and curls her eyelashes, does her eyeliner twice over, then outlines and fills in her lips with a deep burgundy. She thinks of these as her weapons of mass seduction. She works slowly, methodically, timing it so she doesn't arrive too early in her anxiety not to be late.

It's a classy do in the national theatre foyer. Wee cardboard boxes—the kind Chinese food used to come in—are filled with veggie sushi, two chopsticks sticking out of the top of each one; a selection of chocolate truffles dusted lightly with icing sugar are beautifully arranged on Depression-era plates. Suzanne roams, bumping into people she knows and their friends. She pulls out her most vivacious self and makes small talk and jokes. She meets an interesting man: her body type (or at least taller than her) and single (or at least not wearing a wedding ring), and her hopes rise. But then, within two minutes, he mentions—gratuitously, it seems to her, "My wife refuses to come to these events any more. She says they're pretentious." He knew what I was after, Suzanne thinks, finding his response to her vaguely insulting and presumptuous. She reminds herself that there's no shame in being single.

Later, a second potential tells a long story about his old dog who is literally on her last legs then, inadvertently, Suzanne is sure, refers to his wife not being able to carry the pooch down the porch steps. "Man looking for affair, not quite sure how to go about it." Bastard, she thinks and wonders if his wife knows. Wonders, in her own case, why she didn't for so long. I should have, she chides herself. All the signs were there. But I was complacent, smug. Maybe if I'd caught on sooner, it would have been easier to work things out. She considers this. Maybe not. It's a question of trust. She excuses herself to refill her wine glass.

A third man seems promising. He owns a funky advertising agency downtown and is refreshingly easy to chat with. They share a half-hour of casual banter. They seem to have a lot of mutual acquaintances, including Greg: "Never mind six degrees of separation," he says, "in this city there's only about two degrees."

She smiles and draws her hand through her cropped hair. He's taller than her, nice body type—slim. Then it gradually dawns on her that he is gay. Not in the stereotypical Greg way, but gay, oh yes. It is the little things like the attention to detail: the paisley purple shirt and matching string tie, three rings and carefully ironed trousers. Eventually, her suspicions are confirmed when he mentions The Outlook, a gay bar downtown that Greg has taken her to a few times.

Hopes up, hopes dashed. And so it goes in mini-cycles at every social event. The process makes her dizzy. Each time, she goes home with an empty notebook, feeling progressively less at ease with herself and her place in the world as a single woman. She would never admit it to anyone, but like her mother, she feels that she is measured by the male company she keeps. Measured by whether she can *keep* male company. When she told her mother that she was splitting up with Michael, she wasn't surprised. "Well, at least you didn't have kids," she said. "I am sorry, though, Suzanne. I know what it's like to be cheated on." And then she told Suzanne that her father had bought a Mazda Miata—"Mid-age crisis. Maybe he'll be leaving her, too." She said this almost hopefully. She's still so bitter, thinks Suzanne, and hasn't moved on a bit. I won't be like that, she vows.

Suzanne takes solace in her documentary on Maura Kerby. That, at least, is going well. She cleared her bulletin board and pinned the Can-film acceptance letter in the centre. Funding—cash—her starting point for a story board that is gradually forming. The very fact of it makes her arm hairs stand on end. She's setting up a shooting schedule with Kerby for January. And she's working on her script, doing more research, phoning Kerby every Thursday evening to get more background and details. She has also contacted Kerby's parents, teachers, and mentors—the head curator at the National Gallery and two pre-eminent art critics—and arranged times for pre-interviews in the fall. But despite the demands and satisfaction of all this, she is still hounded by her need for a man.

The day after the book launch, she calls a girlfriend SOS. Christina treks in to meet her and Erica at Echoes.

"After a few dozen of these events, you start to lose momentum. You lose heart," says Suzanne. "You wonder what to do next. How much more skin you can show."

They discuss and diss numerous options. "What are your chances of meeting a guy at a bar?" Erica asks. "Who's hanging out there anyway? Drinkers. Guys on the move. And why are they there? Hoping to get laid."

Christina snorts: "All men want to get laid. Straight. Gay. Single. Married. They're hardwired for it. Hard and hardwired."

"Getting laid wouldn't be so bad," says Suzanne. They laugh. But, she thinks, what I really miss is that skin-on-skin thing. The contact. Connection.

"I heard something about Michael," says Erica to Suzanne. "I don't know for sure if it's true, but probably . . ."

"Go ahead," Suzanne says quickly but in a flat tone, her deliberate effort to show it doesn't matter. But it does. The less she thinks about him the better.

"I wasn't going to tell you, but then I thought it would be better if you heard it from me, a friend, rather than being taken by surprise."

Suzanne nods.

"Well, you know Cari-Lynn, the tarot-reading granola at work? Well, she's a friend of a friend of Angie's, and she says Angie has moved in with Michael. At his new place on Third Ave."

Suzanne laughs too loudly. "Well, that didn't take long, did it! I wonder how long till he cheats on her, too." Her heart has accelerated into overdrive.

"He's thinking with his little head," says Christina. "I'm so sorry, Suzanne. This can't be easy for you." She reaches across the table and covers her hand.

Suzanne holds Tina's hand, feels the warmth and strength of it enveloping her own, and she lets down: "He kept saying it was over between them," she murmurs. Tears spill down her face. She dabs at them with the pink flowered cocktail napkin then sips her drink to stabilize herself. I should've tried harder. Met him half-way. Slept with him. Maybe I called it quits too soon. Calm, she urges herself. Be calm. It was over. You know that. Her mantra works for a second, but then she feels mercurial anger mounting by degrees through her body. Anger at him for lying again and again. At herself for being duped, for allowing him to hurt her again. I'm an idiot, she thinks. A patsy.

"At the very least, he should've been honest with you. He should've had the balls to tell you they were shacking up," says Christina.

"He was probably seeing her the whole time we were suppos-edly trying to get back together," says Suzanne. "He's probably been lying all along."

"Oh, I don't know," says Erica, "he seemed pretty sincere when you guys were trying to make things work. At least from how you described it. He probably went back to her after you guys split up."

"Yeah, I'm sure that's right," says Christina.

"He probably found it rough being on his own. Lonely," says Erica.

"I expected him to play the field, you know, date a bit," says Suzanne. "But to jump right into another relationship, it's . . ."

"Pathetic," says Erica. "He didn't even give himself time to recover, to reflect, and learn from what happened. He was too anxious for something permanent, settled."

So am I, realizes Suzanne. I could just as easily be the one who moved in with someone. He just beat me to the punch. This thought calms her.

"I never knew he was so insecure," Erica continues. "And he's missing out on all the fun, the dating, the flirting."

"But it's really scary, too," says Suzanne. "Putting yourself out there on show, and what if you're rejected . . .?"

"It's not rejection," says Christina, "not when they don't really know you. It's just looking around. It isn't a judgment of you per se. It's about their tastes, about what they're looking for."

"Besides, you're gorgeous and talented," says Erica. "If they don't want you, it's their loss and your gain. You deserve someone who's gaga for you, girl."

Into the second martini when everyone, including Suzanne, is tired of talking about her dating prospects, Erica says: "Well, sweetie, it seems to me it's time to switch into high gear and, as I've said before, find a new nail to hammer the old one out."

"I know you have problems with it, Suzanne, but why don't you look into the internet dating thing," says Christina. "Teresa, a teacher at work, tried it, and she's dating a guy who's interested in opera, same as her. See that's the thing. You can specify what you're interested in, you know, films, documentaries, maybe even kiddie lit."

"It's strange," says Erica. "We try to plan everything in our lives: we get a degree so we can have a good career. We try to save dough to buy a car or make a down payment on a condo. We use expensive face guck to ward off old age. But when it comes to romance, we leave it all up to chance. And end up as SIW-WIDs—Single Income Women, Working Instead of Dating. What's with that?"

"If I was single, I'd totally go for online," says Christina. "It's a minimal risk. You communicate through the site, but not directly, so you can get out at any time. And you don't give out your full name, or number, or anything unless you're comfortable. And if you want to meet just go to a coffee shop."

Well, maybe not a coffee shop, Suzanne thinks, remembering Liam. Damn he was delish—but whacked.

"I don't know." She thinks of her parents. Their marriage seemed solid, but then it disintegrated. Maybe if they had been better suited to start with . . .

"There's a chapter in the book about it," says Erica. "You should check it out. I marked it with a Post-it."

"Didn't you say you were going to return that thing?" asks Christina.

"The track's closed for the season," says Erica.

Lame ass excuse, thinks Christina; the casino's still open. But she decides not to pursue it, at least not for the moment: we have to focus on Suzanne.

They order another round of martinis. Suzanne tries an Amber Gamble: Goldschlager and apple cider. It's delicious. *Gamble*, she thinks, half-listening to Christina talking about the painting she's thinking of doing; something about a young woman morphing into an older one. *I don't want to gamble, but this internet thing seems safe—although awfully prosaic.*

Late that evening, she checks out the section Erica marked in *The Book of Love.*

E-dating: The New Community

If you think internet dating is the last refuge of the despondent, think again: this is the modern meeting place.

In the not so distant "good old days," the options for meeting potential partners in person were more plentiful. You were set up by a relative or friend, went to dances and parties, fell for someone from school or your community. Nowadays, we live hundreds, if not thousands, of kilometres away from relatives, and many of us are relative newcomers to our communities. We're busy with our careers, and in the midst of the technological maelstrom of e-mail, the internet, video games, DVDs, and a hundred TV channels, we're not getting out as much. No wonder we don't meet anyone.

Fortunately, the technology that is robbing us of face-to-face opportunities also presents a new option: computer dating services, where you are exposed to hundreds of people and can pick and choose. It's like catalogue shopping. Some love this calculated, controlled approach to romance, but others are holdouts for the vagaries of love the old fashioned way. But really there's nothing new about the screening in e-dating. People have always screened: he's too short, she's too tall, they have the wrong occupation or religion. Online dating facilitates the selection process and increases the odds of success; you can find out at a glance whether a person might be suitable.

According to some studies, most people email with a prospective date three to four times before talking on the phone. The correspondence can be a lot of flirty fun while you learn about the other person. Think of it as technological foreplay. The average first contact to first encounter is seven to ten days. But don't forget to play safe with some simple precautions (see page 152).

And, if at first you don't succeed, internet date again. There is no failure; think of it as a party, flitting from one person to the next until you meet someone interesting. The more new people you meet, the better your chances.

It still seems too calculated to Suzanne. But then again, her current strategy is obviously a dead end. Suzanne was resisting e-dating, but then she caved.

So instead of trying to find a freelance cameraman and sound guy for her Kerby documentary, Suzanne spends an entire evening online, searching for a promising dating site. She dismisses the cheesy and obviously sex-driven ones such as Whole lotta lovin' and Sexploration, MANouever and Passion Quest, but not before checking out the listings available to non-members and laughing at some obviously ancient photos of men sporting mullets or wearing shirts with the long, pointed collars from the early seventies. It's amusing if nothing else. Finally, she settles for SoulConnect, a site for singles who want relationships as opposed to casual sex or whatever. It takes two evenings and much of a work day daydreaming to fill out the questionnaire. Finally, she posts under the moniker:

CapitalWoman

LAST BOOK READ

The Eyre Affair, by Jasper Fforde. A hilarious, inventive sleuthing adventure through the pages of fiction. LOL guaranteed.

(She considers putting down something highfalutin', even if she hasn't actually read it. Something like *A Short History of Time*. If I were truthful, I'd put down *Alice in Wonderland*, but the message is all wrong: childish, dreamer, and worse still, in the parlance of some literary critics, demonstrating a predilection for kiddie porn.)

MOST HUMBLING MOMENT
Admitting to myself that online dating might be a good option.

(This is her most recent humbling moment. Liam being the precursor. And Michael before that.)

BEST OR WORST LIE
"No, really, it's okay."

(Vague enough, a bit funny, she thinks. We've all said this.)

FAVOURITE ON-SCREEN SEX SCENE
Lady and the Tramp—the scene in the Italian restaurant where they're eating spaghetti. Okay, it's not sex, but it's romantic as anything. Even if it is about dogs.

(She remembers watching a porn movie with a lover one time: *Debbie Does Dallas* or some such thing; she can't recall the title, but she remembers the sex afterwards was fabulous. She can't put that down though—she'd just get pervs.)

IF I COULD BE ANYWHERE AT THIS MOMENT
Down the rabbit hole with Alice.

(Aka in bed with a great lover. And if he gets that, she thinks, I am interested!)

SONG OR ALBUM THAT PUTS ME IN THE MOOD
Van Morrison's "Have I Told You Lately?"

(Too romantic? She considered briefly, Frank Sinatra's "Fly Me to the Moon." Her mom and dad used to put it on the turntable and dance around the cramped living room while she watched, amazed that they never bumped into anything.)

FIVE ITEMS I CAN'T LIVE WITHOUT:
Collection of Grimm's fairy tales
Waiting, by Maura Kerby
Rocket-shaped Martini shaker
My best friends (not things, I realize, but I definitely can't live without them)
My 1999 Audi (a few miles but still perky!)

(Vibrator?!)

FILL IN THE BLANK:
<u>A wink</u> is sexy.

<u>Your hand on the small of my back</u> is sexier.

IN MY BEDROOM YOU WILL FIND:
An incredibly comfy bed that's easy to get into and difficult to get out of, neat stacks of trashy magazines (to help me sleep), and trashier scripts that I have to read for work (to put me to sleep), a beat-up but awesomely comfy overstuffed chair, clothes arranged according to colour and season in my closet, reproductions of Edwin Holgate's *The Bathers* and Emily Carr's *Above the Trees*. Two alarm clocks—just in case.

WHY YOU SHOULD GET TO KNOW ME:
I'm a fun-loving woman who makes her living in television and film documentaries. I believe in celebrating birthdays for weeks, drinking martinis and pondering the meaning of life and love with my pals, being first in line at the buffet, avoiding people who talk about their cats, spending rainy days at the art gallery, exploring passion, and getting a kick from champagne.

(Got the Sinatra in after all!)

WHAT I'M LOOKING FOR . . .
A kindred spirit who makes me laugh. A man who has unpacked and sorted his emotional baggage and isn't intimidated by a confident woman. My wish list of attributes includes: curious, romantic, passionate, and self-aware/self-confident.

She checks her e-mail dozens of times the first day, hoping for a response of some sort. On the second day, she tries to log on, but the IT people at work have blocked access to the site. She is mortified and hopes it's not because of her. Just as well anyway, she thinks, I should only check at home. On Saturday, Erica sends her an e-mail with a link to an article about evil online dating stories. "Shurely shome urban legends?" she writes. "Take note, but don't let it deter you!" Suzanne reads about the hapless woman who started e-mailing a man who was "working out of the country on business." The two built a rapport, chatting online for hours about literature, art movies, kayaking, and themselves. Then after a couple of months, an e-mail message she sent came back blocked. She checked her in-box, and there was a message—from his parents!—warning her to stay away from him because he was only fifteen! There are other stories about women meeting men who were married or had totally misrepresented themselves (nuclear physicist turned lab tech turned unemployed wannabe). There were women who agreed to be picked up at home on their first date and wound up being stalked. Idiots, thinks Suzanne, then she thinks of Liam and relents. The vagaries and desire of the heart foster such lapses in judgment.

She sits down at her computer with a cup of coffee on Sunday morning. There's a response, and her heart leaps as she checks out "U2?".

Capital Woman,

I laughed at your missive: self-deprecating, yet self-confident, a seemingly contradictory, but winning, combo. I, too, love fairy tales (although my touch-football teammates don't need to know) and Alice (especially the caterpillar scene, which is hysterically funny). As you'll see from my write-up, I'm a working stiff—a chef at a mid-range market restaurant, but I'm also taking courses towards my masters in political science, so I do have another "intellectual" side (if you can call politics intellectual—sometimes I wonder). I love to travel when I can afford it and have recently returned from Havana; it's stunning, not only in terms of the landscape and political history, but also the people; everyone I met was just so, so kind, almost naive. Beautiful.

Tell me a bit about yourself. Where have you travelled recently? What is your favourite meal? What do you want in a relationship?

Waiting,

Doug

Suzanne clicks onto his write-up and checks out the photo: he has most of his hair (male-pattern baldness) and is a bit overweight but in a good way, a way that affords some latitude for her imperfections. His vitals say he has green eyes, but he seems to be on the short side. She hauls out her calculator and converts the metric: he's a good two inches shorter than her. She'd always joked that height doesn't matter once you're in bed, but now the chance to eliminate seems so easy. *I might as well go for what I want. More hair would be nice, too. And a chef? Not too ambitious from the sounds of things.* She stares at the screen, at his photo. Her coffee grows cold. She checks out his e-mail again: "What do you want in a relationship? That's what Liam had asked! Suddenly she feels hot, beads of sweat dot her forehead, and her heart races.

I can't do this. It's so calculated. I want the romance.

Idiot! she thinks. *You knew that when you posted. This is the way, the modern way.*

But what would I wear? Say? Do? What if he turns out to be a dud, and I've invested all this time and energy? How many more disappointments can I handle until I become one of those women; like Joanna in accounting: doing her hair in an elaborate bouffant every day, makeup, perky suits and still hasn't had a date in years. The single woman. To be pitied, incomplete without a man, the other half. One of the army of hapless heterosexual women. Like Mom.

She picks up *The Book of Love* and scans the introduction to the chapter on dating, pausing to read fully the final paragraph.

Burdened with these heavy expectations of romantic love, it's hardly any wonder people have difficulty connecting. We are so worried about whether Trevor or Tanya will make the mark, whether they'll be able to come through with **all** the goods (impossible!), that we spend our time obsessively assessing them (too tall, linear, old, poor, etc.). Dates become auditions; second dates, the call back. We miss out on the best part: the uncertainty, the flirting, the unexpected playfulness, and fun of romantic love. Surprise yourself.

Suzanne closes the book. Foster's right, she thinks, but the stakes are so high. What if I don't find anyone? What if I do, but it's too late to have a baby? What if? What if I just worry obsessively and never find anyone anywhere anyway? That worrying can't be attractive. "The uncertainty, the flirting. . . . Surprise yourself." Okay, Dr. Foster! For the first time, she finds herself seriously considering this possibility. It dawns on her that this is a game. I'm free to play if I obey the rules, especially the golden rules: be true to yourself and don't expect it all from one person. Don't fall for the fairy tale fallacy. Romance might come, but just as likely something else will emerge: some other relationship such as friendship or acquaintanceship, even. The worst thing? I'll have some great stories to tell Christina and Erica, she thinks. My online chef is probably a good guy; someone I could be friends with, yak with about kiddie lit. Maybe he could introduce me to his friends and his life. Maybe the gay guy from the launch would be a laugh.

"Me 2," she types.

Pursued by Furies

CHRISTINA REACHES ACROSS THE BED to the other side's cool sheets then remembers: Don had a breakfast meeting. She opens her eyes, blinks, and is instantly overwhelmed:

up kids shower dress hurry lunches breakfast kids bus drive teach lunch teach drive kids piano/soccer/hockey supper homework marking kids lesson plan bed.

Ten minutes more, she thinks, pulling the duvet over her shoulders. If I had the energy, I'd get up earlier and paint. For a little while. She sighs and shifts to her side. She envisions the painting she is working on: herself, standing in her kitchen, wooden spoon in hand, stirring a pot on the splattered stove. She can see the colour of her dress. Last Sunday, she'd found the perfect tone of turquoise then applied a layer of acrylic gel to add texture. Jarring, yet pleasing against the yellow of the kitchen—a visual metaphor for her domestic discordance. In the picture, the kids are playing Go Fish at an old grey Formica table. Don? His foot is entering the scene. She is planning another painting of herself with Erica and Suzanne at a bar downtown, sipping garishly coloured cocktails—pink ladies perchance or grasshoppers—all of them wearing elaborate funeral hats, the hats they plan to wear to their husbands' funerals. Imagined. Other paintings are mapped out in her sketch book—teaching, working in her garden. If I ever get around to them, she thinks then checks herself: at least I have a studio now.

She returned from the conference in August to claim the spare room—a room of her own—moving the kids' toys into the family room and basement. The contractor's price was too high, and Don wanted to wait until they could afford a proper renovation, but she told him she couldn't wait. He complained that the kids' toys would always be underfoot, but he didn't make a big fuss.

Not that he ever does, she thinks. He's classic passive aggressive. Although he didn't complain, he couldn't seem to find the time to help her shift things around, so she did it all in a one-weekend frenzy. Still, she thinks, he keeps the kids entertained while I paint.

Sunday mornings are her time, even though it always takes her a couple of hours to get into it. She's spending an awful lot of time cleaning her brushes. But then it happens—the gorgeous turquoise—and, if she's lucky, she'll get an hour of good work out of the three.

I've found a bit of time, she thinks, but it's not really enough to find that spark. She recalls the documentary about duende saying that, like an ancient rite of passage, artists cannot progress without danger. Risk, she thinks. Arthur, she responds. What would have happened if . . .?

She glances at the alarm. Two more minutes. She gets up anyway: better than lying about, whining.

The three friends meet at Erica's apartment for an Italian feast she has prepared: "Just 'cus November's a haul," Erica declared. They linger over homemade cannelloni, an uber-garlicky Caesar salad, and a full-bodied Amarone—Suzanne's contribution.

"Hey, Erica, I've been meaning to ask, how's it going at *The Star*?" says Christina.

"You wouldn't believe the gossip and the back-biting. It's horrific, a vortex of pessimism. But thankfully, I'm not in the newsroom too much. Usually a few half-days a week. And I've found a couple of nice people—women editors, plus my boss. He's a curmudgeon, but he's smart and funny, and he's okay with me working at home—makes me keep track of all the evening hours and all of that. It's nice to get paid decently for writing."

"And is it difficult writing a column every week?" asks Suzanne.

"Not at all. I meet all sorts of people—it's really opened doors for me. I get interviews on the first call. It's way easier logistically."

"So, it's good?" asks Suzanne.

"Well, yeah. I mean I just started, but so far, I love it. And I don't miss the organic gig at all. I gave all my boring work clothes to St. V. de P. Man, what was I doing there?" She shakes her head.

Christina laughs: "I always thought pantsuits were a bit incongruous for a rock music critic."

"Yeah, I know. I feel like I've finally found what I really want to do. At first, I thought being a full-time art junkie was superficial and sorta selfish, but Thomas says, and I agree, that music helps a lot of people; that what we're doing is important. Besides, it's better to let someone who's passionate about organic foods take that job. I mean, I always agreed with what they were doing, definitely, but they found a real keener to replace me. She's outgoing and persistent. I hear some doors are opening up on the Hill. Good for them, I say."

She pauses to sip her wine. "Hey, Suzanne, you haven't given us the latest installment in the cyber-dating saga."

Suzanne smiles. "I'm surprised it took you this long to ask. I arranged to have a coffee with Chefy boy after he'd already cancelled twice—which should have been a sign."

"Yeah, 'Dead End,'" says Christina, and they laugh.

"So, after two cancellations," says Suzanne, "he has the audacity to turn up twenty minutes late."

"Hey, that's my trick," says Erica. "Guys aren't allowed to do that."

"Sexist sow!" says Christina.

"Twenty minutes late," Suzanne continues, "AND he's got this sweat-stained Douglas Tavern ball cap pulled down on his head with hanks of greasy hair sticking out from under it."

"Eew," says Christina. "What did you do?"

"I talked to him, or I tried to, but he was so defensive about his job, so insecure. I was out of there in a half-hour. I'm thinking maybe I'll try speed dating . . ."

"That *was* a speed date," says Christina, smiling.

"Speed-*hating*'s all the rage in the UK," says Erica. "It's all about finding your common ground based on the things you hate."

"Nothing like a shared hatred to start you off in a positive direction," says Christina. She takes a deep breath. "I could use a little positive injection into my love life," she says. "I'm so pissy with Don sometimes. Snarky. It's the tone more than the words. Lord knows, he'd never say anything, but if he did, I'd lose it."

Suzanne and Erica exchange a quick glance, surprised as much at what she is saying as the fact that she's saying it at all. Disclosure's not her strong suit.

"So, lose control then," says Erica. "Maybe that's the way to find out what's behind this."

"I'm never happy, it seems. I have a studio space now, but not enough time and energy — just those few hours on Sunday morning. I'm drowning in minutiae."

"Screw the dust bunnies!" says Suzanne.

"They're already dust bison!" says Christina. "Anyway, I have a cleaner every second week now, so that's not the issue. There's nothing else to be cut. I won't cut into my time with the kids. Don and I have no life together anyway, which isn't good . . ."

"Can't you go back to part-time?" asks Erica.

Christina shakes her head. "I did the math. It doesn't work: two cars, a mortgage. I'm a friggin' hostage to that house."

"Move!" say Erica and Suzanne in unison.

They laugh. Christina smiles.

"Don loves it there. When we moved in, he said we'd see the kids graduate from high school from that house. He grew up in a suburban palace in Hamilton — his parents still live there."

"Yeah, but if it's the underlying thing that's making you unhappy . . ." begins Erica. "Don wants you to be happy."

"Catch him post-coital and break the news. They usually agree to anything at that point," says Suzanne.

Christina smiles but thinks, yeah, and that's the other problem.

Christina cannot bring herself to talk to Don. He's changed or is changing, she thinks. She never used to lack for spooning or cuddling, but now when they say goodnight, he gives her a peck on the cheek and turns his back to her. He's preoccupied with drawing plans for refinishing the basement for the kids' playroom. He's decided to do it himself after all. Though he wouldn't do it when I asked for my studio, she thinks angrily.

The evening with Erica and Suzanne was an anomaly; they are both so busy these days, and she hates going downtown twice in one day. She decides it's time to make some friends in her neighbourhood as part of her life makeover. Studio—check. Neighbourhood friend? Hmmm. She digs up Pat's number, the woman she'd met at the school book sale, and invites her over for tea, although she's thinking of serving wine. Pat asks if she'd mind coming to her place instead; it's easier with Leah, her newborn. Christina had forgotten she was even pregnant. I'm so self-absorbed, she thinks.

She arrives with a predictable fall bouquet of orange and yellow chrysanthemums and bulrushes—all she could find at the mall—and a board-book version of *Runaway Bunny* for baby Leah. The kids are in bed. Pat kisses her on both cheeks, thanks her for the gifts, and for the phone call. "I'm so glad to see you! Rob's at work still, and I'm drowning in diapers and dishes!"

Christina laughs. "I know what you mean. Norris was barely two when Vita was born. It was pandemonium for years. I can't imagine having three, including a newborn."

They step into the living room, and Christina is taken aback by the beigeness of the décor: couch, walls, wall-to-wall. Even the prints on the walls are in muted, nondescript tones. And everything is so pristine, so tidy, as if no one even lives there. Christina wonders what she's doing there and can't think what she and this woman could possibly have in common. The tea things are out on a tray, along with a plate of homemade ginger cookies. Where does she find the time? wonders Christina. They sit down, Christina pouring while Pat nurses Leah, her breast modestly covered with a green paisley shawl.

"Does she sleep well?" asks Christina.

"I wish! Three hours at a go, max," says Pat. "I'm sleep deprived already, and who knows how long this will go on. Rob's great, but when you're breastfeeding—well you're the main event!" She talks for a while about her other two children, her boys, and how they've taken to the new baby, then takes a sip of her chamomile tea.

"I'm so tired of the baby chat. Tell me about your job. You teach art, right?"

And so Christina tells her about the inner-city school she works at, the immigrant kids and shortage of ESL teachers, the art projects, and the joy the kids get from them. She doesn't mention her own work, her painting, and wonders at her reticence. Is it too personal? Am I ashamed of my lack of productivity? Christina glances at a painting beside the window, two clowns on bicycles with big wheels, and feels exhausted at the thought of the effort it would take to explain her own work. And the attendant lack of appreciation.

"And how do you find the commute?" asks Pat.

"Horrific!" Christina says emphatically and a bit too loudly. Pat stares at her. "But I'll get used to it," she adds to temper the statement. She longs for Erica and Suzanne, friends who already know her story, her feelings. Friends who are onside.

"I know. It's frantic, isn't it?" says Pat. "But I love it out here. It's so peaceful. And the schools are great. I have to admit, though, I really miss work." She shifts Leah to the other breast. "She's a dream baby, but then I think of my office, my staff working for someone else . . . We're researching a brief about online publishing rights. I'm missing all the fun." She sighs. "And I still regret the CEO job. I had a fair chance of getting it—I'd been there eleven years—and well, who knows when it will come up again."

"That's a shame," says Christina, "although you never know what else will happen." She recognizes what Pat is saying and thinks of how different her own life could have been. Not that she regrets her choices. Don, Norris, and Vita. No, not exactly regrets, but an unfulfilled longing.

The visit is cut short by Pat's youngest waking from a bad dream. They hurriedly say goodbye at the front door, agreeing to keep in touch. As she walks home, Christina thinks she probably won't call again. Pat's nice and interesting enough, and we're both frustrated in our careers, but aside from that, we don't have much in common, she thinks. She's a corporate wonk turned quasi-reluctant super mom. I'm trying to be an artist. She'd be another distraction. As if I don't have enough. No, I won't call. I don't have the time. I need to paint.

When she gets to her house, Christina feels oddly wakeful. She quietly unlocks the door and goes to the couch in the TV room. She leafs through an art book she'd borrowed from the school library. It contains works she had previously passed by that now strike her as potentially relevant. She looks at old Flemish masters' depictions of daily life: house interiors, people playing cards or eating a meal. She flips page after page, looking for something useful for her work then closes the book.

She shuts her eyes, leans back in her chair. Her mind feels crowded and numb. Slowly a picture emerges . . .

She's in her kitchen, but it's not the same. Her old kitchen table is there—the red Arborite one with the rust-pocked chrome legs—covered with half-squeezed tubes of paint. And there's the easel with yet another self-portrait. It was her mantra, her passion. An exploration of the varied roles women adapt to, the defining reincarnations of the female self: student, lover, artist, mother, teacher, wife. She looks at the self-portrait: it's her style, yet she doesn't recognize it. It is her younger self. There she is cleaning a paint brush, unruly hair framing her face, no makeup, an old shirt covered in splotches and smears of paint, clear blue eyes looking directly at the viewer. The gaze is piercing; the look, questioning. She notices there's a canvas behind the one she's looking at and pulls it out. Also a self-portrait, but here she is older, more matronly, with a single string of pearls set against a pale blue twin-set, her hair coiffed into a tight French twist. There are dark semi-moons under her eyes and stars of wrinkles exploding off the corners. The gaze is off to the side, refusing direct eye contact. Don comes into the room, and she hides this older self behind the other painting so her younger self faces out. Don comes up behind her and slips his arms around her waist. "How's my Frida?" he whispers into her ear. She smiles. "Like Mona, Mona," she whispers and feels his smile in answer through her body.

She is interrupted by the sound of ticking. I must buy a quieter clock, she thinks. She pulls on her fleece jacket as she steps out onto the back deck and inhales the cold November air. The full moon illuminates the sameness of the neighbourhood. Gold blotches flicker and stare at her from the back rooms of the surrounding houses. In the building behind their house, she can see the shadowed profile of a person watching television. The late news, she supposes. But maybe Seinfeld reruns. No one is outside, of course. In the distance, a car with a bad muffler passes. It's all so orderly, she thinks, so controlled. Fences reigning in each yard, demarking every tiny kingdom. Lawns cut to within an inch of their lives. No clotheslines—there's a by-law. Don's used to it because he grew up with it, she thinks, but not me. She remembers the house where she was raised in Cabbagetown—downtown Toronto before it was really trendy. Her family never owned a car, much less two. They took the College streetcar or walked everywhere. They even hiked to the grocery store with a wire cart on squeaky wheels that embarrassed the hell out of Christina. Her dad's woodworking shop was in a converted garage out back; his drafting table and books were crammed into an attic room. There was lots of action on the street: bums (as her dad called them) panhandling outside the local shops, masses of rowdy students roaring around late at night, rowing cats mating, raccoons knocking over garbage cans. In the thick of things. They never questioned where they lived. It just was. She remembers her mother saying one time, when they ventured by subway into the north of the city to visit some friends, that she sometimes longed for the quiet of the suburbs.

"It's an *åndsfortærende*," her dad said in Danish. "A soul-destroying place," he added in English for Christina's benefit.

Her mother must have agreed, because after he died, they

moved to a cheaper place, an apartment on the outskirts of the Beaches still close to the city's centre. It's a good thing he never saw this house, thinks Christina. He really would have given me a hard time. She can just hear him declaring in his distinct Danish accent: "This is a place that contradicts creativity." She feels separated, outside herself, an observer. Suddenly, her chest is heavy, her throat constricts. Reluctant breaths rise and stick in her throat. This is my home, the place I live. The back neighbour switches off the television and lights. She inhales the night air. Blows it out in a white cloud like a smoke signal. I can't stay here. She has no doubt about it.

She is intensely relieved by her decision, and all the next day her head dances with art: new compositions, patterns and techniques to try, books to read, old friends to talk to. She thinks about sticking swatches of her mother's fabric on the canvas and integrating them into the background as wallpaper or upholstery or, more boldly, as clothing. Mixed media—paint on canvas is so passé. All these ideas flit through her mind, then she hits a wall when she thinks of telling Don. How can I possibly tell him that I want to move again? How do I approach such a loaded conversation? She meets Erica for a quick after-work coffee.

"Tell him how you feel," Erica says. "Tell him how it's impossible for you to create in that house, in the 'burbs. I mean, you made a mistake. You haven't—please don't take this the wrong way, Tina—but you haven't been yourself. That time you told me off about Hugh . . ." She shakes her head. "That was way over the top, even if it was partly true."

"I know. I'm sorry, Erica. I was really belligerent."

"I'm glad you see it. It illustrates what I've been saying. You *need* to do art. I've seen it in you before, during teacher's college. If you don't do your art, it hassles you."

Christina nods: "I remember reading somewhere that if you don't respect the muses, they will turn and pursue you in a frenzy. I know you're right. I was trying to be *Chatelaine*-meets-*Art World*, some media mogul's notion of the modern woman who can have it all. But what I also wanted was to be like Maura: living on the cheap in some loft in New York City, painting until three in the morning, and talking art over a bottle of two-buck Chuck."

"Are you jealous of Maura?" asks Erica.

"Yeah. It's hard not to be. And it's even worse now with Suzanne doing this documentary. I keep thinking that it should've been me. I can't talk to Suzanne about it."

Erica puts her hand over Christina's. "One difficult conversation at a time," she says. "There's a good chapter in *The Book of Love* on resolving conflicts."

"Have you read the whole damn thing?" asks Christina, grinning.

"Cover to cover," she replies. "So much of it is spot-on." Erica pulls it out of her oversized red carry-all and hands it over. Christina accepts it, grateful for her friend's concern, for her friendship, and decides not to say any more about returning the book.

After changing out of her work clothes, Christina grabs a minute to read. She finds the chapter on marriage, subsection: "Getting off the war path." Such hokey subtitles, she thinks.

> Marriage is an institution that functions surprisingly well. But as Mae West so aptly put it: "I'm not ready for an institution." We have a love-hate relationship with the idea of marriage. On the one hand, embracing its practical aspects, primarily the financial and emotional stability it provides, particularly for raising children. On the other hand, resenting the day-to-day mundane sameness of it. A sustainable marriage requires mindful living, and that includes deciding what you can and cannot live with and taking a considered path towards addressing it.

Christina glances up at the alarm clock: 5:10. Time to make dinner. She skims Foster's words of advice.

. . . best way to fight? . . . study of 130 newlyweds[4] . . . the happiest marriages are those in which the wife offers complaints in a positive, gentle, even humorous way, and the husband . . . offers a neutral response . . . from an evolutionary approach . . . when women complain, men, who still want to protect and provide for women, hear: You're a failure. And they feel shamed and weak; they withdraw or hide. Women . . . interest in groups and talking, see this silence as a threat . . . hyper-sensitive to distance, isolation, and neglect.[5]

Behind every criticism, every blame and every judgment lies a desire. "All a woman has to know is to tell the guy: 'I love it when you . . .' or 'It makes me happy when you . . .' In other words, go right to the desire."[6] Articulate in a positive way what you desire and be prepared, if asked, to offer suggestions on how to get there.

---

4   J.M. Gottman, J. Coan, S. Carrere, and C. Swanson, "Predicting marital happiness and stability from newlywed interactions," *Journal of Marriage and Family* 60 (1998): 5–22.

5   P. Love and S. Stosny, *How to Improve Your Marriage without Talking About It* (New York: Broadway, 2008).

6   M. Schatzker, "We need to talk . . .," *The Globe and Mail*, sec. C1, March 10, 2007.

But what about sex? Christina wonders as she chops bok choy for yet another chicken stir-fry. How do you talk about that? How do you start? Not so much where to put this or that. I'm sure we'd still know our way around, but we've lost the emotional place. The plateau where our loving begins. We've lost our way through disuse, disinterest, dis . . . Where are those green onions? But I can't talk to him about sex. He wouldn't talk; I know that. It's beyond talk. We need to fix the other things first.

The red pepper's gone soft and fuzzy.

Friday evening she comes downstairs after tucking Norris and Vita into bed. Don's sitting in front of the television, which is blaring another banal cop show, and writing in his notebook. She asks if he'd like a drink: a Cuba libra.

"Sure," he says, "but I forgot to buy the coke."

She's so used to him "forgetting" that she's stopped counting on him. Yet, I keep asking, she thinks. We're both being passive aggressive.

"I bought some today. And limes."

"Oh, great," he says absentmindedly, underlining something in his notebook.

She carefully prepares the drink—three ice cubes, a double shot, juice of half a lime, and topped with cola. She nestles a thin slice of lime on the edge of each, brings them to the couch, and sits down.

"Cheers," she says, forcing herself to smile.

He takes his drink. "Cheers yourself."

They each take a sip.

"Do you have a minute to talk?" she asks, noting the pounding in her chest, and wonders if he can see her breasts moving.

"I'm not really watching this." He switches off the television, closes his notebook, and unscrews his pen. "Damn thing," he mutters.

She takes a deep breath. "It's so peaceful after the kids are in bed, and it's just you and me."

He puts the pen with the notebook and smiles at her: "Doesn't happen very often, though—we're both usually scurrying around till all hours."

She wills herself not to complain.

"That's sort of what I wanted to talk about." She takes another deep breath: think positively. Start with what you like. "You know, the things I love most are spending time with the kids and you, and painting, but I'm feeling a time crunch, Don. And I know you feel it, too. When we lived downtown, I walked to work and only taught half time, so I had loads of time and energy for the kids and for you, and, if I'd wanted, my painting."

"I don't understand. You have a studio now and Sunday mornings. Plus you have a cleaning lady," says Don.

Christina thinks: *I* have the cleaning lady, as if that's *my* responsibility, but she lets it slide. Choose your battles, she thinks.

"Yes, and that helps a lot, Don. Don't get me wrong, I do appreciate all of that. And the house is spacious and beautiful, but here's the thing . . . we both work so hard to support it that we don't really have time to enjoy it. We moved here, or at least I did, for the kids, but now, during the school year, we're both so friggin' busy that we hardly see them. I don't get home until five-thirty or so, then there's this whirl of dinner and homework and stuff. And the weekends aren't much better."

"What are you saying?" he asks. "We can't afford for you to go half time." He pauses: "Are you talking about moving again?"

She sees his body stiffen. She takes a sip of her drink to buy some time, calm herself, so she won't snap at him or whine.

"I think we moved here for the right reasons. Better school for the kids, safer. We wanted that. We both want what's best for the kids. But I think we went too far—literally. We're both so isolated. All our friends are downtown and that just seems like such a haul at the end of the day. I'm exhausted after the commute in all that awful traffic."

He crosses his arms over his chest: "You knew you'd be commuting when we moved."

"But I didn't realize . . . it's soul destroying," she blurts. "An hour each way on the 417." She shakes her head. "Not to mention the effect on the environment. And the lost time . . . "

"I don't understand why this is a big revelation to you," he says. "And if you hate it that much, apply for a transfer to a school out here so you can work closer to home."

Damn, she thinks, I was hoping he wouldn't bring that up.

"It's not that easy, Don. There aren't that many art teacher positions, and there's a waiting list. It would take years." She takes another sip. "Can we just step back a minute and look at the big picture . . . our life, our limited time before the kids grow up. Can we change somehow to make this work better, not just for me, but for all of us?"

"You *do* want to move. I can see through all this mumbo jumbo, big picture stuff. You've been reading that damn book, haven't you? Listen, Tina, you know I love you, and I love the kids to bits and I think—I *know*—this is the best place for us to live. We have a lovely house, good schools, peace, security. All that. I really like it here. I feel at home."

"I don't," Christina retorts, and though she'd vowed not to, she tells him what she's concluded. "I grew up in downtown Toronto. I hate the Disney-esque, neat and tidy sameness of all this. I miss living in a real neighbourhood, where houses have makeshift additions and overgrown gardens, and you live next door to single moms or senior citizens. I miss all that—the diversity, the realness of it. And mostly, I miss not having enough time to live my life, my art, fooling around with the kids. Going out with you once in a while."

"You should have thought of that a year ago."

She notes that he is flushed now. Anger? she wonders. He never gets angry. I'm whining, she thinks. So much for following the friggin' book and staying positive.

"So you want to move?" he says evenly, staring at her.

"Yes," she whispers.

A shard of silence pierces the room.

"We could move into the west end," she says quickly, "somewhere halfway for both of us. A compromise. There are nice neighbourhoods there, too. With good schools. I could take the bus to work, and we could ditch the second car. Get a smaller place with a smaller mortgage."

"Have you even thought this through, Christina?" he says, his voice rising. "Have you thought about how much it costs to sell and re-buy? Thousands. Five, six grand minimum. And then there's the disruption for the kids and paying for the actual move. *We're* happy here. It's only *you* who isn't!"

"Okay, maybe," she concedes to placate him, "but I *can't* live here for . . . what . . . fifteen years? I just *can't*." She feels a tear escaping and brushes it roughly away.

He grabs her wrists, twisting them slightly in his large hands. "Can't you think of someone besides yourself for once?" he says, giving them a final twist, then throwing them down. "You disgust me!"

He strides from the room. She sits riveted to the couch. Her heartbeat thunders. She hardly hears him slam the front door.

Hears her heart. Hears the car start. Stunned, she rubs her wrists, stares at the red rings like bracelets. His hands are stronger than I thought, she realizes with a shock. Where did that come from? Stunned, she slumps into the couch, staring limply at the blank television screen. She has never glimpsed anything even approaching violence in him. It's a one-off, she tells herself. I pushed him too far. But she feels alarmed as much by his words as his actions. She considers phoning Erica, but knows she'll be out somewhere with Thomas, and besides, she feels ashamed. What could I say to her anyway? How would I explain . . .?

She sits immobile on the couch until after eleven, replaying the conversation in her head, cursing herself for not handling it better, for not having that flirty, coquettish thing that other women seem to have. The thing that allows them to get their way. She considers calling him on his cell and even dials the number but hangs up before it rings. "Screw him," she murmurs.

She propels herself off the sofa into bed where her anger inexorably turns to fear. What if he refuses to move? I can't stay here. I just can't. And I don't think it's all that great for the kids either, living in a mono-culture. She remembers the little toughs in their designer clothes and Pat, who is so smart, and yet resigned to her lot. What if Don asks me to make a choice? Him or me. That's what it comes down to: being true to myself, to who I am. An artist, an inner-city person, involved, vibrant, social. What the hell was I playing at, thinking I could live out here, work full time and still be okay, still have time to do art? How could I be so deluded? And now I could lose it all. The thought shocks her. This could go either way now, she realizes. We've reached a point. Her heart speeds up, she feels hot, her mind races. She shakes her head and goes to the bathroom, drinks a glass of water, then peers at herself in the mirror: I'm an idiot. I never should have agreed to move out here. She crawls back into bed, tosses, turns, resolves to push all the "what ifs" out of her mind. It doesn't work—she replays scenes, extracts different endings—but eventually she finds her way to a sleep that is deep and dreamless.

She wakes next to him and is surprised at her relief: he wouldn't just leave, she thinks, but obviously, some small part of her thought he might. He smells of stale beer and cigarettes—although he gave up smoking before Norris was born. When she pads back from the toilet, he is awake.

"Could you get me an aspirin, Tina?"

She hesitates a heartbeat, suddenly angry at him: how dare he treat me like that, twisting my wrists, walking out.

"Of course," she says. Serves you right, she thinks.

He pops the pills and downs the glass of water.

"I should know better," he says, wiping his mouth with the back of his hand and collapsing back onto his pillow. "I met Roger at our old pool hall downtown. You know, I haven't seen him in nearly six months. It was a blast. I had to take a cab home, so we'll need to go get the car."

She sits on the edge of the bed. She can hear the television downstairs and recognizes the cacophony of cartoons. The kids are up and taking advantage of the lack of parental supervision to log a bit of TV time.

"Did you win at pool?" she asks.

"Not a chance," he says, grinning. "Oooh, that smarts!" he says holding his head.

She ignores him, straining instead to hear the TV. It must be the *Road Runner*, she thinks. All that violence. "I've known for a long time," he says then pauses, ". . . that you weren't happy. I knew I was taking a chance, moving out here, but I really thought you'd like it, the peacefulness and space and everything."

"What was that all about last night, grabbing me like that," she says.

"I'm so sorry, Tina. I really am. I lost control, I was just so, so angry with you. I thought we'd talked all this out. I thought you knew what it would be like out here."

Lame justification, she thinks. "I thought you were going to hit me."

"Oh, gawd, so did I, for a second there," he says. "So did I. That's why I left."

She says nothing.

"I've never done anything like that before. You know me, Tina. I'm not like that . . ."

"Like what? A wife beater?" she is suddenly enraged.

"I'm not violent. Please forgive me, Tina. It won't happen again. I promise."

"The kids must be hungry," she says, pulling on her dressing gown. She shuffles downstairs and begins fixing breakfast for Vita and Norris, allowing them to continue watching Wylie E. Coyote get squashed for the umpteenth time. She's not sure what she should do. She's reasonably sure his aggression was a one-off, but she needs to think about it and doesn't want to give in too readily. She wants him to know how serious this is. She also recognizes that she's now holding a lucrative bargaining chip.

They pick up his car downtown, and he takes the kids to do the groceries, while she goes home, puts in a load of laundry, tidies the kitchen. She briefly considers his sincerity, the likelihood of a repeat, then shakes her head. The day roars past with chores and errands, ending as it began with both of them in bed.

She tells him she forgives him and acknowledges that it's totally out of character, but there's one caveat: "Please, please don't ever do something like that again. You scared me."

"Of course not, of course not," he says. "I was so riled up. I'm so sorry, Christina. I love you. And the kids. I want us to live happily."

"I do, too," she says.

"But not here?" he says.

She hesitates before carefully choosing her words: "I've never lived in the suburbs. I know a lot of people love it, and you grew up in them, but I couldn't even imagine how displaced and alone I would feel. And working full time. And commuting. Don, it's just too much for me. And if I'm stressed out, that's passed along to the kids, so it's not good for them either. I also take it out on you. I'm sorry for being so snippy with you lately."

"That's 'cus you love me," he says, the cadence of his voice making the statement of fact more of a question.

She laughs. "That's true."

"So let's sit down with the accounts and figure this out," he says.

"Really? You're sure?" she smiles at him.

He nods. "There must be a way."

"Thank you, Don."

She snuggles up to him. He puts his arm around her.

"You know," he says, "this probably would be easier if we were, you know, doing it. I feel so distant from you . . ."

She holds her breath; she really doesn't want to talk about this now. Somehow naming "it" makes it worse. Nameless, their lack of intimacy isn't quite real; she can believe they are just going through a short phase or a lull.

"Seven months," he says. "That part's always worked for us before . . ." He strokes her bare arm.

He seems genuinely perplexed, and her heart goes out to him. Seven months, she thinks. I had no idea.

"I was trying to understand it, too," she says. "It says in *The Book of Love* that women need to feel good before having sex, and men use sex to feel good. So, when life gets stressful, you want to, and I don't. I thought that was too simplistic at first, but actually, it makes a lot of sense. I don't feel good right now."

His hand shifts to her clavicle, his finger outlining the dip and contour.

"I'm unhappy, too," he says. "I married you, and now all we do is raise kids together. It's like a corporation or a business agreement. We're not close. I mean, look how long it took for you to confront me about the house, though you must have known for ages."

"Sort of," she allows, "I couldn't quite admit it to myself. It seemed so selfish—just like you said. And then I saw how it was affecting me and the kids and you . . ." A tear escapes, and suddenly she begins to cry. He brings her to his chest and kisses her sweetly on her lips. Arthur's kiss flashes in her mind, her vulva swells and she feels guilty, but then thinks what the hell. She feels his arousal, too, feels like she's watching him, both of them together, as he continues stroking her back, moving down to her buttocks. Slow circles and soft exclamation marks. Then Vita cries out in the night—"Mom! Mom!"—and Christina leaps out of bed, glad of the release.

chapter eleven

Est-ce aimer?

THE DOOR BUZZER RINGS at 2:25. Five minutes early, but Suzanne has been ready since two, killing time by reviewing the technical requirements for her documentary. It is her life now. Everything else is on hold: painting the bathroom, taking her new Pratt print to be framed, even the search for a boyfriend—she hasn't cruised the SoulConnect website for weeks and has put the speed-dating idea on hold. She realized she needed some time out, away from the emotional ups and downs of dating, time to recover properly from Michael. And besides, the documentary deadlines are looming. She's arranged to film Maura Kerby in early February, which is less than three months away, and she has a million things to do: hiring crews, renting equipment, revising the script.

Her boss set up this meeting between her and his long-time colleague, Gerard Levesque, the lead cameraman on some of the very best Canadian documentaries about artists, such as *Leonard's Loves, Atwood's Antics, Gould Unglued*. Hiring him would be a coup, practically a guarantee of a distribution deal. Maybe even an award. He liked the documentary proposal, but there's the little problem of money. Suzanne hopes he'll settle for less than his going rate.

The buzzer rings. She presses the intercom button: "Gerard?"

"Oui, c'est moi!" he says. She hadn't expected French. But of course.

"Come on up," she says and buzzes him in.

She plumps the cushions on the chairs. Glancing in the mirror, she licks her fingers, smoothes down a strand of hair, then applies another thin layer of red lipstick, pressing her lips together as she hears his light tap on the door.

She'd heard he was good looking but had not expected this:

He's handsome in that artsy, craggy, older man way. She's weary of pretty-boy small noses and coiffed hair. Gerard is all man: big nose, sculpted face, fine lines around his brown eyes. Longish grey and black hair. Not so long that it requires a pony tail—which is decidedly passé—but long enough that it curls under at the bottom and can be pushed behind his ears. Long enough to be unruly.

"Gerard?" she says, more question than statement.

He smiles. White teeth, open, friendly.

"Suzanne," he says decisively, looking directly into her eyes and holding out his hand.

She takes it.

He holds her hand gently—a nanosecond too long, she wonders—and she lets go first.

She invites him to sit in what used to be her living room, now her production office: two overstuffed club chairs primed at chatting angles on a worn Persian carpet, a melange of composite bookcases lining a wall, computer perched on a fifties teak desk, and next to it a second-hand filing cabinet that she had painted bright red. Her files are colour-coded: green for finances (green = $), red for script (red = passion/creativity), purple for marketing (purple prose), and pink for production (nice alliteration).

She fetches them each a coffee. They sit down in the comfy chairs, and she tells him about the project, the first in a series of documentaries she's planning about the emerging group of Canadian realist artists. How did they arrive at such a place? What is their story? What drives their passion? She's starting with her favourite artist, Kerby.

"She paints scenes of everyday life," Suzanne explains. "A woman reading in bed, a couple doing the dishes, a teenager listening to music. But she exaggerates the proportions at the locus of action—the hands, mouth, eyes, ears—to emphasize the sensual, and by doing that, she reveals the emotional."

Suzanne hands him a portfolio of prints.

"They're much more impressive in real life," she says. "Most of them are quite large, two metres across or more. The National Gallery has two, but there's only one hanging right now. Aside from that, you hardly ever see her work because it sells right away. It's too soon for a retrospective, and she's only had one show at a public gallery. She's in her early mid-career, you know, a work-in-progress. I think it's good timing for a documentary."

Gerard holds up one of the prints: "Her work is amazing. I love her palette, those intense reds, blues, greens. And the perspective is so unusual."

He looks up at Suzanne and smiles: "What did you have in mind?"

Rather quickly it turns out as she'd feared. The pay she can offer is about half his going rate; too low for him to accept. Besides, he's already booked during the scheduled shoot, which can't be changed because Kerby is only available for shooting during the second week of February.

To hide her disappointment, Suzanne begins gathering the cups.

"Don't feel discouraged," Gerard says. "It's a wonderful project."

She stops and looks at him.

"I'll give you a recommendation," he continues. "I know a good guy. Paul Fletcher. He's a real up-and-comer. And I'll give him a hand with angles and logistics and what not. I'd like to contribute. Gratis, of course."

"Executive cameraman?" she says with a smile, vying for that all important credit line. His name on her bill would be a coup.

"Sure," he says. "The visual opportunities will be incredible. I really wish I could be your main man . . ."

"Me, too," says Suzanne.

He catches her eye and smiles then laughs. She smiles too.

"Look," he says, "why don't we go to the National Gallery and look at her painting and brainstorm a bit? Then let me take you to dinner, you starving filmmaker."

He scoops up her hand and kisses her finger tips. She holds her breath, glances into his eyes—such a deep brown—before looking away, suddenly shy. She is unaccustomed to finer attention from men. She understands sex and need but not the nuances that precede it.

"So not exactly a professional relationship?" she asks.

He laughs again. "Not exactly."

He pauses.

"You're very beautiful." And he puts a finger under her chin, raises her head so she's looking at him. "Your face. The curve of your cheekbone. So tiny and delicate."

Suzanne wills herself to hold his gaze, although she feels the blood rushing to her face like in junior high that time when Derek, who she'd had a crush on all year, finally asked her to dance.

"Thank you," she stammers. "I'm not used . . ."

"Vous êtes très gentille," he says.

And she smiles at him. There is a slight tremor in her hands as she takes the cups to the kitchen.

The gallery's permanent exhibition space is practically empty; everyone's attending the Christopher Pratt retrospective. Suzanne tells Gerard she's seen that exhibit three times. It fits into her thesis about the Canadian penchant for accessible art, a predilection that's evident in the works of artists like Emily Carr, Edwin Holgate, and Kerby.

"Their paintings of familiar scenes prompt the viewer's memory," she explains, paraphrasing from her Can-film funding proposal. "They give the viewer a sense of place, which is a uniquely Canadian concern. We're all about the 'where am I?' Where is my place, my community? It stems from having to band together, to help one another, in order to survive in this brutal climate."

She pauses. "What do you think?" she asks him.

"I completely agree," he says. "That's the difference between the Americans and us. They're all about the frontier, every man for himself. Their mantra—and you see it in their literature all the time—is '*who* am I?' I mean, take realist art. In the Canadian tradition, it depicts small moments that root us in place. Our home, for instance, or our town. For me, it's through those seemingly simple moments that we can appreciate the bigger, complex picture."

"I know exactly what you're saying," says Suzanne. "I see

Pratt's jelly jars and I remember when I was a girl, sitting under the maple tree in our backyard with my mom, cutting strawberries for jam. Then I remember how I adored her in those years, how she was my world. So that one image allows me to re-imagine another place, and that takes me to the bigger place: my personal narrative."

They talk about the need for art to be accessible, and he recounts his recent frustration with an Anselm Kiefer exhibit at the Museé d'art contemporain de Montréal.

"You had to read these pretentious three-hundred-word statements before you had any clue what a piece might be about," he says. "The spontaneous emotion of the thing, the feeling it evokes, was gone. The works were intellectual. Period. And that's fine and interesting, but it's one step removed. If you can capture the intellectual by isolating the emotion, bien! Now, that's powerful!"

"Here's the Kerby," she says.

They consider the painting of a naked, middle-aged woman lying, partly covered in a double bed, the other half of which is still tightly made. Her slightly enlarged hands hold a book; the cover depicts a man and woman embracing: a bodice-ripper. The woman looks beyond the book past the viewer into her empty bedroom. You know she is alone.

"You can feel her longing and disappointment," says Suzanne. "It's in her eyes, the way she holds the book, her nakedness—she's exposed."

"And the humour. Look at that cover," he says pointing to the exaggerated embrace.

Suzanne smiles and absorbs his profile. She knows she won't wait long with him. There is a vibe between them, a current. We're on the same grid, she thinks.

Over dinner at Swish, she learns he is fifty-eight and never married. Not a good sign, but then his career has been his overriding concern most of his life. He's travelled all over the world, living for years at a time in Paris, Barcelona, and London. He speaks Italian, Spanish, German, and of course, French and English. He's so sophisticated, she thinks.

The more he speaks, the more she is drawn to him, but the feeling is tinged with unease. Is he too old for me? she wonders. She remembers laughing with Erica about a section in *The Book of Love* that said women have basically planned the colour scheme of the nursery after just one date. She and Erica agreed it was partly biological—that deceitful oxytocin effect—but mostly practical: if it doesn't pan out in your imagination, well, why waste time on something destined to disappoint? Of course, there were exceptions, especially when Suzanne was younger; men she slept with for the sake of good sex, like the water polo player with his outrageously buff torso and shoulders, and the cyclist with the powerful calves and rock-hard butt. Gerard is definitely not that sort of man, but neither is he the other kind. The husband-father kind. She does the math: twenty-five, she realizes. Twenty-five years older than me. And even by candlelight, she sees the wrinkles bracketing his eyes, the commas around his mouth. A part of her wishes she weren't so attracted, wishes she could steer things to a mentor-type of relationship. But the line has already been crossed.

These thoughts flit at the edge of her mind. She knows, but she doesn't want to know. She wants to believe in potential, is attracted to the idea of it. And his attention, his obvious interest in her is flattering. Freud's old saw pops into her head: Men desire women. Women desire men's desire.

Over cognac, he holds her hand across the white tablecloth. With anyone else this would seem like a cliché, something to laugh about later with Erica and Tina, but with Gerard, this simple act is infused with romance. He brings her hand to his lips, kisses the inside of her wrist in that most tender place.

"Too fast for you?" he asks, looking up at her while cradling her hand.

Suzanne smiles. "Too unfamiliar," she says.

"You're beautiful, talented—I'm sure there are many oppor-tunities," he says.

"A few," she lies. "No one of particular interest." (True.)

"And so," he says, "can I see you again? Demain, tomorrow? Please say yes."

And she laughs. "How can I say no when you put it so nicely?"

He walks her home, gently tucking her hand onto his forearm, an old-fashioned gesture that reminds her of her parents—when she was little, of course, before her dad bolted. The "unpleasantness," as her mom still calls it. Suzanne invites Gerard up for a nightcap, but he says it's late already, and he has an eight o'clock breakfast meeting. He walks her to her apartment door, embraces her shoulders with his hands, and slowly kisses one cheek, then the other. Approaching her again, he gently nibbles at her upper lip. She feels the surge of blood between her legs. He takes her mouth. His tongue slips in, tracing her teeth, then slips out to seal her lips in a kiss.

"Tomorrow," he says.

"Yes," she whispers.

"Goodnight."

And he is gone, leaving her leaning heavily on the door frame then fumbling with her keys. Tomorrow. Perhaps the most romantic word ever.

She replaces the batteries in her vibrator and gives it a go before their second date, hoping this might hold her to a third, maybe even a fourth. She wants to give herself time to get to know him before physical intimacy, like the Foster book suggests. But it doesn't work. Alcohol is a contributing factor—more for her than for him. Alcohol and soft light to ease the harsh reality of his old skin. Not so much his face, which she finds so attractive, so manly with its chiselled lines and crevices. No, she needs to soften her view of his body: the puckered skin, its elasticity shot; his concave chest and drooping old-man breasts; the folds around his neck like a baby's, yet not.

But with an alcohol infusion and dim lights, she finds him to be a wonderful lover. Nothing fancy. At least not the first time. Just touching, kissing, caresses, then the sudden arousal and soon after, the need. Then penetration. Her on top because his knees are a bit dodgy after years of crouching holding a camera. She straddles him, leaving their hands free for stroking, holding. Afterwards, he cuddles with her—Michael always reclaimed his personal bubble—and she cuddles into him, loves the skin-on-skin, the warmth, and intimacy. After a few weeks, he wants to be on top and holds her wrists down, shouting her name as he comes powerfully inside her. She wonders at the quantity of his come, which seems to linger in her for days despite vigorous bathing. The feral smell wafting by her when she least expects it: in the midst of a meeting at work or as she prepares dinner. The smell prompts a physical memory that makes her breath catch.

The nights and weeks become a month. They sleep together at his apartment when work schedules allow, go to films, meet his friends for cocktails or dinner—never her friends; he doesn't ask, and she is not ready to share him until she feels their relationship might be going somewhere. Secretly, she fears that her friends will tell her the obvious.

So she holds him apart from her personal domain. He is part of the film, her advisor and mentor. She can't imagine now doing it without him. Much of their conversation revolves around details—angles, lighting, settings. She absorbs everything, even taking notes as they sit on his sofa, sipping French red wine.

Suzanne admires the simplicity of his apartment. No open newspapers, no smudged glasses half-filled with water. Everything hugs the ground in the spacious living room: a low-lying Scandinavian sofa, Arne Vodder credenza, Finn Juhl armchairs. Her favourite space is the bedroom with its pale grey and blue walls that somehow refract the light, making the space seem large *and* intimate. Gauze curtains whisper across the room, reveal the balcony where they smoke post-coital cigarettes. She luxuriates under the crisp white sheets in the king-size bed.

They never speak of the temporal divide between them, although sometimes when he's talking about the things he's done—attending Woodstock, the opening of *Raging Bull*, meeting Robert Altman—she sees the years between them and wonders if he does as well. When her desire for a child comes to mind, she puts it on hold like everything else in her life. After the documentary is finished, I will decide, she thinks.

There is no talk of love on either side. Sometimes, when they're making love, she feels an urge to utter the words, feels like she does love him. But, she worries, what if he doesn't respond in kind? Or worse, what if he confronts me about it? Is the feeling even real? Or is it gratitude posing as love?

She wonders whether it counts if you say you love someone while you're screwing.

One Friday evening, she comes back from her bathroom ablutions, and instead of welcoming her with an embrace, he's lying in bed turning pages in *The New Yorker.* She climbs into her side of the bed, expecting him to put the magazine down, but he doesn't.

He turns a page.

"Is something wrong?" she asks.

"I want to finish reading the cartoons," he says, flipping another page.

She lies down beside him, waits a few minutes, then cuddles up next to him.

He puts down his magazine and takes her in his arms. "You're always there," he whispers.

"What do you mean?" she asks.

"Don't get me wrong, Suzanne, you're great." He strokes her cheek. "But you're always so eager. I don't get a chance to show you that I want you. It's part of the game. I pursue you, you resist, I chase a bit more—it's fun."

With her heart sounding an alert, she pulls away to look at his face for signs. Is this the swan song? she wonders.

"We have fun," she says defensively.

"Of course, of course," he says, "and flirting, playing will add to the fun. You're a wonderful, attentive lover, but I'd like a chance to crank it up a notch, to pursue you."

She immediately flushes: "Pursue or control?" she demands.

He shrugs, "For me, when we're in bed together, it's about making love." He kisses her forehead and slips out of bed. "I'll be right back," he says, heading down the hall to the bathroom.

She pulls away from the warmth left by his body. Of course this is about control, she thinks. He's never complained about my enthusiasm before. He's probably threatened by my sexuality. Or maybe not. He doesn't seem to be. Is this part of the game? Am I too serious about sex? She considers her preoccupation with technique, the books she's studied: *The Joy of Sex, Tickle His Pickle, Sex Tips from a Gay Man for Straight Women*. They taught me the thrust of it, she realizes, but not the parry.

She shifts in bed, suddenly finding it too firm.

For me, it's all about getting to sex, which leads logically to commitment. Maybe. Premature sex, a shortcut to short-term relationship. Was that in the book? But I'm too impatient to enjoy the journey. Maybe I'm afraid because it's rough, uncertain. Dangerous. Maybe I'm the control freak! she thinks. Maybe what he's asking for is normal and healthy. Maybe it *is* supposed to be playful.

She hears Gerard coming down the hall and lies on her side, arranging the sheets so they show the contour of her hip, the dip of her clavicle. The lit candle he carries illuminates the contours of his face, and she feels desire surge. He gets into bed and reaches out to touch her. She lies still, unsure what is expected. But in the unexpected, she finds new pleasure with him.

As promised, Gerard is helping Paul, talking to him about angles, double takes, lighting tricks to create drama and mood. Suzanne asks his advice about sets and scheduling and is amazed at how much he knows. The Kerby shoot is due to begin in two months, and the logistics are never ending.

His schedule is packed, too, and she finds herself spontaneously offering to pick up the computer game he wants to give his nephew for Christmas.

"You're so gentille," he says.

She feels a flush of pleasure: "It's who I am."

"I just hope I don't corrupt you," he laughs, caressing her shoulder.

The store is impossibly busy. She waits twenty minutes for service only to find the game is out of stock. Then she drives across town to a second store to get the damn thing. She waits in line again, wishing she were at home revising her script, wondering why she has adopted this role with him. Just how far would I go to please a man, to gain and keep his affection? she wonders. How much would I give? Then she remembers that he is helping with her film.

But would he be helping me if I wasn't sleeping with him? she reflects. What does this mercantile exchange make me?

Her turn at the cashier comes at last, and she pays for the game.

The gals decide to meet for a late boozy lunch. It's their escape a few days after Christmas, but at the last minute, Erica has to interview a musician, so it's just Christina and her.

They chat about Christina's new painting, the one with the three of them drinking in a bar. So far it's a preliminary sketch.

"Art imitating life," Suzanne says. "I hope I'll be wearing something divine that I couldn't possibly afford."

"Actually, I'm thinking of painting us all naked. You'd have to pose, so I don't know how you guys feel about that. But it seems right for the painting. We expose ourselves to one another through our friendship."

"I've never posed nude. I don't know. It might be fun. Can you add an inch or two to my bust?" She laughs.

Into the second martini, Suzanne talks about the film and inevitably, about Gerard.

"So," says Christina, "Gerard's obviously too old for kids, so he's not a long-term prospect. What do you want from him besides sex, of course, and help with the film?"

Suzanne is instantly defensive. "I don't know for *sure* that he's too old," she says. "I mean we haven't talked about that. It's way too soon. It could work out."

"Let's do the math," says Christina. "Fifty-eight plus eighteen: He'll be seventy-six when your kid graduates from high school. Probably older. Do you want that? Knee replacements, puberty, and menopause all at the same time?"

Suzanne laughs. "Well, when you put it that way . . . but he's really such a wonderful, intelligent guy. We never stop talking when we're together, and he's great company. And you know the best thing about older boyfriends: there are no parental units to contend with. They're all long gone."

Christina laughs. "Yeah, I remember Michael's mother. Talk about a drama queen." She takes a sip of her martini. "I'm just looking out for you, girlfriend. I mean, if all you want is some fun and passion, fair play. But what if you fall for him? How would you feel about not having a child?"

"We haven't talked about lo . . ."

"Would you like anything?" The stealth waitress has materialized at their booth. Suzanne notices they are alone in the restaurant; all the ladies-who-lunch have left, presumably to continue their retail therapy. Christina orders two Cosmopolitans. Before heading to the washroom, she reaches into her purse and hands Suzanne *The Book of Love*. "It's your turn," says Christina. "I still feel guilty about keeping the damn thing, but I have to admit it's got some bon mots."

Rather than think about what Christina has said, Suzanne opens to the book's table of contents and turns to a subsection on insecurity.

When a child is consistently and demonstrably loved, it often results in life-long feelings that they are loved and of value. In short, it gives the person an inner sense of security, a constant place from which to engage the world. In the absence of this inner security, a person may place excessive importance on their romantic relationship; external love makes them feel loved and valuable and secure. For these people, the world is an unpredictable place in which they have to constantly strive to ensure they are loved. This can lead down two equally dysfunctional paths:

1. **Co-dependency**

   Rather than a relationship with depth and true intimacy, this person has an all-consuming desire to have his or her need for security and love met. Sex is frequently an affirmation of this.

2. **Inability to commit to a relationship**

   These individuals honestly don't know what commitment means because their parents didn't commit to them. Or, they know what commitment means, but it terrifies them because it makes them vulnerable to hurt. One defining characteristic is that, as adults, these people consistently choose to leave a partner before that partner leaves them.

This last phrase buzzes her brain. She considers her serious relationships. There were not so many really, just one in high school and a few at university, then Michael. Piecing them together like a jigsaw puzzle, a picture emerges: she's the one who has always left. And Michael? She remembers thinking, at the time, that she was making a pre-emptive strike by leaving him before he left her—at least physically left her—but emotionally he was already gone. So that was different, she thinks, relieved. I have made some progress. But the need for love and for sex, that's another thing entirely. Suzanne has never doubted that her childhood left her damaged. Shaking her head, she runs her hands through her newly clipped hair. Damn book. Stay in the now, she wills herself and takes a sip of her cocktail.

Christina returns, bumping her hip on the table, jiggling the brimming Cosmopolitans. "Whoa!" She sits down heavily.

"So. Let's look at the facts," she says rather loudly in the nearly empty restaurant.

Here it comes, thinks Suzanne.

"He's not daddy material," says Christina, "and you want to get moving on that front. You're attracted to him, but because of this timeline, you aren't in love with him. Am I right?"

"Maybe . . ."

Christina holds up her hand like a traffic cop, leans in, and whispers, "The question is how many times can you fuck a guy you don't love?"

Suzanne frowns. "Come on. That's a bit harsh, Tina. We've only been together a few months. Give it some time. Of course, it's sexual now. I've been gasping through a drought."

"Oh, don't we know it!" laughs Christina. "We've been hearing about it for months. But Suzanne, you know he's only the rebound . . ."

"Yeah, well, maybe. But maybe not. I don't know where it's going. I'm just enjoying the ride."

Suzanne dislikes her situation being reduced to the level of schoolyard banter: Are not. Are too. She suspects Tina's bluntness stems not only from genuine concern but also from jealousy over the documentary, which will, after all, celebrate Kerby's success. Suzanne knows that Christina is wallowing in self-recrimination: I should have . . . I could have . . . Poor Tina, she's so hard on her artistic self. But that's just how she is. Suzanne understands this, and even if she didn't, she would still accept her friend the way she is.

"I'm going to let things be as they are for now," Suzanne says. "I've had enough change lately. I'm happy for now. You haven't said anything about you and Don. Did you sort out things? Are you feeling more kindly disposed towards him?"

"Yeah, we had a sort of blow-out and now it's coming together slowly . . . It's hard to talk about because it's sort of a work-in-progress right now. Soon though. Soon."

"You know you can always talk to me, Tina," says Suzanne. "Or Erica. Sometimes I think you hold things in too much."

Christina sighs. "Yeah, maybe. It's complicated."

Suzanne lets it go.

Sleep is still elusive. Sometimes reading doesn't even work, and Suzanne resorts to watching late-night television. Early one morning, she catches part of *The African Queen*: the scenes where Bogart is trying to put the moves on Hepburn. It's only natural, he tells her.

"Nature, Mr. Allnut, is what we are put on earth to overcome," Hepburn replies with inimitable haughtiness.

Suzanne laughs out loud. As Bogart pulls *The Queen* up the river, Suzanne begins to nod off and thoughts swirl through her mind: Such a slog, going up the river, overcoming nature, the sexual imperative. Which always fades. Adding intimacy, knowledge. Caring. Mom and Dad were too busy working. Mom never stopped moving. They never went out alone together. Neither did Michael and I. Not often anyway. And when was the last time I asked him about work? When did he ever ask me about Kerby?

She jerks fully awake and switches off the television, makes her way back to her bedroom, tosses a bit, then switches on her light to read a bit from *Grimm's Fairy Tales*.

At least, at Gerard's place, she can sleep. One night after making love, she lies in his arms, and he begins talking.

"Suzanne, I'm really very fond of you, and I love spending time with you, but I don't feel like we're a couple. There are huge parts of your life I know nothing about. I don't know any of your friends. I've only been to your apartment a few times. It's like you're keeping me in a separate compartment."

She is startled by this seriousness.

"Am I?" she asks to buy time.

"You know you are," he says, pulling away from her to look her in the face. "What are you afraid of, my sweet one?"

"Of being hurt," she says without thinking.

"Ah, aren't we all." He strokes her cheek. "I think romance—amour—is like good art. You have to suspend disbelief and go with the narrative. I know it's only been a few months, but I'd like to be closer to you, to know you better—to at least have the potential to love you, Suzanne. Your fear, is that what holds you back?"

Suzanne feels she is teetering on the edge of a precipice.

Michael, her mother and father, other lovers and friends are all crowding behind her. A slight breeze, a strong breath could push her into an abyss.

"Tell me," he whispers.

She swallows hard. "You're too old," she says, startled by how harsh it sounds and instantly mitigating: "I feel you're too old for me. I want a baby . . ."

"But not too old to fuck?"

She jerks upright: "Gerard! It isn't like that. What a word!"

"Isn't it? Isn't this fucking? You take my penis into your mouth, yet you won't let me into your life."

Suzanne gathers the sheets to cover her chest.

"Maybe it's too soon for me, too soon after Michael," she says. "Do you want a baby?"

"So, what have I been? A stop-gap until the ideal father material comes along?"

"No, no, it isn't like that at all, Gerard. Please. I really like you. You've been a wonderful friend. And lover," she adds, stroking his arm.

He softens. "I didn't mean to be so harsh," he says, "but it isn't very flattering to hear that I'm old. Too old."

He gathers her back into his arms.

"You didn't answer my question," she whispers, "do you want a child?"

He sighs. "About ten years ago, I really wanted to have a baby, but my partner at that time couldn't conceive, and in the end, even though we went for counselling and talked endlessly, it drove us apart. It was a very sad time. And now, well, I really can't see having a child at my age."

"That's what I thought," Suzanne says. "I think I've known that all along. I never made a conscious decision, but I think I kept you out of the rest of my life because I sensed that this relationship wasn't going to last. I was afraid that if you were really part of my life, knew all my friends and all of that, it would make it harder to extricate myself. Harder and more painful."

"Extricate?" he says. "I don't understand. We'll stay friends no matter what. It's important to stay friends. After all, who knows you better than your lovers? Those who have seen you at your most vulnerable, at your point of climax, in deep sleep, when you wake up? If we lose those connections, how can we hope to be understood? Don't push me away for that reason, Suzanne. I'll always be your friend, and I mean that."

In that moment, she feels relief even though she knows the love affair is winding down. Knows, in fact, that it never really *was* in the first place. But instead of feeling loss, she feels she has gained a male friend to balance out all the femaleness in her life—and a mentor, which is what she wanted all along.

"Funny, isn't it," she says, "we seem so well suited. I mean on paper. I was thinking about it the other day. If someone was looking at our CVs, they'd say, 'Those two are well matched.' And we do have a lot in common, but it isn't there, you know, the impetus to love."

"Not for you at any rate," says Gerard. "Est-ce aimer?"

She is silent. I've been so selfish, she thinks. I never once considered that he'd fall for me. "I'm sorry, Gerard."

"Moi, aussi," he whispers and kisses her gently at her hairline.

chapter twelve

St. Single's Day

To: <u>Christina Andersen</u>; <u>Suzanne Beaulieu</u>
From: <u>Erica Savone</u>
Re: Party time!
Ladies, I wanted you both to know at the same time; hence the
e-mail. I'm escaping the perilous world of dating — Thomas and
I have decided to move from LAT to live-in! I'm uber-nervous
and desperate for some Pollyanna pep talk and poignant
pointers (are you lovin' the alliteration?). I'm moving into his
place — it's so much bigger than mine — on April 1st. April Fool's
Day. Hope that isn't an omen! I'll make the middle bedroom
my office for writing and mucking about. A room of my own
as per the dictates of Ms Woolf, but, still, I'm feeling pangs
about giving up my cozy apartment and, more importantly,
my time to be alone. On the other hand, I'm at his house
four days (nights!) a week anyway, so no biggie, right? Wrong!
Yikes! I've definitely got the jitters. Let's meet to celebrate
(commiserate?). How does next Friday evg look for y'all? It's
Feb. 13, St. Single's Day; how apropos!
Love,
me
*"By all means marry. If you get a good wife [or husband], you'll be
happy. If you get a bad one, you'll become a philosopher."*
— Socrates

In midtown Manhattan, Suzanne perches uncomfortably on the
edge of a bed in a cut-rate hotel room, sifting through her e-mail.
She has only two days left to film Maura. The main interviews,
the seemingly endless Qs & As, are finished, but she still has to
shoot Maura in her studio, painting and talking about a work-in-
progress — the impetus for ideas and the process of work. Two

days. And what if Maura's in one of her moods and picks over every detail, rewords questions? Please no, thinks Suzanne. She scrolls down the e-mails: none from Maura, which is a good sign. She clicks open and reads the missive from Erica. Damn, she thinks, Erica has all the luck. But she immediately corrects herself. I had a good chance with Michael and I'll have others. She's trying to be optimistic, to not appear too anxious or needy, and hopes that in adjusting the outward appearance, the inner will follow. Over time. Erica's words have started to run on a loop through her mind: Give yourself time to recover or it'll come back to bite you on the butt twice as hard. Suzanne started therapy last month and has decided to take the year off. A year for me.

"I'm going to take an angst-break and try to pull the documentary—and myself—together," she'd said to Erica over a quick coffee before leaving for New York.

"I think that's a really wise idea," said Erica. "And you'll be really busy with the doc anyway. I can't wait for the opening."

Why didn't she tell me her big news? wonders Suzanne. There I was spilling my guts. Maybe she was afraid I'd be jealous. I am jealous.

She rereads Erica's message and replies:

To: <u>Erica Savone</u>; <u>Christina Andersen</u>
From: <u>Suzanne Beaulieu</u>
Re: Party time!
Erica: Good for you, darhlink! Not sure if I can add any bon mots given my dubious track record, but I'll happily parry and party with you both. Back from NYC Thursday night; keep me posted re. time and place on Friday.
Hugs,
Suzanne
Muse Inc.

Christina is scrolling through e-mail in the family room. She should be making dinner, but the kids are seemingly content watching *Papa Potato*, a French cartoon; it's obnoxious—

particularly the cloying songs—but at least they're learning some French. She scans the column of senders, looking for a message from their realtor and a response to the offer they'd made on a house that morning. She knows it's too soon, but she's been thinking about it all day and is more convinced than ever that it's the perfect house for them. It's just off Main Street in an up-and-coming neighbourhood and it's within their price range. Nearly downtown but safe and clean. Plus it's around the corner from a really great school. And she loves the house itself: a forties wartime bungalow with three kind-of-small bedrooms upstairs, but the owner is a handyman and has extended the kitchen into the large backyard, added a family room, a big deck, and converted the garage into an insulated, heated woodworking shop with windows on two sides. It's a small space but has great light and is separate from the house: perfect for her studio. Even Don's excited about it.

"It's so close to everything," he said. "I can pop onto the highway to work and I'll be going the opposite direction of the traffic; it'll be a breeze."

She finishes scrolling. No e-mail from the realtor—not that she really expected one.

She opens Erica's e-mail: Good on her, she thinks. He's a great guy. She finds herself positively grinning. "Just hope she doesn't want any sex advice from me," she mused aloud and frowns. There hasn't been a replay of her almost-night, though Don did mention that they should try to get away for a weekend before the move. "Just the two of us, if you know what I mean," he said, winking. She smiled: "Maybe at Easter. It's a long weekend." But they haven't made any definite plans. She sighs. Then types:

To: Erica Savone; Suzanne Beaulieu
From: Christina Andersen
Re: Party time!
CONGRATULATIONS, Erica! And calm down. Thomas is a great guy—loving, thoughtful, communicative, and he's a lucky dog to get you, babeliciously together woman that you are! I'm so,

so happy for you.
Friday sounds great. I'll try to collect my marriage witticisms
by then — such as they are.
Wishing you lots of love and happiness together,
xxx Tina

"Here's to you and Thomas!" Christina hoists her martini glass in the air.

The other two women meet her to clink as a trio.

"And to good karma!" says Suzanne emphatically.

"I'm takin' everything I can get—karma, prayers, toasts!" Erica says.

They sip their cocktails. They've all ordered a new concoction that Suzanne discovered at a New York bar: Lake District. It's equal parts of chilled gin and sparkling apple cider (alcoholised, of course) with a generous zest of lemon.

"Elixir of the gods," says Christina, licking her lips.

"Hey, I heard an excellent one yesterday," says Erica. "You know that gross saying, 'Why buy the cow when you can get the milk for free?' The female corollary is 'Why buy the entire pig for a little sausage?'"

The women laugh.

"Speaking of which," says Suzanne, "are you still all jittery about the LAT to live-in?"

"I'm slowly getting my head around it," says Erica. "I haven't lived with anyone for at least ten years, since university, and that was with roommates. I've never lived with a guy. It's a huge change, but my pragmatic side says it's the logical thing to do. It's so hard to find the time to see each other now. I work two nights a week minimum, and he's always got sessions or meetings with musicians in the evenings. At least this way, we can spend more time together."

"Sounds like you're still trying to talk yourself into it," says Suzanne.

"Maybe . . ." Erica shrugs.

"Have you worked out who does the laundry?" asks Christina. "I know it sounds lame, but it was the one useful thing my mom told me when I married Don. Start as you mean to go on, she said. Think about what it will be like beforehand, work out all the potential stumbling blocks, differences of standard, taste, and mood, plus a whole lot of differences you can't even imagine. It's best to do some pre-emptive peacekeeping—especially when the motor's still purring—and anticipate the mines."

"Survival strategies!" says Erica, laughing.

"Exactly! I don't know that I followed it, but I'm sure Mom did—she and Dad were pretty simpatico. I think it's good advice. Yours for the taking."

Erica smiles: "Accepted."

"You're a sly dog," Suzanne says to Erica in a deliberately casual tone. "I didn't know you guys were thinking of moving in together."

"We weren't. It just came up on Monday . . ."

So that's why she didn't tell me, thinks Suzanne.

". . . well, he brought it up, he even got down on a knee. It was hilarious," continues Erica, "and I figured, what the heck, it's time I took the plunge. I'm thirty-three—a spinster according to my father—and everything seems right with Thomas. I figure I've marinated in his eyes long enough—you know, strike in your prime! as Auntie M would say," she laughs. "And now, with this new job, well, the timing seems good."

"I'm happy for you," says Christina. "You and Thomas have so much in common, and you seem so comfy together. Plus he's really sweet. That dinner he made for us all—that fish thing—that was sublime. Nothing like hitching up with a good cook!"

"How long have you been going out?" asks Suzanne. "Eight months isn't it?"

Erica nods and pops an olive in her mouth.

"Michael and I started living together after three months—definitely too soon."

There's a pause. Christina and Erica each search for something to steer the conversation away from Michael, fearful of a replay of the demise of Suzanne's marriage. She's slowed down now, definitely. She doesn't go on a Michael-tear *every* time they meet, but it doesn't take much to trigger it.

"I have some news, too," says Christina. "Don and I are bidding on a house. It's a sweet little forties bungalow just off Main Street."

"Excellent!" says Suzanne. She reaches across the table and grasps Christina's hand. "The trio reunited. What's the place like?"

Christina describes the house and neighbourhood.

"There's another bidder and we've had to raise our offer twice already, so we'll see. It's smaller than what we have now—less to clean and less space for all the crap—but we can barely afford it. If the bid goes up again, we're sunk. As it is, I'm going to sell my car. And we'll downsize, get rid of some of the furniture and all of the junk. Sheesh, I thought it was bad on the last move, but now we've expanded to fill the new house, so it's worse than ever. I've already packed seven boxes of toys for St. V. de P. Where did they all come from? Are they breeding in the closets? It's depressing. And I have to pack them up on the QT or the kids go nuts—'You can't give that away! I need it!' one of them inevitably whines. Even though they haven't looked at the thing in six months. The tyranny of the kiddy consumer."

"I know what you mean about the stuff," says Erica. "The thought of merging and purging when we move in together—it's brutal. Should we keep my dishes or his or both? My stuff's generally better quality, mostly because Mom's foisted all her cast-offs on me for years, but he has lots he wants to keep, too. Sentimental value or his fifties fetish. It's cool stuff. Fiesta Ware and an Eames chair. Well, it's a knock-off, but a good one. And it's all so suited to his house."

"Great house for kids," says Christina.

Erica sips her Lake District, buying some time.

"Yeah, well, the jury's still out on that one," she says. "I'll see how I feel in a year or so. I'm going with the gut. Besides, we have to get to know one another before we toss a baby into the fray."

"It sure mixes things up," agrees Christina. "But it's also the most creative thing I've ever done."

"Just for starters, I'm looking forward to living together," says

Erica, anxious to change the subject. "So, how's the documentary coming along, Suzanne?" she asks.

Christina feels envy rise. She hasn't thought about Maura or the documentary in months, not since all the moving talk began. It's weeks since I picked up a brush, she realizes. I'll never get enough done for a show.

"It's coming," says Suzanne. "I'm heading into the final edit now. Some of the scenes are just great. Maura's so articulate. I feel like a doofus next to her, asking these inane questions, and then she spouts these pearls. There's this one scene at the MoMa, where she talks about the need to create, how miserable she feels if she doesn't pick up a brush or pencil at least once day."

"You know about that, Tina," says Erica.

Christina nods. "So when do we get to see it?" she asks.

"Probably in a month or so. I'm taking the first two weeks of March off to whip it into shape. I've got to finish quickly. The rental on the editing suite is going to kill my budget. I've also run into some snafus around song permissions. I want to use the Leonard Cohen song, "Anthem." I love that line, "There's a crack in everything, that's how the light gets in." To me, that's the heart of creativity. The broken thing. The crack that allows illumination. It's the perfect song, but getting permissions is really a hassle, and it looks like it's going to be pretty expensive, too, so I may have to go with another tune."

"Do you want some help?" asks Erica. "Thomas and I know lots of up-and-coming musicians who'd be thrilled to be on a soundtrack and would probably do it for a song, excuse the pun."

"That might work," says Suzanne, nodding. "It's all about original art, so why not have an original song as well? I may take you up on it. I'm looking for something upbeat and artsy about the artistic process, the highs and lows."

"I'll talk to Thomas. I'd love to do it," says Erica.

Maybe I should do something to help, too, thinks Christina. Art direction or oversight . . . something. But there's no time. I guess I don't really want to help, she realizes.

At the end of the evening, Suzanne opts to walk home. "I need to clear the cobwebs," she explains.

Christina gives Erica a lift to Thomas's house. It's a clear, crisp night. Exhaust hangs in clouds at the sides of buildings, behind cars. Cold. They're halfway there before the car's heater kicks in. Their chatter keeps their minds diverted, but as they approach Thomas's neighbourhood, there is a pause in the conversation.

"You know," says Christina, "I found all that talk about Maura really hard. I hate to admit it, but I'm really jealous of her success."

"No surprise there," says Erica. "Everyone envies Maura to one degree or another. I envy her. I mean, she comes out of nowhere and goes straight to the top. It's unbelievably lucky. Sure she's talented, but so are you, Tina. You're last portrait, you in the kitchen with the kids—it's stupendous. I just love it."

"And Don's foot. Don't forget his foot!"

Erica laughs. "Now that's presence!"

"I am logging the hours," says Christina. "Well, usually anyway. Two nights a week plus Sunday morning, but I'm so far behind. I'm competitive, you know. That's what it is."

"'Go slowly. Go carefully. Be patient.' That's what my mom used to say about growing good tomatoes. It seems to apply to nearly everything."

Christina laughs. "Good line," she says and pulls up between snow banks in front of Thomas's house. The porch light is blazing and the kitchen light shining.

Thomas meets Erica at the door, wiping his hands on a tea towel.

"Hey there, media star, how are the gal pals?"

Erica smiles and gives him a greeting kiss. "They're great, and you?"

"I'm roasting pecans—gotta check 'em—I'll be right with you." He dashes off to the kitchen.

Erica kicks off her boots and hangs her coat, wondering for the hundredth time about "Man, the new woman," as she and Suzanne have dubbed the metrosexual. Roasting pecans, indeed.

What would Dad say?

She follows him into the kitchen. He's wearing purple flowered oven mitts as he pours the nuts from a hot cookie sheet onto a tray.

"The gals are happy for us," she says. "They also gave me some advice about us moving in together."

"Nightcap?" he asks, holding up a bottle of tequila.

She nods: "Bueno."

He places a shot glass in front of her.

"Tina says we should start as we mean to go on. You know, splitting chores, managing money, and all that."

"Sounds good," he says. "It's relatively easy to sort that stuff out. And it's one less thing to bicker about." He laughs, but she is quiet.

"I don't mean to make light of it," he continues, noting her silence. "I know it's a really big step, especially given that neither one of us has ever lived with anyone before. It's almost like marriage."

"Oh God, don't say that, Thomas! Not that there's anything wrong with marriage," she adds quickly, "not for some people anyway, but for me, well, I don't know." She pauses to think. "There's something about that contract. It's like a licence to neglect. The business of the day-to-day—vacuuming, buying groceries, cleaning the bathroom—all that stuff takes over. And all the romance, the need to pay attention to your partner, to talk—all that seems to get lost in the shuffle. That's what happened to my parents. And to Christina, too, really. Though in her case, she realizes it. I mean it's so insidious."

"My parents are happy enough, I suppose," says Thomas. "A little dull . . ."

Maybe we should stay as LATs, she thinks. Maybe that's best for me.

"Every couple is different, of course," he says. "I guess you have to go with your gut."

"And what's your gut saying?" she asks. "I mean, you asked me and everything, and it was very romantic, but are you having second thoughts?"

Why can't I admit I'm the one who's second-guessing the decision? she wonders.

"I guess my only hesitation, the only thing that I wonder about is kids," he says.

Erica's heart races.

"Every time I bring it up," he continues, "you do a dodge. I was thinking about it today—don't get me wrong, I really do want to live with you—but I was thinking that we should decide whether we want them before we get truly enmeshed. I love you, Erica. And I want to have a child. With you. I want to see that red hair on our child."

He leans over and strokes her head. Erica casts her eyes downward, leans gently into his hand. She wonders if he can hear the thumping of her heart.

"Have you thought about it, Erica?"

"I'm . . ." She straightens up in her chair, sips her drink. "If I was going to have a child, you would be the father. It's not that. It's just . . . well, I never thought I would. I love my life, my work. How could I keep doing it? What am I supposed to do, breastfeed at clubs? It seems so incongruous with who I am. Now there's you; there's us. So now I'm not so sure . . . I'm thinking maybe, maybe we should."

Thomas touches her arm. She softly lays her finger tips on his hand.

"It's going to get really complicated if we move in together and then disagree on this," says Thomas.

Erica breathes deeply. "You're right, we should get it sorted. Do you think we should wait a bit? Give ourselves another six months? That'll be enough time for me to figure it out. I want us to start really solidly."

"Me, too," he says squeezing her arm.

"Okay, it's a deal, then. Six more months," she says. "Let's drink to it."

He pours them each another shot, and they clink glasses.

"We're not so bad as we are," he says, smiling.

"Not too shabby at all." Erica grins. She feels hugely relieved. Go slowly. Go carefully. Be patient, she thinks.

Christina opens the front door quietly in case Don's already gone to bed. She half-hopes that he has, so she can have a cup of tea in peace. She has so little time alone—but there he is at the kitchen table, tapping away at his laptop.

"Hey, honey," she says, trying to sound cheery and happy to see him, "how's it going?"

"Just plugging away on this report on the new software," he says without looking up from his screen.

"Going well?"

"Not so bad," he says.

"Tea?" she asks, plugging in the kettle.

"Sure. But no caffeine. So, what sort of highjinks did you ladies get up to? Have some fun?"

"Yeah, they're such great company. Erica's all pumped about moving in with Thomas, and Suzanne's nearly finished her film. I've really missed getting together with them. I can't wait until we move back into town . . ." She puts two bags of ginger-lemon tea into the once white teapot. "Hey, that reminds me. Any word from the realtor tonight?"

"I forgot to check the e-mail."

She frowns. "How could you forget, Don? It seems like you're always forgetting things this past year or so. Groceries, making appointments . . ."

"Have I?" he asks.

"Don, please don't take this wrong. I'm trying to understand you, that's all. I've noticed you have this sort of passive-aggressive thing going. You agree to do something—like phoning a repair guy or picking up the dry cleaning or whatever—you agree, maybe because you don't want to argue, but then you sabotage it, by 'forgetting' to do it."

"I'm busy, that's all," he says, walking over to the computer. "I've got a lot on my plate. Be fair, Tina. I do tons of stuff around here."

Tina hesitates. Maybe he's right, she thinks. She gets out matching blue cups.

"She's answered," he says. Christina rushes to his side and bends down to read the e-mail.

"Shit!" she exclaims. "Five thousand more. They went up five thousand. Oh, Don, can we do that?"

"Five," he whispers. "We'd have to go up at least a couple of more and that would bring us to seven or eight. All over our budget. I mean if you want to go half time and all that . . ."

"But, it's not that much! Gawd, I really want that house. Maybe I could ask Mom. I know she has some squirrelled away."

"We'd have to pay her back, too. It's all the same. It isn't a problem getting the money, Tina. Hell, the banks will loan us as much as we want—even more. The problem's in the monthly payments. It's already going to be tight . . ."

"But how much difference can eight grand make?" she asks. "Over twenty-five years, it won't be much."

"It'll bring us twenty grand over what we initially aimed for. Let's keep looking."

"Yeah, but another place might need renos. Or repairs. This one is good to go. New roof and furnace. A studio. We can do it, Don. We're both good with money. And it's the perfect place for us."

"It is perfect," he agrees. "You really want it, don't you, honey?" his tone softens.

She nods.

"Okay, let's make one more bid—just the eight grand, though—and that's it. Agreed?"

She shakes his hand, smiling crazily: "Yes! Fingers crossed . . ."

He types their counter-offer to the realtor while she pours the tea, adds a teaspoon of honey to his, and places the cups on the table. She feels guilty for accusing him of being passive-aggressive.

"Don, I didn't mean to pick on you before. What I was saying about not doing stuff. I know you do a lot, but I guess my point is, if you don't have the time to do something, I'd rather you just said so instead of leaving me thinking you will and then being disappointed. And you bottling up your frustration and then exploding."

"Once in ten years. Come on."

"I know, Don, but I can't help thinking there was something more to it, something underlying it: anger, being fed up . . ."

"Sexual frustration," he says.

Ah, that, she thinks, taking a bird-sip of the too-hot tea to buy time. She wraps her hands around her cup, stares into it. She knows it's unfair of him to link the two, a diversion, really, to make her feel that his bad behaviour was somehow her fault, but at the same time, she knows the lack of sex is an underlying issue.

"I remember watching the film version of *Cat on a Hot Tin Roof*," he says, "with Elizabeth Taylor and Paul Newman. Great acting, maybe 'cus it wasn't acting. Anyway, there's this scene where Big Mama's talking to the Elizabeth character and Big Mama pats the bed saying, 'This is the foundation of a good marriage.' I've always thought there was something to that."

"Me, too," she says.

She pauses and takes another sip of tea, then continues: "I don't know what happened, Don. It sort of crept up on us. For a long time—since Vita was born, actually—I've been feeling frustrated because I didn't have the energy to paint. Then we moved out here, and I started working full time and, well you know how I've felt. But you've been great. You helped me make some time, and we're moving. And now? I don't know. It's like we've fallen out of the habit of making love. Like, I've forgotten how. The intuitive sexuality is . . ." Gone, she thinks, but cannot bring herself to say it.

Don reaches across the table, lightly touching her fingers.

"Maybe we're both living in our heads too much," he says.

"I've read about it in *The Book of Love*," says Christina. "Maybe we're not paying attention to our emotions and our bodies. We're both young, Don, and in love with each other. Sex has always been wonderful between us. Well, at least for me . . ."

"And me," says Don. "Definitely."

There is a pause between them.

"Come upstairs with me," he whispers.

She nods, stands, and begins gathering the cups.

He touches her arm: "Leave that. Just come with me."

He holds out his hand, and she takes it. He kisses it then leads her upstairs.

As she takes off her bra, he embraces her from behind, cupping her breasts and gently caressing them. She closes her eyes, wills herself to relax, to be in the moment. She turns to him for a kiss, but all he offers is a peck, then a second, then one on her neck. She feels his hardness against her soft belly, but she feels no desire. Nothing.

"Let's lie down and cuddle a bit," she suggests.

He holds her for a few minutes, stroking her arms, her breasts, thighs, then his hand wanders up, looking for the portal, but she keeps her legs closed. I can't do this, she thinks, but says nothing. She wills herself to open her legs, but she is dry to him. The more she wills herself into the moment, the less she is. After several minutes, she turns on her side, to face him: "Don, let's just rest a bit. I can't force this."

"Whatever," he says, jerking his hands away. He turns his back to her. Not wanting him to feel rejected, she begins to stroke him along the contour of his back, but he shrugs her away. They lie together. He switches off the bedside night light. She lies in the dark, trying not to listen to the sound of him masturbating next to her. He comes with a slight grunt, like relief, like a bowel movement. He gets up to wash. She pretends to be asleep but stares into the darkness for a long time before drifting off.

In the night, she has a dream, a sexual dream. She is aroused and wanting, then opens her eyes to find Don sucking her breast, his hand between her legs. She comes fully awake with a start: "Oh . . ."

"Shhh," he whispers, "I love you, Christina."

The bed is warm and comforting, his shape, his body, familiar, yet exciting. He enters her easily, beginning a slow rhythm, pausing as her desire grows, in the old way she has loved, then starting again. Building. She comes with a force she'd forgotten. More. She wants. Then he comes with a shout, pushing inside her.

He holds her in the nook of his arm, and she toys with the

damp curls of his pubic hair, wondering why she resisted this. She smiles to herself—a Mona Lisa smile—and settles into his warmth, his even breathing like a lullaby, lulling her into a dreamless sleep.

Suzanne walks home quickly but can't keep pace with her racing mind. She arrives at her apartment overwhelmed and muddled with details from her busy week in New York with Maura. A bit of a control freak that one, thinks Suzanne. Well more than a bit, a shitload. Maura endlessly advocated for certain shoots, certain paintings. Sometimes Suzanne took her suggestions and other times not. Differences in opinion became the subjects of seemingly endless debate. Suzanne stopped short of saying, point blank, this isn't a collaboration, it's my documentary. I may have to confront her about artistic autonomy, she thinks. I'll have to ask Gerard how to approach that. She glances at her watch: 11:15. Too late to call him now. She wonders if he has a new woman in his bed and gives in to a pang of jealous sexual longing before she shakes her head. A year, she thinks. I promised myself a year on my own so I can sort all this mess out. To love well, one must be well. Such an obvious fact, and yet look at me these past months, she thinks, repeating my mother's romantic obsessions, investing so much in potential relationships.

Inside her apartment, Suzanne puts water on to boil for tea, recalling the after-supper ritual of her childhood. Her role was always to set out the china teapot with the little blue flowers, matching mugs, and the sugar bowl with a little chip in the lid. Her mom would fill the kettle, plug it in, and scoop the loose Earl Grey into the tea ball while her dad put the Digestives on a yellow plate—always the same one. Then they moved to the living room, drank tea, and told their stories about family and growing up on farms, and sometimes, when she pleaded, they would tell the story of how they met. That romantic tale that she so loved. Mom can't let it go. Still calls herself Mrs. Beaulieu.

"I'm tried of being a victim of my past," she told her new therapist. "All my life I've hooked up with one man or another. I spent most of last year desperately searching for a Michael replacement.

I'm tired of measuring myself by the male company I keep. Just like Mom."

"For the first twenty years, you're a victim, for the next twenty, you're a volunteer," the therapist opined, as if quoting from somewhere.

Suzanne sits at the kitchen table scanning the table of contents of her expensive Everyman's Library edition of *Grimm's Fairy Tales* but isn't lured by any of them. Sipping her chamomile tea, thinking that a little shot of rum would set it on its feet, she leafs through the newspaper, and her eye is caught by an obit.

Jean E. Foster
MSc PhD
Couples Therapist

Surrounded by family at her Ottawa home. Beloved friend of Terry Dollard. Dearly missed by brother, Roger and nieces Stacey and Sandra. Pre-deceased by her husband, Jonathan Rowley. Highly respected relationship and couples psychologist. Gibson Bros. Funeral Home, Sat., Feb. 14, 2008. Visitation 2 to 4 pm; service 6 pm. In lieu of flowers, please send donations to the Canadian Cancer Society.

Omigosh, she thinks, circling it with a red pen: *The Book of Love*. It's got to be the same woman. Psychologist, counsellor. And the wake's tomorrow. I wonder if we should go. And what should we do with the book?

She fires up her computer and sends out an e-mail, alerting the others.

In a flurry of e-responses and phone calls, they agree to meet at the funeral home at three to return the book.

"It was never ours," writes Christina. "We should have returned it in the first place. What if for some really strange reason it's the only copy? We have to fess up."

Erica feels a twang of pure annoyance and thinks, Tina used it as much as I did. If she really thought it should've been returned, she shouldn't have had anything to do with it. Easy for her to take the high road now.

"I meant to return it," she types, "but I think we've all used it this year for one reason or another. Besides, better late than never."

She's right, thinks Christina guiltily. It was helpful.

"The important thing is to give it back," she answers. "Let's all go to the wake."

Erica and Suzanne agree.

"I'll bring the book," responds Erica.

I'm the one who took it last spring, she thinks, and I decided not to turn it into the lost and found. I'm the one who'll have some explaining to do. Fair enough.

The parking lot is full, but luckily three cars are pulling out. Christina snags a choice spot near the main entrance and steps through the snow. A flurry of couples is coming through the doors, and she waits for a break in the action before nipping in. The entrance foyer is full of people coming and going; there is muted conversation, a stifled yawn. She's hanging her coat up when Suzanne and Erica burst into the room, chattering. They stop abruptly when they remember where they are.

Erica grabs Christina's hand: "We're dolts," she hiss whispers.

They take off their hats and gloves and hang up their coats.

"Have you got the book?" asks Christina.

"Right here," says Erica, patting her black-leather purse. "I'll give it back. I'm the one who took it."

"What will you say?" asks Suzanne.

"That we used it and learned something. Is that okay?"

Christina nods.

"I don't know about learned," says Suzanne. "Entertained, maybe."

"Well, I'm not going to tell him that!"

"Who?"

"Her 'friend,' the partner, Terry. I'll give it to him," Erica whispers.

"Come on. Let's go," says Suzanne.

The petticoat on Erica's taffeta black skirt swishes as they walk down the hall. Suzanne's brown high-heeled boots click on the tile. Christina rummages in her purse for an awol mint but can't find one. She clicks it shut.

Pockets of people are gathered here and there, but the shiny black coffin stands alone. They approach slowly.

Erica leads the way, feeling a surge of sadness: it's like I knew her, she thinks. She's been a wise friend to me this past year.

A gilt-framed photograph of Foster is balanced on the closed bottom half of the coffin. Erica pauses to look at it and sees the likeness of a plain woman. The dark hair is peppered with white and pulled severely back from the round face. She notices that the eyebrows could use a good threshing, but is more quickly drawn to the eyes below them. They are wide open and kindly, and the mouth, in spite of the thin lips, is formed into a lovely, warm smile.

Suzanne glances at the photo, noting only the peppered hair and the nondescript polyester scarf in red, grey, and black knotted at her neck.

Christina notes the ordinary woman but is taken by the flowers. Numerous bouquets and heaps of yellow roses cover the coffin lid. Must have been her favourite, she thinks.

None of them looks at the actual body.

The family is lined up to the left of the coffin. First in line is a middle-aged woman with jumbled, cropped brown and grey hair. She is wearing a black business suit that is slightly too big, as if it were borrowed. Erica walks up to her.

"I'm sorry. I don't know you," says the woman.

"Oh, I'm, I'm looking for Terry. Terry Dollard," says Erica.

"That's me."

Simultaneously, all three think the same thing. Is Foster gay?

Suzanne does a double take: not a bad looking woman, Terry.

Good bones. A little makeup would bring out her eyes. She looks familiar somehow . . .

"We're sort of clients," says Erica, "but we never met Mrs. Foster. Maybe we could talk for a minute when you're free? Later if you like."

"I hardly know anyone here. They're mostly Jean's former clients. Roger can take care of them."

Terry walks over to a large, teddy bear of a man with a clipped grey beard, and says something to him. He nods. She gestures to the women to follow her into an adjacent side room. It's furnished in vintage funeral parlour. A faded burgundy paisley chesterfield and two over-stuffed, solid burgundy armchairs give an air of worn elegance; grey textured wallpaper and a generic pastoral scene in an ostentatious gilt frame complete the picture.

"My feet are killing me. How do women walk in these things?" Terry says, gesturing to her pumps. "Have a seat."

Terry slumps down in one of the armchairs, crosses her leg, one over the other, then remembering her skirt, re-crosses them at the calves instead. Erica takes the armchair next to her and introduces herself and her friends, who are seated primly on the couch. Suzanne peers at Terry and suddenly remembers: She was with Foster at the racetrack. The women were sitting just behind them that warm May evening just before Erica found the book.

"Just to clarify," says Erica, "you're the one who was closest to Mrs. Foster?"

"Yes, I'd say so. We've been living together two years now — since her husband, Jonathan, died. We're old friends from college."

Not gay, all three think.

"We have something that belongs to Jean," Erica continues. "I found it at the racetrack last May, and, I'm ashamed to admit it, I kept it. It seemed so interesting. It is interesting. And helpful."

She pulls the book out of her handbag and passes it to Terry, who practically snatches it from her, then turns it over in her hands.

"Omigosh! When did you say you found this?"

"Last May at the racetrack."

"I knew it!" she says. "I phoned the lost and found about a dozen times. Why didn't you turn it in? Jean was frantic."

Erica turns fire-engine red: "I, we, well, we started reading it, and we were all going through personal stuff, and it was so useful, pertinent . . ."

"You should have turned it in. You really should have," says Terry sternly. "Jean looked everywhere for it. I ordered two advance copies as sort of a surprise and incentive — she was having such a hard time finishing the book after her husband died — then we lost one at the track, and she hated the idea of this imperfect, incomplete version being out there."

"We're so sorry," says Christina.

"It's my fault," says Erica. "I'm the one who walked off with it. You're absolutely right. I should have turned it in. I was selfish."

Terry doesn't seem to have heard. She flips through the book.

"Jean started making final revisions. She switched around a few chapters before starting in on the text." She shakes her head with a small smile. "She was impossibly meticulous. I was beginning to think it would never be done. Then she got sick last November . . ."

"We're so sorry for your loss," says Suzanne.

"She was a loyal friend, a lifelong friend," says Terry. "I don't know how I'll manage . . ."

There is a pause. Voices filter in from the adjoining room.

"And the book," says Erica, "will you publish it, do you think?"

"I don't know. It's not really complete. I'll have to talk to Roger, her brother. Maybe I should get an editor."

"I can help you with that," says Erica. "I'm a journalist, and I know some people in the book biz. Here, let me give you my card."

"Thanks," says Terry, taking the card. "It would be so much easier if Jonathan were still alive. He was her co-author really. She always said so. Writing didn't come naturally to her, but he encouraged her. She used to talk to him as if she was counselling someone, and he'd tape record her. Then she'd use the transcripts to help her write, and he'd review the text with her. Maybe that's why she couldn't finish it: it reminded her of him." She sighs. "Sometimes I think her grief brought on her illness. I know that's silly from a scientific point of view, but I can't help but think she died of a broken heart."

Tears well up in Suzanne's eyes.

"That's so sad," she says.

Terry shakes her head: "Well, even if the book doesn't get out, she still has a legacy. She was an excellent couples counsellor—just look at the turnout here." She gestures toward the main room.

She pauses, staring at the book's cover. "I'm glad you found it useful. It confirms my opinion about it." She pauses. "I'd better get back in there."

They all stand. Erica offers her hand, and Terry shakes it.

"Thanks for being so understanding," says Erica.

"And our condolences," adds Christina. "We only had the book to go on, but Jean seemed like a wonderfully wise woman."

"Yes," Terry says so quietly that all three women lean in towards her. "Yes, she was."

The friends pause in the vestibule of the funeral home as they pull on their coats and gloves.

"Well, that went better than I expected," whispers Erica.

"Yeah, I thought for a minute there that she was really going to give us hell," says Suzanne.

"I need a drink," says Christina. "There's a pub at the corner. Shall we go for a little pick-me-up?"

They step outside into a swirl of snow.

It's a genuine pub, dark, slightly sour smelling from spilled beer, but a welcome retreat from the cold. Rather than risk botched cocktails, they order pints of draft beer.

"So, what did you make of that?" asks Christina.

"It's such a sad story," says Erica. "I wish I'd returned the book sooner. It might have made things easier for her."

"How were you to know?" says Suzanne.

"Yeah, and I'm sorry to have lost it now," says Erica. "It's sort of like losing a friend, an aunt or something."

"Oh well, there are three grateful readers. That's not such a bad record," says Suzanne.

"Three?" says Christina, eyebrows raised. "I thought you were unconvinced."

"It had some bon mots. And it got me into therapy. You know: 'an unexamined life is a life half-lived.'"

"I hate beer!" says Erica. "My bladder's the size of a peanut. Back in a flash." She makes her way to the back of the pub.

Christina takes a sip of her pint: "You know, I'm glad I caught you alone for a minute, Suzanne. I've been thinking about something, and I want to 'fess up. When you first told me about the documentary last summer, I felt hugely jealous of Maura and of you for pursuing what mattered most to you."

Suzanne laughs. "You're jealous of me! That's rich. I've been jealous of you for years—Vita, Norris, a loving husband."

"Don't kid yourself, Suzanne. We have our share of problems. Squabbling, different views of things. I thought I'd never get him to agree to this move. And now we're dickering about logistics. And for a long time, our sex life was kaput. Now, though, things seem better." She flashes to last night, the comforting warmth of his skin, his even breathing. "There's an ebb and flow to marriage that I'm coming to accept. I used to think it was this sort of straight progression. Now I realize it's two steps forward, one back, another sideways—all confounded by trying to make and keep space for yourself."

"But you've done lots of painting. Especially since the fall," says Suzanne.

"I have you and the documentary to thank for kick-starting me. After all these years, I'm still jealous of Maura. As Erica says, who wouldn't be? She's had such fast and fabulous success. But I'm not jealous of you now. I'm pleased for you. And I can't wait to see the documentary."

"Ah, the subtexts of friendship," says Suzanne. "It's a bit of a dance as well, don't you find? Step forward, step back."

Christina smiles: "Cha, cha, cha!"

Erica sits back down at the table: "Speaking of dance, Thomas and I have done a side-step. We've decided to wait a bit before moving in together."

"What?" says Christina. "But I thought it was all settled."

"We want to do it, but it seems too soon. We have to sort out the kiddy question first, before we get any further."

"Are you coming around to the idea—of kids, I mean?" asks Christina.

"Maybe. A year ago I would have said No, end of story, so that's a big change. I need a bit more time to decide."

"Well, I think you guys are perfectly matched," says Christina. "I'm sure it would work out wonderfully. And the kids would be adorable."

"I wish I'd made a copy of the book," says Erica. "There might be something in there to help me out."

"Well . . ." Christina pauses for effect, "I do have something from *The Book of Love* for you both to keep. I photocopied it when Suzanne loaned it to me last summer. It's a great chapter called 'Making Love Last.' I think it's the best one."

"Making love last," says Suzanne. "Seems to me that's key."

"Yes, well, it's like you said, Tina, about starting as you mean to go on," says Erica. "I think when you move in with someone you immediately establish certain expectations about how you will be, and how you will live together. I mean obviously you can't mitigate against all the uncertainty or make all the decisions up front, but certain basic things need to be in place."

"Like children," says Christina.

"And housework and sexual frequency," says Erica. "The whole package."

She takes a sip of her beer.

"Here's to sustainable love," she says, raising her glass.

They clink.

". . . and to sustaining friends."

CHAPTER 13

MAKING LOVE LAST

Love does not consist in gazing at each other,
but in looking outward together in the same direction.
ANTOINE DE SAINT-EXUPÉRY

Summing Up

Our expectations of romantic love as a foundation for marriage are too simplistic and, hence, unrealistic. Women, in particular, ascribe to the "happily ever after" scenario promulgated in everything from fairy tales to sitcoms. And men aren't much better. But the fact is that 37 percent of marriages that began in 2003 will eventually end in divorce. Governments are beginning to recognize how this is tearing apart the fabric of society. In Texas, legislators passed a law in 2007 that waived the marriage-licence fee for couples who take a premarital class and doubled the fee for couples who don't. In Germany, couples must wait three months after acquiring a marriage licence before getting hitched.

With good reason.

The ideal of romantic love is mired in the beginnings of the love relationship, the most sexually charged, fleeting period when we are most attracted to one another. This inevitably dissipates, and it is at that point that either the relationship fizzles or slowly unravels, or that we begin the real work of love. Once limerence fades, you must have something more than the fact that you're in love to keep it going and growing.

And so the question is: How do you make love last?

The simple answer: work. I know no one wants to hear that, but if we don't understand this basic fact, we are forever doomed to disappointment and disillusionment, and the need to start over again and again.

That work begins with yourself, with self-awareness and recognition of your needs and your responsibility for meeting them. The result of this is a true acceptance of your separateness. Couples comprise two people with two lives and all that entails: career, friends, hobbies, volunteer work, reading, entertainment — the list is as individual as our thumb print.

Asking one person to play an integral part in all these areas is untenable — and ultimately boring. The kiss of death. A relationship perseveres because you're interested in what's going to happen the next day and your partner's an interesting person to share it with. It's therefore vital to have something to help you grow individually: your career, volunteer work, hobbies or passions, sports, etc.

Dr. M. Scott Peck, the author of *The Road Less Traveled*, one of the twentieth century's most famous and arguably most useful self-help books, defines love as the will to extend one's self for the purpose of nurturing one's own or another's spiritual growth.[1] Spiritual growth, in this context, can be loosely defined as striving towards and meeting our full potential. According to Dr. Peck, the act of nurturing another person's spiritual growth has the effect of nurturing one's *own* growth.

At the same time, in genuine love, the distinction, the separateness between the two is always maintained, respected, and nurtured. In other words, you support your love partners for who they are — not your idealized notion of who you *wish* they were (often replicas of ourselves).

What this means, in practical terms, is that you must nurture and support, but at the same time, not expect everything from the one person. My grandmother used to tell me: "Don't put all your eggs in one basket." If that basket is marriage, it will break under the weight. It is not realistic, possible, or even desirable to have all your physical, intellectual, and emotional needs met by

---

1   S.M. Peck, *The Road Less Traveled* (New York: Simon & Schuster, 1978).

one person. But you are responsible for seeing that they are met, by yourself and by others (including your lover, friends, relatives, colleagues, etc.).

One of the side effects of adhering to the above is that it frees one to live one's life, rather than succumbing to some gradient of the co-dependent relationship (see page 185), which is essentially a relationship prison that limits who you see, what you do, where you go, etc.

Separateness requires mindful living: living in the present, instead of worrying about a past you can't change and an uncertain future. The idea is to enjoy every morsel of your time together and apart. Otherwise, it's not well spent. And we only have so much currency.

I've deliberately kept this section short and have provided a synopsis of how to make love last, as a sort of top twelve tips.

Epilogue

In this book, I have delved into the realm of romantic love. But the fact is, love extends in many directions. Ancient Sanskrit and Persian languages have more than eighty words that we translate in English as one word: "love." We are limited by this verbal paucity. The price of the cult of romantic love is the devaluing of the community of friendships—and other types of love—which can give our lives so much meaning. But that is a subject for another book. The pursuit of happiness will, inevitably lead you well beyond this particular book of love (and its monastic view).

Top Twelve Tips
for Enduring Love

1. Nurture your inner sense of security, your constant place from which to engage the world. And, in the process, you can take responsibility for all your needs and find ways to meet them. Don't expect that one person can meet them all. Cheerfully accept your partner's limitations and your own.

2. Make time for each other. Develop every-day good habits, like eating together every evening, or talking for twenty minutes before going to sleep. Go on a date at least once a week and talk about yourselves, your desires, fears, frustrations, joys. Between dates, connect physically at least once a day. This doesn't necessarily mean having sex; it could be a kiss, a caress, a hug, holding hands. These "pleasure points" allow couples to feel connected throughout the week, instead of pleasure-pressuring their date night, weekends, or vacations.

3. Find and nurture the interests you share: gardening, music, cooking, whatever. Make time for the pleasure of a shared passion, which will bring you closer.

4. Divide and share domestic tasks equally and do them willingly and without complaint. Many a relationship has succumbed to the tyranny of the dust bunny.

5. Keep the sexual motor running. Sexual intimacy allows you to put aside stressors and reinforce the emotional connection. Don't talk your desire to death; make time to do *it*. Add some play to playing around. This can be as simple as buying a pair of lace panties and as elaborate as meeting your partner at a bar and pretending to be strangers. Be inventive and surprising, and have fun.

6.   Apologize sincerely when the situation merits it. The corollary to this is to forgive what you can. Psychologist Robert Enright[1] described four stages of forgiveness: uncover your anger or hurt and acknowledge it to yourself; decide how you want to forgive your partner; try to understand what motivated them to act in such a way (e.g., stress, guilt, resentment); and, finally, look deeper and try to find the redemptive meaning in the experience.

7.   Don't go to bed angry. I remember reading this in a *Dear Abby* column as a child, and even then, it made sense. Going to bed angry allows the issue to fester and grow in importance. Instead, communicate well and as positively as possible, then, at least, you'll fight with less friction. Keep your sense of humour. Also keep in mind that communication doesn't only involve speech: write a note or give a big hug.

8.   Be nice. Treat your partner with the same courtesy as you would treat your closest friends. John Gottman, a psychology professor at the University of Washington, can predict which marriages will dissolve based solely on the number of kind and unkind interactions. When the ratio falls below five to one, he sounds the death knell.[2]

9.   Be grateful. Think of things you appreciate in your partner. There's a human tendency to focus on what's not there instead of what is there with questions such as: if only he would do the dishes, while forgetting that he's spent the last month building a fabulous deck; or if only she would lose ten pounds, then I'd get my sex drive back, while forgetting that

---

1   S.M. Peck, *The Road Less Traveled* (New York: Simon & Schuster, 1978.

2   J.M. Gottman, J. Coan, S. Carrere, and C. Swanson, "Predicting marital happiness and stability from newlywed interactions," *Journal of Marriage and Family* 60 (1998): 5–22.

she has a wonderful verbal repartee. Remember that feelings of love travel in cycles: sometimes you're on a high, and at other times, not. This is normal and natural.

10. Be an active listener. Be engaged while your partner is talking to you, not doing a suduku at the same time. Listen, wait until he's had his say, then ask questions about how he's doing, feeling. Ask what her plans are or what his problems are. Make useful comments, or offer empathy or sympathy. Ask for elaboration. Be interested.

11. Performance appraisals. Review how you're doing on a regular basis (once per month works well). Begin with what's working best, and then, get down to the prickly issues. Set goals and review progress at the next session. Use this as a time to not only tell your partner what you need, but also how you can succeed individually and as a couple.

12. Celebrate the big and the small stuff. A garden plan finished, a promotion, a finished work project — marking life's successes builds intimacy. Don't forget to ask for details of why this makes them happy; it will help you understand them better and, at the same time, allow them to understand themselves.

Sources

Bajramovic, H. Personal communication with author. Ottawa, 2006.

Chernick, B.A., and N. Chernick. *In Touch: The Ladder to Sexual Satisfaction*. London, Ont.: Sound Feelings, 1994.

Comfort, A. *The Joy of Sex*. New York: Crown Publishers Inc., 1972.

Durex. "2005 Global sex survey." *The Ottawa Citizen*, November 9, 2005, sec. A1.

Gottman, J.M., J. Coan, S. Carrere, and C. Swanson. "Predicting marital happiness and stability from 'newlywed interactions.'" *Journal of Marriage and Family* 60 (1998): 5–22.

Hendrick, C., and S.S. Hendrick. "A theory and method of love." *Journal of Personality and Social Psychology* 50, no. 2 (February 1986): 392–402.

Klusmann, D. "Sperm competition and female procurement of male resources." *Human Nature* 17, no. 3 (2006): 283–300.

Kurzban, R., and J. Weeden. "Do advertised preferences predict the behaviour of speed daters?" *Personal Relationships* 14, no. 4 (2007): 623–32.

La Giogia, G. "Intimate info." *Canadian Health* (January–February 2008): 54.

Lee, J.A. "Love styles." In *The Psychology of Love*, by M.H. Barnes and R.J. Sternberg, 38–67. New Haven, Conn.: Yale University Press, 1988.

Love, P., and S. Stosny. *How to Improve Your Marriage without Talking About It*. New York: Broadway, 2008.

Macneil, S., and E.S. Byers. "The relationships between sexual problems, communication and sexual satisfaction." *The Canadian Journal of Human Sexuality* 6, no. 4 (1997): 277–84.

Michael, R.T., J.H. Gagnon, E.O. Laumann, and G. Kolata. *Sex in America: A Definitive Survey*. Boston, Mass.: Little, Brown Co., 1994.

Peck, S.M. *The Road Less Traveled*. New York: Simon & Schuster, 1978.

Post, S., and J. Neimark. "Love across time." *Oprah Magazine* (June 2007): 65–66.

Schatzker, M. "We need to talk . . .," *The Globe and Mail*, March 10, 2007, sec. C1.

Thanks

NOTHING OCCURS IN A VACUUM. Over the years I've been blessed with wonderful mentors and teachers, including Douglas Glover, Isabel Huggan, Frances Itani, Prof. Gerald Lynch, Carol Shields, Matt Cohen, and Audrey Thomas. I also owe a debt of gratitude to Jerimiah Bartram, Mark Frutkin, and Gabriella Goliger, and to the Ottawa Writing Group for their thoughtful critiquing of parts of this book. Thank you all. I extend an extra heartfelt thanks to my first reader, Dr. Miriam Shuchman; to my diligent editors, Leanne Ridgeway and Beverley Humphries, and the talented team at GSPH; and to my husband, Stuart Kinmond, who has taught me much about love.

— *Barbara Sibbald*

About the Author

BARBARA SIBBALD was shortlisted for the 2007 Ottawa Book Award for *Regarding Wanda* (Bunkhouse Press, 2006). Her short stories have appeared in eleven literary journals and two anthologies, *The Company We Keep* (BushekBooks, 2005) and *Winning Shorts* (General Store Publishing House, 1995). A journalist by profession, she has won the Canadian Association of Journalists' Investigative Journalism award and was twice cited for the Michener award for Meritorious Public Service Journalism. Her work has appeared in *The Globe and Mail*, *Ottawa Magazine*, *Ottawa Citizen*, *Chatelaine*, and elsewhere. Barbara lives in Ottawa, Ontario, Canada, with her husband, the visual artist Stuart Kinmond.

www.barbarasibbald.com